A New Leash on Life

by

Cassandra Joelle

Dedicated to my mother, the original armchair detective.

And to my Sophie, my unfailing companion for fourteen years and who was the best dog ever. Until we meet again.

CONTENTS

CASSANDRA JOELLE

<h1 style="text-align:center">CHAPTER 1
READY FUR LOVE</h1>

"One more piece. Just one more," I bargained with myself as my eyes were nearly closed. It was already past 11 at night, but I was making so much progress on this puzzle, it was hard to find a stopping point. Feeling a second wind, I reached for the puzzle box to remind myself of its level of challenge but instead saw my phone illuminate and grabbed that instead.

'1 Notification from FindMeChristianDate.com' flashed across the screen. My heart sank as my finger tapped to see what it was. While it was loading, I pictured my wedding speech.

"Imagine my surprise, all those months ago as I was sitting up late in my little apartment, working on a puz- err, my master thesis, and I virtually met my husband for the first time." The crowd cheered and we were clinking glasses when my slow internet finally loaded revealing I had no new matches or husband waiting in the wings, but rather my free trial period had expired, and if I didn't pay $159.99, my account would be closed by morning. "Bye-bye, dating

website." I plugged my phone into the charger and made my way to bed.

BEEP. BEEP. BEEP. I awoke from a deep slumber to a horrible sound. My arm couldn't find the alarm clock in the darkness. Tearing off my sleep eye mask, I realized I'd rolled over to the other side of the mattress and was grasping the air.

Beep. Beep. Beep. Whack!

I called out to my voice-activated virtual assistant: "Virtual assistant, find a better alarm clock that isn't so… rude."

"*I've added an alarm clock to your shopping list and compiled a list of alarms that are popular among shoppers, along with the features of each.*" The answer echoed through my small apartment.

"Thank you," I smirked at the ease of technology, yet remembered it was also the reason why I was so tired and rolled over into the pillows. The down feathers greeted my face, poking my eyelids.

"*Studies have shown that by regulating your circadian rhythm, waking up naturally can be achieved.*" There she goes again, always wanting the last word.

I lay in bed for a few more minutes, depleting all the extra time I had before getting ready for church. I only had myself to blame for my exhaustion, staying up too late and the disappointment of the Christian dating website. I've never contacted anyone in its three-month free trial period; I just browse the bios and see if anything caught my eye. But without paying, I never saw the profile pictures of any of the men, which was fine for me; I liked the *love is blind* theory anyway.

I groaned at the idea of leaving my comfortable bed, but I tried to barter with myself.

Get up now. I might have time for a few puzzle pieces.

My mind and legs argued with each other. It worked; partially, anyway. I sat up.

Just the life of a 30-something painfully single paralegal.

"I should write that one down for my personal ad title." I laughed at my joke.

I took out my prayer journal in my nightstand with its matching floral pen, reviewing the prayers and praises of the week, while jotting down a new one and speaking it into my heart.

"Dear Jesus,
I believe I am ready for love,
when you're ready to send it to me.
Love, Katie."

I let the memories flood my mind. There had been many attempts at love over the years. As my mother called it, *premeditated attempts at matrimony.* But I tried not to use her crime lingo when speaking of my romantic interests, as it really seemed to turn men off. Personally, I had no interest in true crime outside of the walls of my office, and thankfully, we mostly handled family law. But my mother was another story. She didn't view it as entertainment; rather, she picked up on things from the psychological standpoint of 'bettering her street smarts.'

My *serial* search for love started when I was a preteen trying to call my celebrity crushes on 411 for weeks on end. They weren't my first totally impossible love interest. I seemed always to be drawn to the unavailable. But it could be worse. I could have chosen to marry my incarcerated prison pen pal like so many other women. Not that I have one of those… anymore. I had to stop replying to him once the price of postage skyrocketed. It was only a week later that I saw on the news he had escaped. I kept thinking over and over: I'm so glad I used a fake name. But then it dawned on me: he had my address!

I recall asking my mother what to do in this situation. She hung up the phone, only to appear at my front door a half hour later with a paper bag. "Let me in. We don't have time for dilly-dallying." She emptied the contents of the bag onto my dining room table, holding up a box of black hair dye. "If we dye your eyebrows too, this will make you totally *unrecognizable.*"

"Is that what I want?"

"Of course, it is, Katie. *He's a fugitive.*" "But I never sent him a picture of me. He doesn't know what I look like."

"Well, okay then. If he shows up here, I could answer the door. Maybe he won't want anything to do with an older woman like me."

Wait, I just remembered I had omitted something else. "He doesn't know where I live, though." I sheepishly hid my eyes from her, only then recalling I hadn't given my home address on the envelopes because my mailbox in the house I was renting had been mowed down by a school bus earlier that spring. Who could blame the driver, though? Driving in six-inch heels like she was had to have been a challenge— especially after her recent glaucoma diagnosis.

"So, he doesn't know your name, what you look like *or* your address?" As we say in the biz, '*de facto.*'"

"Well, you didn't let me finish on the phone. I am still *quite* concerned. I am starting to have a real predicament with junk mail. Do you think he is the one signing me up for all these mailers?"

The snooze on my alarm went off again as I reached over and swatted the clock with more force this time.

I scribbled a few flowers down in my prayer journal around today's notes before putting it away.

As the intoxicating aroma of my automatic coffee maker wafted through my apartment and met my nose. "Time to stop dilly-dallying," I announced. I considered skipping the early church service today and attending the later, but then I thought of Judy sitting all alone in the pew with no one beside her. I jumped out of bed, the plush carpet greeting my feet.

Though I was careful not to make church a social hour, Judy kept me accountable. Before we met, my self-consciousness took the wheel. I wasn't terribly shy; I just felt awkward in new places. I used to strategically shuffle in as everyone was sitting down and sat closest to the door until Judy saw me as she walked in confidently and surely and asked me to join her. Thankfully for me, it blossomed into a genuine friendship, and I've enjoyed her quirky wisdom that was as truthful as it was funny. So, for all the reasons I attended, Judy's fellowship was high on the list. For what might seem like an unlikely pair, Judy being 89 and I being 31, we had a lot in common— like we were both single, for one.

Not a week would go by that Judy wouldn't remind me to trust God and his timing for my love life.

"Are you sure that's how the verse goes?" I would tease her.

But she knew well the battles of loneliness, having been a widow for nearly half of her life. She would always tease me that if I didn't start putting myself out there, I would be the bridesmaid at her wedding instead of her at mine. She loved to tease me; our sense of humor was another common ground we shared.

I looked out the window to see how I should dress, as it was common for Judy and I to grab a light lunch after the service. She loved to walk to the bistro that overlooked the town square, rain, or shine, so we could "husband watch," as she called it. It was important I came dressed appropriately for both the lunch and the jaunt. Although it was a short walk, there was nowhere to hide from the elements. She would playfully scold me if I wore something utterly drab or too plain, but she always encouraged me to be myself. "I know the right one for you is out there, dear, but he might not notice you if you're wearing *that.*"

The weather looked bleak with a side of cold, as usual, this time of year. I would need to dress warmly and wear something waterproof i.e., *unflattering.* I cringed, thinking how my hair would react to the humidity.

Shaking the worries out of my mind, I made a small pot of coffee and threw a piece of bread in the toaster. I didn't normally eat so lightly, but I only had a few minutes before I needed to get out the door. The smell of the coffee energized me, awakening my eyes, and I gulped it down while I buttered the toast and ate it in the hallway on my way to the wardrobe.

Quickly washing the sleep off my face, I grabbed my toothbrush and started scrubbing my teeth while I picked out a bright green sweater, gray skirt with black tights, and Mary Janes to wear. It was closer to frump than high fashion, but I didn't feel like it was *that* hideous. And besides, the shoes were as functional as they were *comfortable.* I looked at my reflection in the tall mirror on the back of my closet door. My dark mane was frizzy but shiny. Brushing out my hair, I was relieved I had a full bottle of dry shampoo that gave it body *and* made it smell like some weird chalk flower.

I swiftly dabbed on a little concealer under my eyes and a peachy-colored blush to my high cheekbones, using the same blush as an eyeshadow. It brightened me up instantly and enhanced my honey-colored eyes.

I felt refreshed, but then I remembered the rain outside. Grabbing the gray rain slicker from my coat rack near the door, I peeked at my reflection in the mirror and shook my head at my color choice, instantly dulling my outward appearance into a gray, shapeless *potato*. I took a photo of my bizarre ensemble and made a silly face, sending it to my mother. She replied immediately:

You look cute, but the color could be better?
(Typing)
(Typing)
(Typing)

Finally, her follow-up text came through.

Or better yet, keep that one. It hides your figure and beauty. Surely, you wouldn't be the first choice for an abduction wearing that.
(Typing)

Good thinking on the shoes, too.

Gee, thanks. I slid my phone into my pocket. I liked these shoes.

CHAPTER 2
NEIGHBORHOOD WATCHDOGS

"Dear Jesus,

Thank you for my eyes to see that this color is wretched on me."

Yes, the color couldn't have been worse for the raincoat, but it was such a good deal that I made yet another fashion sacrifice for functionality. Still, I felt the color drain from my face, again calling my virtual assistant. "Virtual assistant, buy a raincoat that doesn't make me look so dead."

"I didn't quite catch that. Would you like me to add a raincoat for your head to your shopping list?"

Laughing at the fumble, I grabbed my keys and Bible bag, glancing inside to make sure my highlighters, colored pens, and sticky notes were inside as I set out the door.

I raced down the steps, my shoes sloshing in the puddles being flooded out by the fat raindrops. They hit my head like nickels. I still do not own an umbrella, despite living in the Northwest, but I kept meaning to find one that's durable and won't turn inside out at the slightest hint of wind like my last one.

I almost holler to my virtual assistant, but I remember I am in public now, where talking to yourself is not considered normal. I jetted to the covered parking and breathed in relief when I reached my car.

Umbrellas can be triggering for many fears, since I live in the Pacific Northwest and it's an accessory staple, but there is one scenario that really takes the cake. Of course, there is nothing more embarrassing than when your umbrella has a malfunction. You can be looking cute as a daisy, waiting at a bus stop when a gust comes up, and then you're holding a metal rod with spikes sharp enough to poke everyone's eyes out if the wind shifts because it's turned into a weathervane. Now, you must quickly announce why you no longer need the bus so that you can fix the umbrella in private, as it's bringing generational shame.

"Oh no, I forgot I have to go home."

As people sighed in relief, watching you and your maiming tool flee, they whispered, "If her hair gets any frizzier, it may break off completely."

Not that I would know because, *of course,* that's never happened to me.

My car is freezing. Turning over the engine to my ten-year-old SUV, my teeth chatter as I wait for the heater to kick on, noticing the windows fogging up immediately. The wipers go haywire, and the radio is three times the volume it should be for this time of day, blasting out a crooner from the early 90's. It's one of those songs

I'll always be able to belt out the chorus, but the rest of the lyrics I'm stumbling through. This doesn't matter as I'm generally not singing around people unless I'm at church, and thankfully, there we have lyric books and overhead projectors.

I laughed as I was reminded that the last time I was in my car was Friday night after work, and I was in a much different frame of mind then. The high hopes of a peaceful weekend staying up late and not being in my work cubicle was exciting. I enjoyed my job as a paralegal, as I loved the research factor, but I had more than a few coworkers who I found nosey. I didn't know why they cared about my quiet life, considering they would all go out on the town almost nightly, and if they really did care, why was I never set up with their single friends? Well, there was one setup. But it wasn't really my fault how that went down.

I still shudder at the thought of that ill-fated setup, except now with my cold car, my body is nearly convulsing. I might be ready for a relationship, but I was not looking for something casual. I want marriage or nothing at all— settling is not an option. The dreadful attempt of a co-worker I didn't know to marry me off was shortly after I started my job at the law firm. Nancy, the woman who worked next to Clark, said her nephew was single and that I was *'just his type,'* which she said with a wink. I wasn't sure what to make of it, but I was flabbergasted to be described as anyone's type who didn't know me because I'm quirky. I just don't get to know people that fast and vice versa.

She showed me a picture of him. It was an action shot from his school sports days.

"He was a big-time college baseball player. He is a little older now, of course– around your age." Nancy beamed while looking at the photo, but as hard as I looked, I couldn't tell what he looked like. "This probably isn't the best picture of Jake. But I promise, he's adorable!"

I stared at the photo some more. He was wearing a baseball helmet covering most of his face from the angle of the shot. Instantly, I'm reminded of the cute guy I met on the train when I was 18. He'd been wearing cargo shorts, sandals, a V-neck, and, most notably, a football helmet. He was quite cute under the helmet, so I decided to look past it instead of questioning the *reasons* someone might be wearing such a thing. Afraid of getting hurt? Obsession with the game? Clinical insanity? But at 18, naivety ruled, and I still shuddered at the thought I gave out my phone number to that guy. *At least he never called.* Who was I to judge? After all, I'd only been riding the train to go to an underground speakeasy holding a combo knitting class & intensive group therapy session to fight our aichmophobia, the fear of sharp objects. "*BYO Knitting Needles,*" the poster said. What could go wrong? Quite a bit, it turns out. But that's a story for another day.

Katie's Words of Law
Negligence
Ideas that needed more common sense than one's ability to

execute.

"Can I give him your number?" Nancy asked, holding the company directory to show me she already had it. I nodded hesitantly, aware that I was brand new to this work environment and suddenly willing to go against my nature to make a good impression. "Sure…" but I wasn't *sure,* as I watched her text Jake my phone number. He texted me shortly after that and wanted to pick me up that evening for dinner. And since Nancy vetted him profusely, it was the *only* time I'd let someone pick me up at my house. Partially because my mother hadn't let the fact that I gave out my home address to someone I didn't know, nor would she ever let me live it down; the other reason was, well: *I hadn't had a date since.*

That night, waiting for my blind date, I kept looking out my door to see if he had arrived, since I didn't have a window overlooking the small parking area. Two neighbor ladies who often sat outside surveying the happenings were in their usual chairs. At ten after, I finally just went out there for good, locking the door behind me and heading down the stairs.

"Hello," I called out to them, thinking it would be rude not to acknowledge them canvassing every move I made.

"Hi!" One lady enthusiastically called back.

"Are you waiting for someone?" The other woman asked.

"Yes, I have a date, actually." I felt my cheeks blush at the thought. I didn't mention it was a blind date, though I instantly wished I had when I saw the car pull up.

From the pages of Katie's Dictionary:
blind date
blīnd dāt
noun
A forced coupling of two people who haven't met in the wild because they have nothing in common.

"Oh no," my neighbor lady let out. I felt the same panic as I heard a high-pitched *whir* sound coming from a nearby car— one of those noises that generated feelings of doubt before stepping into a vehicle.

She turned to her friend and asked loudly, "Is that him?"

As if her friend would know, despite the fact I caught them up to speed at the same moment. The ladies straightened up their postures as the car turned the corner and, sure enough, pulled into our loading area where I stood. One of the ladies took a picture of his car, which I assumed was for my Dateline special. I couldn't see that well at night, and the headlights blinded me when I turned my head to look. But I could've sworn the car was totaled.

Fear washed over me. Who wants to hear *'Oh no'* when their blind date is being described? I robotically walked to the car since I didn't see him getting out or anything.

"Have fun," one of the ladies called out, but I didn't hear any hope in her voice.

So, this man I didn't know picked me up fifteen minutes after he said he would, in a half-eaten silver Honda. I looked at him, his eyes wide and pointed, but I couldn't find any words as I gaped at the car.

At first, he didn't get the problem, but then he followed my eyes and nodded. "I just borrowed this from a friend." Reacting to my surprised expression, he stammered out, "I have an Audi, but it's in the shop."

"Oh." I wasn't sure if he'd ever heard of a rental car company, but despite my better judgment, I got into the smashed car, and we sputtered away, the fragrance of fast-food lingering.

"I'm sorry I'm late. I got you an apple empanada." He handed me a crumpled-up paper-wrapped fried dessert from a fast-food drive-thru.

"Thank you?"

I didn't have any intention of eating the dessert, considering it was unsolicited and half *unwrapped,* so I set it on the dash. I looked at him through my peripheral vision. He was sandy-haired, fair-skinned, and a little chubby. I didn't have a problem with that, but he was no athlete. I think Aunt Nancy may have elaborated a little when giving me a description.

"Just gotta get gas first," he muttered.

We pulled into the fueling station, and I could see the extent of the car's damage under the bright lights. I felt like it would be safer for me to exit the vehicle while he filled it up in case it exploded. I stepped out of the car and talked to him over the roof.

"Did you wreck on the way over here?"

He looked confused, so I motioned to the crumpled front end.

He shook his head. "No, that was yesterday. It wasn't my fault; I was out in the boonies, and a wild turkey ran out into the road."

"All of this from hitting a turkey?"

"No, it caught me off guard, and I swerved into a ditch. I'm just glad it's still drivable."

"Wow, I bet your friend is really upset."

"Who?"

He turned and went inside to pay, so I decided to sleuth. I reached into the car and opened the glove box to pull out the vehicle registration. *2008 Honda Civic. Jake Halstad.* I shoved it back inside, knowing this was the first *and last* date I'd be going on with Jake.

He returned, pulled the fuel pump, and jumped back in the car. He gassed it out of the lot and down a dimly lit side street, "Where do you want to go for dinner?" he asked me while simultaneously turning *up* the radio. It was a blaring sports broadcast. Not a moment later, he turned what remained of *his car* into the Olive Pit.

"I was thinking of the Olive Pit."

"Sure. " I did like the restaurant, and at least I'd get a decent meal.

When we got to the door, I grabbed the handle, expecting him to take it from me and let me walk ahead. Instead, he breezed in, shuffling sideways to fit into the small opening I had created.

The hostess, whose station was overlooking the parking lot, looked at me with very concerned eyes.

"Can I help you?" she asked, as if she was ready to call me a cab and let me out of this date, here and now. I should've taken her up on the offer.

"Two of us," Jake was scanning the restaurant when he saw something he liked. "Can we sit in the bar?"

I didn't know they had a bar. I hope he's not a heavy drinker.

The waitress led us to a table in the dark bar area, and I sat first. Jake followed, staring blankly ahead, asking, "Can you move over to the left?"

In doing so, I peeked over my shoulder and saw the baseball game flashing behind me. I didn't mind him not speaking, though. Without the intense rattling of what was left of the front end of *his* Honda, I realized just how high-pitched and nasally his voice was. This wasn't a *voice* I could hear for the rest of my life, *no matter how much he ignored me.*

When the waitress came, he ordered a salad.

"A salad?" I asked, "At the best pasta place in town?"

But he didn't hear me because someone had just hit a foul ball, and he hollered out in protest.

I ordered an extra cheesy plate of ravioli, shaking my head at my horrible date. He barely touched his salad, but he ate 13 breadsticks. When the bill came, he put down a little over half the amount in cash. I wasn't expecting him to pay. In fact, I was relieved because it didn't set any burden of going out again. I gladly put my card on top of the cash, and the waitress sorted it out.

The biggest surprise of the night was not his car, lack of conversation, or genuine disassociation with reality. It was when he went to drive me home afterward, only to ask to come back into my apartment with me.

Um, what? No, thank you.

He may have implied he just needed to use the restroom, but appearances are important when you are a single woman. Plus, as my mother instilled in me from a young age, he could've been a serial killer.

I returned to work the next day only to find my entire office laughing it off that I wouldn't let my date use my bathroom, and he ended up having to pull over on the side of the road. "I don't see how that's my problem or my business. There was a restroom at the Olive Pit." The office went into a real uproar after that one.

Then, there was one coworker who hit on me once. I think so, anyway. *Greg.* A perfectly normal guy— worked in the mailroom— but chewed gum. I don't just mean a piece, but many pieces at once. Multiple wads of gum, all chewing simultaneously, creating a horrendous brown color. He approached me one day and complimented my watch, but my eyes went straight to the heaping mass of gum in his mouth.

"I like your watch." *Smack, smack, smack.*

"Um, thank you." I couldn't take my eyes off the gum.

"I like big faces." He pointed to the watch.

I laughed a little at the random phrase.

Just then, he attempted to blow a bubble with the gum, but it got out of control, popped, and stuck to his nose. I was about to ask him if he suffers from crippling TMJ, but he pushed away his mail cart with no response as if nothing ever happened. Later, at the dreaded water cooler, I was refilling my bottle when someone asked me if Greg and I were *a thing.*

"What? No! Why would you say that?" If the look of disgust on my face wasn't rude enough, my tone sent it home. I barely even knew the asker— Cynthia from Indiana. And I only knew where she was from because she had some sports team bunting on the outside of her cubicle.

"Because he said you were interested in him."

"Well, I'm not." I scoffed it off, no need for further correction, but found it increasingly disturbing that because I said *thank you* when he commented on my watch, that being the only two words I'd ever directly spoken to him, he thought I was interested. My mother also accused Greg of serial killer-dom and warned me not to walk out in the parking lot after work alone since I might have a stalker.

"He's delusional." she'd say. "This guy— what's his name? Ted? He's created a fantasy land in his *mind*–a place I'd never want to go— that you two are *together.* "

"It's Greg."

"What is?" My mother was only half listening as I could hear her clunky, long acrylic nails pounding away at the keyboard. I assumed she was pulling up profiles of like-minded criminals.

"His name is Greg."

"Whatever. You need to steer clear of this guy. Does he have access to your personal things— phone, water, house keys? Maybe you should consider changing jobs. This guy, Ted, could be pretending to charm you, but really, he's just another *Bundy.*"

"What do you think he's going to do? Poison my water? Make copies of my house keys? Steal my phone and return it later after filling it with pictures of his feet?"

"Now you're starting to get it."

From the pages of Katie's Dictionary:
Paranoia
păr''ə-noi'ə
noun
What every Millennial has since watching the early 1980s production, 'Stranger Danger.' See also: Motherly instinct.

It was then that I decided I wouldn't get in too deep with my coworkers. My mother's increasing wariness of Greg, whom I'd even started calling Ted, wasn't the reason, though. I just came here to do the work that I enjoy. The party lifestyle of this office wasn't for me, but it was a job that aligned exactly with my experience, paid decently, and came with an excellent boss, and, best of all, a three-week vacation every year to do absolutely nothing with it. It was good.

Snapping back to reality, I realized my teeth stopped chattering while waiting for my windows to clear. I quietly said a prayer that the right man would come into my life. I thanked the Lord for my many blessings and letting Him know my life was in His hands. I DO trust His timing! I took a deep breath and saw that I was going to be late, so I backed out of my spot, turned out of my complex, and onto the road.

It was 9:28 am when I reached Three Maples Church, named after its beautiful trees, planted out front, with service starting at 9:30. I'd hoped Judy would be waiting for me inside, holding my spot in the pew. I parked and threw my keys in my pocket, a place I'd likely forget later, and raced up the church steps. The ushers nodded and smiled at me as I entered. Thankfully, I was not the only one living on the edge this morning, as the lobby was still full of people. The music softly started, and everyone slowly shuffled to their seats.

"Well, I suppose I'll call off the search party," Judy smiled as I slid into my seat next to her. "Up late again? Anything to report back?"

Judy well knew I had been browsing a few dating sites, but that was nothing new. I'd been casually looking for years to no avail.

"My new jigsaw is 1,000 pieces that are all the same color, just slightly varying in hue," I smirked at Judy. I knew that would get a rise out of her.

"When I was your age, I was out dancing three nights a week!"

"Oh? I didn't know that! What kind of dancing?"

"Well, back then, my husband's parents were swing dancers. So my husband grew up learning it and very much enjoyed the dance, but he himself had two left feet, and I had no desire to accidentally be thrown through a window. I'd always been more of a country girl, so he compromised and learned to line dance, which we did every Thursday night for the next fifty-odd years. As much as he enjoyed it, I'm afraid he never quite got the hang of it. It all came down to his feet. And boy, were they *odd*."

"What do you mean, odd?"

"Well, his two left feet weren't figurative, dear. It's the reason the military wouldn't take him. Thankfully, he found a great career as a shoe salesman. Foot irregularities are much more common than you know. I remember one client had a size seventeen left shoe. The right was a size ten. They became great friends. He'd started an adult basketball league with my husband; they called themselves the "Flat Footed Flyers.""

"That name!" I laughed it off as Judy went on.

"I know, dear. Word caught on fast that an irregular foot team was forming. At the peak of their league, they had twenty-six players. It was large enough that they could split into two teams, thankfully, because they needed an opponent. So not only were the Flat-Footed Flyers playing, but now we had the Bunion Busters coming in opposition. And my guy recruited them all."

"Wow, he sounds like he was an amazing guy." I took her hand. "While I've never been professionally diagnosed, I've always *felt* my feet were irregular. Maybe I should find a basketball team?"

"Anything social would be good for you, Katie. I only wish the line-dancing place was still around. I'd love to show you my moves." Judy smiled.

I had no doubt she knew how to dance, as her everyday movements were fluid and easy.

"Well, in that case— maybe we should let Pastor Bill know what we want at the next church social. A shot caller for line dancing!" We giggled about our ideas when Pastor Bill came to the pulpit.

"Good morning, friends," a woman we hadn't seen before tailed behind him. "This morning, I wanted to start us off a little untraditionally with a new project that Three Maples has been involved in. I know it is something very dear to all of our hearts. We've been asked for help from a local animal shelter in their efforts to save God's creatures and find them loving homes. I'd like to introduce the Marshall's daughter, Samantha, from the Newtown Animal Shelter. Samantha?"

A woman about my age took a small microphone from Pastor Bill as he remained at the pulpit. I could see the resemblance to the Marshalls, the couple who always sat beside Judy and me every Sunday morning. She had her mother's beautiful blonde hair, and it was tapered into a similar bob. Samantha nodded and, still standing adjacent to Pastor Bill, spoke sure and loud.

"Thank you, Pastor. As he said, I am with the Newtown Animal Shelter. I am here to ask for your help. You see, our shelter is full." A small gasp was heard. Cue the Sarah McLachlan music. Is someone cutting onions in here?

"We have beautiful, loving pets who desperately seek a home of their own. We are so full that we can't take any more in, and the situation is dire for those we turn away." She paused, stammering her words as if she might cry. She looked up at the crowd.

"I ask that if you've ever considered adopting a pet, now is a wonderful time to do so. You wouldn't just be adopting, but you'd be falling in love. Gaining a best friend." Pausing, Samantha pulled the microphone closer to her lips. "You'd be saving a life."

The voice of someone choking up behind Judy and I started off the crowd. We all felt the emotional plea of this woman who was here as a last resort. I certainly felt it, too. Judy and I looked at each other with big eyes, and it was clear we both wanted to do something to help. I just didn't know what that *something* was.

After Samantha spoke, Pastor Bill thanked her, and she stepped down the stairs leading from the pulpit, walked down the aisle, and left. In passing, she looked as emotional as the attendees, and my heart broke for the animals.

Judy leaned into me. "I want one."

I smiled, considering she'd always commented about the dogs we saw people walking on our outings, so I knew she was a dog lover.

"Just one? How about a few?"

Judy didn't say anything as the Pastor started his sermon, a very timely one about kindness and compassion.

"We know that the Lord hears our cries. But He also hears that of the animal kingdom. Open your bible to Matthew 10:29. *'Are not two sparrows sold for a penny? Yet not one of them will fall to the ground outside your Father's care.'* Wow. Isn't that remarkable? Not one sparrow— a small bird that people used to sell for half a penny falls to the ground without Him knowing." Pastor Bill closed his bible and came out from behind the podium.

"The Lord created everything in existence. Think about the grains of sand for a minute. Are any two pieces the same? Have you ever seen a snowflake under a microscope? Have you ever cut open an artichoke and truly admired its intricacy? Or scrape your skin, only to watch your body heal itself? It's enough to make anyone believe in the Lord's existence."

"Now, what about the beautiful animals He has graced us with? We have such diverse beauty all around. From the colorful tropical birds in the jungles, the incredible song of the sea's blue whales, to the Smith's intelligent labradoodle." He smiled at the mention of the rambunctious dog that ran off with the potato salad at last summer's picnic. "They are all God's creatures." Pastor Bill went back to his podium and took the microphone. "And some of them need our help." He smiled at Samantha.

We ended the service with a prayer for the week.

"Our Heavenly Father,
Thank you for this day that you've brought us all here for.

Our being alive is a testament that You are not done with us yet, and we pray that Your path for our lives continues to become clear so that we may follow it and do Your will. We thank You for Samantha, who works tirelessly for the animals, and I pray that we find room in our hearts and homes for the precious creatures You created that are looking for a second chance. That are looking for a family of their own.

May we find them that, Lord.

In Your name, Amen."

The church filled with *Amens* after his prayer, and everyone began standing. I half expected a run for the door to get to the shelter, but everyone stiffly walked in a polite single file. The Pastor didn't stand at the exit doors today shaking hands and kissing babies, but instead, stayed up at the pulpit.

Judy wanted to say goodbye to him, so she told me to wait while she tiptoed up the stairs to talk to him. He leaned in and gave her a short hug. They were both smiling, and she must have said something funny because he was suddenly busting up with laughter. I smiled at Judy, not even needing to know what she said; she was just a joyous person that everyone loved.

When she returned, I waited expectantly for her to fill me in, as she always did.

"He's really worried about the animals, too," she said.

As I looked around the room, I could feel that everyone was solemn and wondering what they could do.

"He and Julie are going over to the shelter later. He said they would pick me up to tag along."

"Oh, that will be fun! Tell him to post any news on the church bulletin website so I can see if they adopt anything." The thought of adopting a pet sent me into flashbacks of the aggressive small dogs my mother always rescued.

"Shall we go to the Bistro?" I changed the subject, taking our minds off the pets. Judy shook her head to my surprise. "I want to, I really do! I love our lunches. But Pastor Bill and Julie are picking me up at noon, and I need to change my clothes." She motioned to her lavender polyester pantsuit and shiny beige shoes. She looked adorable in that outfit, but she was right, it was too fancy for rolling around with dog hair.

"Will you be alright?" she asked.

Her concerned look told me she really did worry for me, given that her social life was more active, and it dawned on me then that I relied on her company more than I wanted to.

"Oh, of course!! You know, I was considering going to that pottery cafe." I had been considering that for the last three years, and now that I'd said it, I had to go or risk being a liar.

"That's wonderful, honey. Make me something pretty." Judy beamed and we both felt better. Off she went in her shiny gold coupe.

As I climbed into my car, I looked over and saw Samantha sitting in the car next to me with her head in her hands. I was within arm's reach of her passenger-side window, so I tapped on the glass. She looked up, dazed, with tears in her eyes. She smiled at me and rolled down her window.

"Hi there. Can I help you?" She spoke as confidently as she did inside– as if she was still representing her work sitting in a parking lot, crying in her car.

"Oh. I'm good… I just saw you... Are you okay?"

There was a pause while she looked out her windshield, now clear from rain. "It's just heavy, you know? I feel helpless."

Looking at Samantha, I felt something tug in my heart.

"I just want them to find homes so that– " her voice caught "– nothing else happens."

My mind went there– to the alternative, the writing on the wall. I didn't know what to say, so I chose something generic. "I know they will find homes. Don't worry, Samantha. You are making a difference."

She smiled and thanked me, rolling up her window and starting her car. She waved as she drove off, as I still sat in the driver's seat of my car, the door ajar, and so was my jaw. I knew the desperation she felt, though unrelated. I longed for a partner. I longed for love.

But what am I feeling right now? Surely, it was not the *desire* for pet ownership, was it? I just wanted to do *something*. Could I have a pet? Technically, yes. But I had never had one of my own or even considered it. The very idea overwhelmed me. Sure, I grew up with dogs, but my mother had always been the one taking care of them. The deeper I wondered just what my hesitations were, I felt like they all went back to my hopefully near-future husband. What if he was allergic to pets? Or worse, what if he already had a colony of hairless cats he was raising?

At that moment, I had a breakthrough that I hadn't reached in all the years of my mother's therapy. My life had been on hold while I waited for a husband to come into it, but I'd grown so comfortable with the mundane routine that I wasn't ready to change it.

Wondering about pets I might have one day with my future husband, I pictured something furry but wasn't sure what it might be. I did like animals, and I always enjoyed seeing them.

I had a friend back home, Ginger, with a cat that she was always gushing over. I recall that the cat was adopted as an adult. They loved it dearly; she sent me a photo the day they brought him home. Things were fine for a week or so. The cat was settling in as far as I knew, but Ginger was a teacher, and when she went back to school in the fall, she found it had started *acting out* around the house. She would come home to wet walls. She thought a pipe had burst in the kitchen, but upon further inspection, she realized it was *cat urine.*

"He's peeing up the walls, Katie."

I laughed at the time she told me because it was truly unbelievable that his spot of choice would be a wall. So, they took him to the vet for help.

The cat was diagnosed with depression and was given medication. I couldn't make it up if I tried. But I suppose humans get depressed. Why wouldn't animals? I just didn't know what a cat living in a beautiful, loving home getting fed *Furball Fiesta* three times a day could be depressed about.

The next time I saw Ginger, I asked her about her cat and how his *treatment* was going. "He is doing great. I realized I couldn't live with the fact I had a cat on antidepressants. So, we hired someone to build a small condo in our backyard with the same carpet and wallpaper, and sure enough, he pees all over it night and day. It sure hurt to take money out of our retirement, but we all feel better now. Problem solved."

Everyone drove off and I was the lone car left in the Three Maples parking lot, in deep reflection of my emotions. I wondered about the families I saw here every week; did they have pets? Was it unusual to *not* have a pet?

We had one and a half dogs growing up. I say that because one was a full-fledged, happy skipper of a dog, and the other one was why guests needed tetanus shots. Both were incredibly bonded with my mother and were always sweet to her. But if you tried to approach my mother, the one would go rabid. Never approach her unless she's put him away in the other room, like a mop bucket. And especially, never show up with a surprise birthday cake and wear a cowboy costume to re-enact a scene from her favorite western; *you will never be able to explain that to the paramedics.*

I enjoyed the fun dog, but the other needed intensive therapy and possibly a baptism. We tried integrating him into society, but the rescue group my parents got him from believed he was from a hoarding case, which explained his fighting for food and territorial ways. But it didn't explain why he was only interested in toys and household objects that were pink.

"I thought dogs were color blind?" I asked my parents after they took Winston, the killer dog, on his inaugural trip to the pet store. All the toys he picked were in the same shade of rose.

"There must be something special about this hue of gray for him." My mother threw her hands up in the air. "But you gotta admit, it makes him even cuter." She reached down and gave him a pet. He perked his head up and took off for the other side of the house, returning a moment later with a pink shaving razor in his mouth, making a beeline for my father.

"Help! He's out to shave my legs!"

My mother watched the chaos ensue, knowing perfectly well she could stop it at any time, but instead, she took another sip of coffee and watched Winston chase my father around the living room.

"Winnie must've gotten into the garbage bin again," she smiled, and I laughed at the sweet nickname. "He just loves to dumpster dive. It's in his nature. They said he had to fend for himself, poor thing!" My mother spoke of her new dog proudly as my father hollered for help that never came.

My mother often talked about the dogs she had in her past. Just last month, when she called, the first words out of her mouth were, "Big Al would've been 28 today." Big Al was a little furry mutt she adopted when I was eleven. He was the sweet one and

Winston's sidekick.

Pulling myself together, I drove directly to the pottery cafe, the one I'd *thought* about going to for years now— only to find it closed permanently. It was vacant inside— the only trace of its previous existence was the name on the windows, half scraped off. There was a sign on the door advertising the building was for rent.

"Now what?"

While leaning on the side of introversion, I planned on— or rather, I *expected* Sundays to be out with the people, as I say, so now I was left a little unsure of my footing.

"Dear Jesus,
I'm not sure what to do here, but I'm lonely. Please send me your comfort.
In your name,
Amen"

Looking to see what else was over in this part of town, I noticed a coffee shop to the left that served fancy juices. *Beans and Greens.*

"No thanks," I know my limits on caffeine and veggies.

There was a consignment store, but the CLOSED sign was lit. I drove around to the large car park behind the defunct pottery store, and what do you know, I found the *Newtown Animal Shelter.* It had a flashing OPEN sign illuminating so brightly it could be seen from space.

I saw Samantha's bright blonde hair inside the well-lit building. I drove a little closer, but not close enough that she would notice me or that I might accidentally commit to something. I saw her inside, smiling at a couple holding a big orange cat. She walked them to the door, and the couple came outside. The cat had beautiful plush fur and was licking its new owner's hand as he carried the cat to the car. The woman was carrying a bag of toys. I noticed a stick with a feather peeking out of the top.

I looked at the couple. They were happy, I could tell. My heart ached for a companion. Why was it so hard to meet someone? How did these people find each other? I heard Judy's voice in my head. "You have to go places to meet people!" But I did go places. Didn't I? I just didn't have the same desire for large crowds and swarms of people that others my age might.

Samantha rushed outside to the couple with the cat. I turned my car off to bring *less* attention to myself, but now I could hear Samantha tell them they forgot their carrier. They laughed and put the plush cat inside, although they realized just how *plump* the cat was, as it took up a lot of space. They all giggled, but Samantha said it was safer for her this way, to which they nodded, and the woman promised to return the carrier tomorrow on her way to work.

Samantha waved them off, the happy family now complete with a new member, when she turned her head and saw me. She looked as if she would start crying again as she ran over to me excitedly. In my shock of being caught, I rolled down my window. "I am so glad you came! I— I'm sorry I didn't get your name earlier."

"Katie," I stammered, as I didn't want to say anything that might upset her again, especially the part about how I came here by mistake.

"Katie! That's lovely. Come on in." She opened my car door for me, and I grudgingly swung my legs out onto the pavement.

"I didn't plan on adopting today. I just sort of found the place by accident."

Samantha raised her eyebrows at my explanation and looked me up and down. I had my car door open with my hand gripped on the handle. I felt that if I let it go, I'd be automatically assigned eleven cats, knitting supplies, a mysterious bodily ailment and a diet requiring prunes.

From then on, Katie was known as the old spinster who smelled like your grandmother's perfume and cat food. She always had yarn in her pocket and could predict bad weather with her left knee. Legend had it she could communicate with felines in their native tongue, and at her call, every cat within earshot would come running. But there weren't enough witnesses to confirm that this phenomenon was real. The neighbor lady said it was real, but without video, no one believed her, and she became the woman who cried cat.

Katie's Words of Law
Appeal
ə-pēl

Formerly known as "no takebacks" on the playground.

Samantha felt my anxiety and put her hand on my arm. "Katie, I know just what you need." She turned, waving for me to follow, which I did, curious as to what that was, considering I didn't quite know myself.

The shelter was immaculate inside and smelled like calming lavender. I pictured a distressing kennel, but there were only a few gentle barks in the background. There were two small wings, each with a long corridor clearly marked: Dogs and Cats. I expected to be led into the latter and for her to hand me some fatso tabby that just wanted to eat and sunbathe, forever sealing my fate of becoming a *cat lady,* which didn't sound so bad since they seemed independent, but she led me to the dog wing.

Standing in the hallway was a man with an obvious athletic build. His back was to us as he wiped down the windows looking out to the back lawn.

"Tommy? This is Katie," she gestured to me as he turned around.

He might have been the most attractive man I'd ever seen.

Samantha was right. She *did* know just what I needed…

"Nice to meet you, Katie." Tommy smiled a white-toothed grin. He had wide eyes and that permanent stubble look.

"I was thinking of kennel 11." Samantha's words were drowned out by my curiosity of this man. Tommy nodded in agreement with her when the front door chimed, and Samantha excused herself to see who was there.

"Follow me, Katie."

My feet floated down the hall after him. I'd go anywhere with this handsome guy.

"Here we are. Katie, this is Dolly."

Before I could blink, he handed me a milk chocolate brown *curly* creature that weighed about five pounds. I looked down at Dolly hesitantly, and by her eager gaze, I guessed she was happy to see me. I felt my head shaking back and forth, trying to quickly get out of this situation before I hurt anyone's feelings.

"Oh, I just don't think I can. I mean– "

This didn't deter the athletic man in the slightest.

"Katie, would you just look at her for a minute?"

I got a better grip on her and held her out before me. Our eyes met, and I couldn't ignore the facts: she was tiny, and I couldn't imagine her needing much more room to roam than my apartment; she seemed very calm, considering I was a stranger and all. But the biggest fact of all: next to this man who handed her to me, she was the cutest thing I'd ever seen.

From the pages of Katie's Dictionary:
dog
dŏg, dŏg
noun
A domesticated creature that you provide all the finer things in life yet can't claim as a dependent on your tax return.

CHAPTER 3
GONE TO THE DOGS

"Let's go into the playroom and let you two get to know each other better, shall we?"

We followed the man into a colorful room with rubber mats covering the floor. There was a box of toys, some water bowls, and large windows showing the outside dog run. Posters of happy customers and their adoption stories lined the walls.

"Here we are. Go ahead and play for a while. Dolly is a bit of a shy one since her owner passed away, but Samantha has a real talent for matchmaking, and I just *know* with time, you two will be inseparable."

Here I was, having an incredibly handsome man talk me into this little curly-haired creature. "Oh, alright, we will just— "

He quickly left the room, shutting the metal door behind him, and both Dolly and I stared at the door for a second before returning our eyes to each other.

The loud noise of the door mechanism made me recall when my mother brought home her current rescue dog.

"You'll never guess what happened today," my mother shouted into the house, and the door caught a gust of wind, slamming shut. "Oh, there there, sweetie. Don't let the door scare you! This is your last stop."

"What's going on?" My father hollered from his chair.

"Come on out, guys. I have a surprise for you!" Mom hollered back.

I had been working on a term paper but happily accepted the distraction. "Okay, I'll be right out. Let me just finish this sentence."

Pounding away at the keyboard, I made a rough ending to the paragraph when a brilliant idea came to mind. I started typing away again when I heard a terrible noise followed by the screams of a grown man.

If you could imagine the noise a rabid animal would make when it received its first eyebrow wax, that's about the shrill volume I heard coming from the living room. I pushed my rolling chair away from the computer desk and launched myself into the commotion.

My father was lying on his back, and my mother was holding a tiny dog who was licking her hand. I was at a loss for words.

"What in the world happened here? Dad, are you okay?"

"He's fine. Little Edward here just felt intimidated, that's all. How was he supposed to know your father is so *clumsy?*

I went over to my dad and offered him a hand up since my mother wasn't assisting. "Thanks, Katie. I have my hands full, as you can see. Isn't Edward as cute as they come?" She was beaming.

"Is that *ours?*" I couldn't imagine her response being yes. Any other response would've been acceptable. *'I've volunteered to take him to the looney bin.'* Or *'No, he's escaped the circus.'* But my father and I groaned in unison when she cried out, "Yes! Meet your little brother, Katie! Edward Fitzgerald. Very regal, don't you think? Maybe he will grow up to be a banker or a lawyer. Of course, he could just be *mommy's perfect puppy* forever, too."

After helping my father to his feet, we both gaped at my mother, who had utterly transformed now that she was holding the little fuzzy *dog.*

"Are you momma's baby?" The dog excitedly wiggled in her arms as she cooed to him.

"That *thing* is a national security threat for all I know. Katie, if only you could've seen how it came after me!" I looked down at my father's legs.

"Dad, you're bleeding!" He was known to need a band-aid if he so much as *looked* at something with a sharp angle, but he was right, this dog drew blood.

"Don't be ridiculous! You just have thin skin. Here, Katie— take Eddie for a moment, and I'll be right back." She thrust the little guy, who we knew had a thirst for blood, into my arms, and I felt the fear wash over me. His body started to rumble, and a slight growl stirred from his throat.

"Hurry! He's about to get me too!"

She didn't hurry. Instead, I swore I could hear *laughter* under her breath. "Found them!" She exclaimed.

"Grab the antiseptic, too." My father hollered back.

"What was that? No, I found something else. Here— Katie's old shin guards from her soccer days. You two have the same legs. I bet they will fit fine." She leaned down and adjusted the strap around his calf. "See? I knew it."

Edward's growl grew louder.

"Someone help me with this guy!" My panic filled the room.

"Just set him down Katie. Let's see these things in action!"

I didn't want to leave my father like that, but I also feared for my neck with him being so close. I set Edward onto the ground, and he went straight for my father's exposed ankles.

"OWWW!"

My mother covered her mouth. I couldn't tell if she was concerned or laughing. "Okay, okay. It's not his fault. He's just decompressing. Come here, *Eddie*. Katie? Better call 911. There's an artery around there somewhere."

My limited exposure to dogs up until this moment was fleeting and *frightening* and only occurred when I was home visiting my parents, so I didn't know how to start with this little dog.

"Hi, Dolly. My name is Katie."

Big brown eyes looked up at me, and she gave a slight wag to her tail, which made me feel guilty for the words to come.

"I'm in a bit of a situation here. You see, I wasn't intending to adopt today and..." Dolly tilted her head. She might not understand what I was saying, but she'd been through a lot in her short years of life— I couldn't imagine she was that old— and for a moment, I just stopped. Stopped talking. Stopped *thinking.* I thought back to church this morning. This was a creature that God created that needed a home. I had a home. I had the time. I had very *little* going on, and honestly, I was lonely. I wanted a husband. I wanted a family. Maybe Dolly *could* help me out of my shell?

The only thing I could do was pray.

"Dear Jesus,
I pray for your guidance here.
I don't know what to do.
In your name,
Amen."

For the first time in my life, I made a *desperately uncalculated* decision, picked Dolly up, and we left the playroom and headed for the front desk. Tommy was nowhere to be found, but I saw Samantha brightly looking up, and in a fluid motion, handed me the adoption forms.

"Tommy said it was a go. I'm so thankful for you, Katie! I've filled most of the forms for you, if you just sign here and here," motioning to the X's she marked, "put an emergency contact here," I scribbled in my mother's name and number. "And one more thing— the terms of our shelter are that you must attend at least *one* first-time pet owner's class. You can bring Dolly of course. There's one this Friday at 6 pm."

I looked down at Dolly, who was staring at me with the whites of her eyes. "Oh, I see. How many people usually attend those classes?" The fact that it was mandatory didn't mean it didn't overwhelm me.

"These days, just a handful. Don't worry, I will be there. You can sit with me."

The promise of a chair waiting for me really quenched the anxious thoughts, and I faked a smile. A jolt of panic pulsed through my body as Katie attached Dolly's leash to her collar and handed it to me.

Just then, Tommy skidded out of the dog hallway with a big grin and came over and *hugged me.* "Thank you for adopting her. She's a real sweetheart."

I was blown away by the gesture. I couldn't remember the last time I hugged a man, and I then realized I'd forgotten to apply deodorant that morning, so instead of raising my arms high and he going lower, I did that weird thing where you lean *into* a hug, half bent over, arms out like a ballerina (and back leg in air)– quite the moment to realize I wasn't *flexible* enough to execute. I lost my footing (since one automatically went upward) and fell into his chest. He laughed it off, "Oh, we got a real hugger here, I see."

Samantha pulled out a well-worn small carrier. "Here is a carrier. Please return this at your earliest convenience, and you will need to get one of your own for your vehicle. Here is a list of a few more items that Dolly will require, along with food recommendations. And if you use this veterinarian," she handed me a card reading *Dr. Michael Wylons, DVM,* "you get a discount on all services for the first three months."

I immediately wondered if he was young and single— maybe Dolly was the missing piece to my love life?

Samantha, as if reading my thoughts, added, "He's very trustworthy and knowledgeable. He's been practicing for almost forty years." *Of course, he has.*

Samantha helped me put a flimsy harness on Dolly that matched the flimsy leash she was already wearing.

"These will do until you can get her a proper one. May I recommend the pet store on 29th? They have a beautiful selection of durable items with prints perfect for this little princess! And they even have some handmade items from local artisans." Her eyes glittered with excitement as she spoke. She handed me a bag labeled 'Essentials.' "Here is some food, reading material, and answers to common questions. Give it a look over. Now," she came around the counter and crouched before Dolly, "How about one more trip outside so we can show your new mommy how to take you out?"

We took Dolly outside to the grass. I was having an out-of-body experience. I tried to tell Samantha this was a mistake. That I was trying to go to the pottery cafe because my 89-year-old best friend couldn't hang out today. That I wasn't sure I could do this. But all that came out as I was hyperventilating was, "What do I do— what I meant— I am having an— accident?" Samantha looked at me quizzingly, trying to piece my word salad together.

"It's going to be okay. You girls will get along swimmingly, I just know it."

My body trembled, and I felt an embarrassing rush of tears to choke back, so I was thankful when another car pulled up. A family I recognized from church arrived with their preteen children. Samantha was beaming and swiftly tucked the carrier handle under my free finger that wasn't hoisting the bag up and thanked me as she turned to welcome the family in.

"Katie," She called back as she held the door for them, "I will see you Friday at 6."

It wasn't a question, and I nodded in reply, my hands full.

Dolly stood in the wet grass, shivering as she waited for us to leave. I asked her if she went potty, and her unimpressed gaze said she was ready. I didn't know how the leash would work, as I recalled my mothers' dogs always struggling with the concept, but I found when I took a few steps, so did she. We slowly made our way to my car. I looped the leash around my wrist while I set the carrier inside, buckling it in around the handle like I saw the cat people do. Surely, that wasn't their first pet, and I didn't hear Samantha inviting them to the pet owner's class.

I reached down and picked up Dolly, who felt a little damp from the grass, and I wiped her off a little with my sweater sleeve. I sat her in front of the carrier, and she quickly hobbled inside, spinning around, and laying on the mat like she'd done it a million times before. So far, so good, I thought as I closed the carrier door.

Generally, the moment I closed my car door, my internal monologue would resume. I blamed it on all the time I spent working in solitude. However, this little dog might have thought I was cuckoo if I started in. But then again, I wouldn't want to be dishonest. I wasn't crazy, at least, nothing in a clinical aspect. I was just regularly crazy. As my mother always said, there are levels to any diagnosis.

I started the car, flipping my rearview mirror down to see her in the back seat. She was still okay. I drove slowly at first, expecting her to have something to say about— anything— but she remained silent all the way to my apartment. It wasn't until I pulled in that I remembered I didn't even know if my lease allowed me to own a pet. A mild panic washed over me. I didn't want to get evicted, charged fees, or have a bad rental history. *This could be an out.* A way to undo the adoption I wasn't prepared for. I instantly felt guilty for thinking that no matter how relieved it made me feel.

But when I got out of my car, Dolly's carrier in tow, I looked around the complex. I saw at least ten dog owners walking around with their pets on a leash. Okay, maybe it was allowed.

Once we made it inside my apartment— now *our* apartment— I set Dolly's carrier down and opened the door. She cautiously walked out and looked around meekly. I opened the bag Samantha had given me and pulled out the kibble and supplies list. In the kitchen, I found two ice cream bowls and filled one with water and the other with her food, apologizing to her in advance.

"These bowls will have to make do until we go to the pet store."

Her eyes perked up at me.

"The store? Do you want to go to the store?"

She didn't do it again, but I decided we would go this afternoon, and I changed into a sweatshirt and jeans with some rain boots as the weather looked like it was about to revert to the ol' soggy foggy.

I went to my closet to search for the clothes and felt my legs weaken. I fell to the floor, and the tears started flowing uncontrollably.

"Dear Jesus,
I'm not sure I can do this.
I wasn't ready for this responsibility.
In your name,
Amen"

My words were broken, and my voice was muffled as my head lay in my hands. Moments later, I heard a tiny body breathing next to me. It was Dolly, and as I reached over to her, she licked my hand.

"Oh, thank you for the kiss." I lifted her up to me, and she started to lick my tears. I cried a little more, but after a few minutes, it was followed by a washing of relief over my body.

"Well, Dolly— " She looked at me when I said her name, "that was my scheduled nervous breakdown for the day. Shall we get on with it?"

I sat her down, washed my face, changed my clothes, and put on a few dabs of makeup. She patiently sat on my bathmat, watching every move I made. "There are a few things we must learn about each other, Dolly. The first is I haven't lived with anyone in a very long time since I moved out of my parents' house. You are my first roommate, but I know I'm not yours. I hope you will give me the grace to get used to you, as I will you."

She stared at me intensely as I applied my makeup. There wasn't enough product in the world to hide my puffy eyes, so I decided to loiter a bit longer until they calmed down.

Picking Dolly back up, I moved our housewarming party to the living room, where I fetched my cell phone and dialed my mom. She answered on the second ring.

"Hi! How was church?"

She lives a few states away and likes to compare notes on Sundays from what we each learned from our sermons. My ear picked up on barking in the distance. I was prepared to start right in about the dog, but then my mother got a chance to speak.

"Hello? What happened? Are you okay? Are you in the hospital? Is this really Katie? IS MY DAUGHTER DEAD?"

"Seriously, Mom, stop." She is known for watching way too much true crime and now can't handle the mundane reality of my life.

"I'm okay, but I have some news."

My mother gasped at the words.

"What? What is it? Oh, or should I say, *who is it?*"

She wasn't the only one hoping I'd called to tell her I'd met the love of my life, and he was about to whisk me off to his Italian villa where his family was royalty. Though the only crowns I'll be wearing in my life would be from Burger King, I'd live in a tent if it meant marital bliss.

I sighed. "Well, I adopted a dog."

My mother screamed and I heard her opening the front door of her house. She paused for a minute, telling me to wait until she saw her neighbors outside.

"Hold on, they are just getting out of their car."

My mother always says, 'hold on' when really, she means 'be quiet.'

"Okay, I'm holding on tight to my couch!"

"What? Hold on, Katie!"

"Bracing for impact! Ahh!"

She shushed me and then made her neighborhood announcement. "I have a grand dog!" She shouted, and I heard clapping. I started laughing at the thought, and I was beginning to feel excited about Dolly. She immediately hit the button for a video call, her favorite way to bombard me. I accepted it, pointing the camera at my new little furry roommate. My mother freaked out again, speaking to Dolly in baby talk, to which Dolly responded well and put her ears back a little. My mother was natural at these things.

"How did this come about, Katie?"

That was a great question.

"Well, at church today we had someone from the animal shelter come and speak. The shelter is full, and they are desperate for adoptions."

My mother gasped.

"I didn't intend to go there," I said. "I just kind of showed up by accident, and they saw me and the next thing I know— "

"I would've done the same thing! I mean *look* at her. She's just an innocent little *floof*."

Looking at Dolly *did* make me smile. I wasn't ready to admit to my mother how overwhelmed I felt.

"Does she have a bed, or is she just going to use that ratty old blanket she's on right now?"

Dolly was sitting on a brand-new blanket from Pottery Barn, but I pulled out the list, reading off some of the necessities, to which she added a few more.

"You'll find a grass pad for your balcony a lifesaver for those early morning and late-night potty breaks."

I listened in amazement as she went on.

"She will need seasonal sportswear since she's so tiny. Clothes are not just funny anymore. They help small dogs retain body heat. You don't want her to get cold."

The word *sportswear* made me think of tennis outfits or the 'older' ladies' clothing section at stuffy department stores. Although I was still too young to shop in that section, I did look forward to the day when shoulder pads and sequins were mandatory. I could dress like a country singer every day.

"Have you considered grooming her yourself, or will you have it done professionally?" *Grooming her myself?*

Katies Biblical Application
"The righteous care for the needs of their animals," Proverbs 12:10

"Oh my. What do I know about any of this? Can't I just get that done somewhere?"

I could barely keep up with my own grooming. Looking at Dolly's curls, I didn't think I could keep them nice by myself. I could barely handle my own hair texture. Though I washed it often, my hair required help that I didn't know how to give. I'd tried styling it several ways, but it attracted frizz.

Once, while at the mall, I saw a woman with her hair woven into two braids with a big thing of fabric intertwined. It was only her and I eating cinnamon rolls in the food court on a Saturday night, so my staring didn't go unnoticed.

"It's called heatless curls. You braid it around a band, and once you take it out, you have movie star hair."

"Thanks for the tip. I gotta try that."

The next day, I did try it, but the only thing I found that could work for the fabric was the belt from my bathrobe. It was a little too comfortable, however, and a few hours later, my neighbor knocked on my door because she'd just returned from vacation and had received one of my packages by mistake. Her eyes went straight to my hair.

"Hi, Katie. "Um," she visibly forced her eyes away, and I was smiling as if I'd forgotten all about it. "I got this package for you, and uh, is that the band from a bathrobe? Young people these days– always setting new trends."

Trying to act natural and not show my embarrassment, I took the package without saying a word, just smiling back and nodding. The next day after work, she was sitting on her porch, the belt from a bathrobe in her hair, pointing at it and giving me a thumbs up.

My mom was still going on about the necessities. "And that's why you should always have an enema bulb on hand. It has more uses than you'd think, and if you need it, you really don't want to have to buy one in person."

Oh my, what did I miss? Time to change the subject. I told her about the mandatory first-time pet owner's class, to which she was thrilled.

"Dolly is really going to open your world up."

We talked for a while more until she agreed I needed to get on with it because Dolly didn't even have a bed yet. She made me promise to send her a picture of what I purchased the moment I got home.

"Wait, Katie DON'T HANG UP!"

I was halfway setting my phone down when I picked it back up, giving a pet on the head to Dolly, who looked very concerned at the hollering. She would learn soon enough that this was very normal behavior.

"Yes?" I said with a laugh. "It's not like you couldn't have called me right back if I did hang up?"

"Okay, fine. But I want to show you my flowers outside!"

I agreed because they were truly spectacular. She walked outside with her camera shaky, and I could see the neighbors were sitting outside in their lawn chairs. "It's a beautiful spring day!" She exclaimed. "I'm showing Katie the flowers."

She's having a full-blown conversation with her neighbor, Kathy, so I have a minute to absorb the images.

There were multiple clusters of fat roses on thorny vines in red, pink, and coral. From the looks of it, she had just laid fresh mulch and cut her grass. I could smell the picture, and it was a heavenly combination of aromas.

I remembered when we moved to that neighborhood, one of those heavily power-lined communities near the freeway. It was nice, though, because a few school friends lived on my street, and then some more just for the summers out of custody agreements. We would ride our bikes all day and night, getting popsicles at the corner convenience store and drinking out of the hose. Sometimes, I would have a group of girls for a sleepover at my house. We would dress up, pretend to do our makeup like pop stars, and sing along to their CDs. We wore hair scrunchies as accessories and had a two-ponytail minimum. Boy bands were the only talking subject, of course. My mom would always have some kind of craft project for us to do, like painting terracotta pots or making critters out of modeling clay.

Once, one of the girls' mothers called while we were painting the terracotta pots. My mother answered the phone, her hands full of the paintbrushes she was cleaning for us so we could try different colors.

"Hello?" Her voice was rushed but friendly. "Oh, hi, Kimberly! Yes, we're here, her hands are full- she's doing her second pot right now." The mother must have heard wrong because she then demanded to speak to her daughter.

"Hi, Mom. No, what do you mean, am I smoking?" All eyes turned to my mother. "No… we are *painting* terracotta pots."

CHAPTER 4
CANINE CAPERS

"Okay, I'm back," my mother flipped the camera back to her face.

"Can you show me the camellia tree?" I knew I had to get off the phone, but the weather there looked warm, sunny, and rejuvenating, and I missed it.

"Isn't it beautiful?" She asked as she showed me the towering tree with stunning white blooms covering every inch. It was taller than their house. "We have the tree trimmers scheduled for next week. It's getting awfully close to the power lines. I'm afraid the neighbors will petition to have it cut down if it takes down the power again. Though I still don't know why Barry was so upset about that– he has a generator, after all. How am I supposed to know his robotic toilet paper dispenser doesn't work on a generator?"

I laughed at the memory. "It's breathtaking. Where's dad?"

"He's watching the game. Too bad he's missing out on this gorgeous weather."

"Tell him about the dog, will you?"

"Of course, I will. Well, you better get on with it, Katie. Dolly needs her things."

I quickly agreed and said I'd be in touch soon.

I looked at the list for Dolly:

Carrier
Small breed food (brands listed)
Harness, collar, and leash
Name tag with contact information
Food and water bowl
Toys for enrichment and fulfillment
Treats for training
Bed
Jackets/sweaters for different types of weather

The last one made me giggle. Sure, I had seen dogs dressed up in the past, but given her size it not only made sense, but seemed mandatory, just as my mother said. She would need at least a coat when she was outside. Just leaving the shelter, she was already shivering. I would try to find something practical.

I let her get a drink and sniff her food for a while before we got ready to leave again. Her harness was still on, so I just had to get her leash ready, and I went for the carrier. Before I could even put my hand on the carrier handle, she had gotten inside. I was impressed by her training.

"Good girl!" I exclaimed.

We got down the steps and made a pit stop on the grass before we went to the pet store. I took Dolly's leash and found that she knew just where she wanted to potty, quickly doing her business before loading herself back up again. I was smiling ear to ear when one of my neighbors, whom I'd never met, came running over to me.

"What a beautiful dog!" She hollered loudly, bringing unwanted attention from everyone else outside.

"Thank you…?" I wasn't sure how to respond. I didn't pick Dolly out of a lineup, nor did I make her with my own hands, but I felt that response was appropriate regardless.

"I'm looking for another dog." She stated. I jumped right into telling her about Newtown Animal Shelter being full to the gills, and she had an urgent call to action written all over her face. "Thank you for telling me! I will go there!" She ran off and I let out a small sigh mixed with a prayer.

"Dear Jesus,
Please help the animal shelter.
In your name,
Amen."

We loaded up into the car as easily as before, and in seconds we were off to the pet store. I took Samantha's recommendation and found the one on 29th Avenue but it was much, *much* larger than I was expecting.

Staring up at the towering super store, I wondered if I would need to tap into my savings before I walked in. "How much can one little doggy need?" I looked back at Dolly, half expecting an answer.

I was about to find out just *how much* a dog needed.

From the pages of Katie's Dictionary:
High Maintenance
high-maintenance
adjective
The smaller the dog, the more it requires to survive.

I grabbed my purse and list and decided to take Dolly in on just the leash so we could try on things, and she walked excitedly into the store. I was immediately greeted by a young staffer, name tag reading *Mitchell.* He dropped down to his knees and put his hand out to introduce himself to Dolly.

"Hello, miss. My name is Mitchell. Do let me know if I can help you," and to my surprise, Dolly lifted her paw to shake.

I gasped at the revelation of her *trick.* With my lack of knowledge, I certainly hadn't considered the fact that little dogs that aren't in shows can learn them. Mitchell laughed at the delight of Dolly, just nodding to me, and walking away, not giving me even an introduction.

As I strolled through the store, I quickly learned the rules of the pet world. Everyone we met greeted Dolly and would ask questions I didn't know the answer to.

"How old is she?" "Is she purebred?" And I only had one response. "'I'm not sure. I got her at Newtown." To which they would always smile.

"That's wonderful. Congratulations."

Then they would tell me about their dog's stats, age/breed/likes, and dislikes, which foods to avoid, and their favorite groomers, doctors, and pet sitters. Since it never got personal, as no one gave any indication of even their first name, asked mine, it became fun. And by the third round of this, I was starting to pick up on cues. "What treats are his favorite? Has she gotten a teeth cleaning yet? Where do you go for nail trimmings?"

I started taking notes from other people's recommendations, and an hour passed when I had the entire backside of our supplies list covered with the standards of other dog parents, and my cart was full. All that practicality talk went out the window, and I had a pink sweater, a purple raincoat, and a pink sparkle collar with a heart-shaped tag with my phone number on it that the chihuahua *Coco Chanel Vuitton's* mom helped me pick out.

I had the essential food, treats, and dental sticks that the pug King Louis III's mom recommended. The vitamins, toys, and food puzzles that Brussels Griffon, *Mr. Dingle's* dad swore by. Then, after seeing another poodle-like dog, *Captain Curly-Q*, his mom recommended and helped me make an appointment for a grooming inside the building, which Dolly would get on Wednesday.

We breezed through the checkout line. Dolly was worn out from all the pets and attention, and surprisingly, I felt energized. I didn't wince when the bill was over $200, either. *Dulce,* the terrier's mom, told me this would be an expensive trip, but if I purchased quality goods, I wouldn't need to replace them. So, she made sure I bought the orthopedic dog bed with self-heating capabilities and matching blankets. I was ready for the blow when the amount came out of the cashier's mouth, and happily swiped my credit card, glancing over at Dolly once more, who was looking back at me with sleepy eyes.

On the way home, we made a pit stop at the Pup Street dog bakery. I couldn't resist the urge to stop in after *Priscilla*, the long-haired chihuahua's mom, told me all about it. That they had human-looking food– but it was all for dogs. Getting Dolly a special treat sounded like the perfect way to settle into her new home.

We pulled into the parking lot, snagging a spot right up front. "We're here," I let her know, as her expression hadn't changed in the least since the checkout line.

I was undoing my seatbelt and gathering my purse when I noticed a very striking man come out of the bakery, holding a small dog similar in size to Dolly. He was walking fast to his car with a bakery bag in his hand. No doubt he bought something for that cute fluffy dog he was carrying. He had dark hair, stubble, and a prominent jaw and nose. He looked like a manly-man type, but the small dog he was *carrying* really brought it home for me. Since I've only been a pet owner myself for a few hours, I was starting to wonder just how long I'd been missing out on things.

He got into his red truck seconds later, and he and the mysterious fluff were gone. Smiling to myself, "There IS hope, Dolly!" I got out of the car, picked up Dolly, and we went to the bakery.

Priscilla's mom was spot on. This place was a wonderland. Frosted cookies, birthday cakes, cupcakes, biscuits, treats of all kinds, in any shapes or sizes you could ever need. I wished some of it was for people. After looking at the menu, I settled on a mixed bag of mini cookies, the smallest size they made.

"-Ello! What can I get for ye, sweet cheeks?" The woman behind the counter was loud and charming, talking directly to Dolly.

"A mixed bag of mini cookies, please. For shapes, I'll take 2 mini hearts, 1 mini princess crown, 1 blue purse, 1 purple pup cup, and… 1 fireman hat because I still don't know what she wants to be when she grows up." I didn't know I had it in me to joke with strangers, but the woman behind the counter burst into laughter. I smiled back, giving Dolly a little pet. I certainly felt a new confidence with her around.

At the register, the same woman rang me up, and I expected the questions to start rolling immediately, and they did. "And what's yer' name, ye perfect little chocolate muff'in?"

"This is Dolly." I hoisted her up in my arms, so she knew we were talking about her.

"Well, nice to meet yew, Doll-ay' P-aw-ton!"

The people behind me in line all started laughing as did I, and it felt good.

Dolly and I returned to the apartment. I could tell Dolly was happy as she plopped into her new bed once I removed the tags. As my mother suggested, I set up the grass pad on my balcony and then sat and reflected on the day. I couldn't have pictured what this day would bring in a lifetime. It was more socializing than I had done all year in just a few hours.

And something else happened while I was at the pet store, but I couldn't quite explain it. It appears I was feeling comfortable in my own skin for the first time in my life— being able to lead with something other than my own insecurities and frizzy hair. I had this little curly dog that everyone wanted to know about, without breaking my personal barriers and limitations. There was a strong sense of community in the pet world, that we were all on the same page.

Maybe having Dolly meant I could be something other than an introverted, jigsaw-loving, husband-wanting shut-in. I was now responsible for someone else's well-being. It didn't have to be about me anymore. And then I realized that's exactly what I wanted all along— relief from the pressures of attention. It's not that I didn't want people talking to me or directing conversation at me, but up until this moment, that was all that ever happened. Because I was riding solo, aka husbandless, thirty-something spinster, her only outing was church to sit with her 89-year-old best friend. But now that I am a dog owner, it's easing me a little more into the waters of society, finding common ground with others whom I have little in common with, and most of all, attending mandatory class(es) for pet ownership. Samantha did note that the first one was mandatory, but I might need several to learn all that I could about the care of my new furry companion.

After sending my mother pictures of everything I bought Dolly as promised, she video-called me. It didn't matter to my mother if I was sitting in a doctor's office, at the grocery store, or at the movie theater– the lady loved to video call.

"Hi. Where's Dolly?" She was concerned when I answered with my face instead of the camera pointed at her new grand-dog. I swapped the camera over to show the little furry creature lying asleep in her new bed.

"Oh, there she is! My angel! Okay, Katie. Leave the camera on her. I want to see her. But I just wanted you to see what I ordered for Dolly. It will arrive this week. I got this small wardrobe with– look at them– MINIATURE hangers! So cute. She will need it because I ordered her some– okay, a LOT of clothes." We laughed as she showed me screenshots of every outfit– princess dresses, footie pajamas, a leisure suit, and an outfit identical to my old private school uniform. I laughed– hard– until I felt nauseous. It was glorious, joyful, gut-busting laughter.

I then decided to check in with Judy, who had no cell phone. It was 3:30 pm, and surely, she was home from the animal shelter by now. She answered on the third ring.

"Hello?" Her voice wasn't as perky as usual, which made me feel like my mother. "Hi, it's Katie. Is everything okay?"

Judy laughed.

"Yes, hi, Katie! I am fine. I just got home, and I feel a little tired, that's all. I went to the shelter with Bill and Julie, and, well, they each got a cat and had me pick out the names, which I thought of Tad and Pole. Not very original, I know. But then on the way home,

Tad or Pole— I, couldn't remember which was which, was pawing at me because the shelter ran out of cages because so many people came, and well, I've got cat scratch fever, I'm sure of it!" The saga of the car ride wasn't outwardly funny, but how she told it had me rolling.

"Are you sure? What does the doctor order for that?"

Judy went on, "Now it didn't scratch me *per se.* But it thought about it, I know it did. But that doesn't deter me because you know I like them feisty."

"Well, I am so glad you made it home in one piece!" Talking to Judy always made my face hurt from smiling.

"Yes, I am too. Samantha told us you came by?"

She surely knew the whole story by now, but I was glad she let me retell it in my own words.

"Yes, it's kind of a funny story really. I was on my way to the pottery place when I saw it was permanently closed. And then I was driving around back, and it turns out the shelter was located right behind it. One thing led to another and next thing I know, I own a poodle named Dolly!"

Judy was so thrilled to hear about the adoption and had similar ideas about Dolly being good for my social life. I promised to bring her over to meet Judy after her grooming appointment on Wednesday evening.

"I've been praying someone would come into your life. Furry or otherwise, this is wonderful news. I am so happy for you, and I can't wait to meet her."

Samantha, Judy, and my mother were all so sure about this pairing, and I felt bad for my hesitation. But it was a big decision, and a sporadic one at that, so I eased my mind and remembered I didn't take any decisions lightly. Adopting a pet was a lifetime commitment. Although, hearing Judy and my mother's excitement sure made it that much more fun.

That evening, I decided to pull out a few toys, but Dolly still seemed tired. It had been a very long day for both of us. I emptied out the bag from Samantha to make sure I saw everything, and there was another piece of paper in the bag. Opening it up, I saw it was information about Dolly from her previous life. I decided to read this on the couch, so I picked up her bed, with her in it, and sat it on my lap. It was not overly intrusive for her or me, but that way, we could bond a little. She was awake but seemed to be relishing the peacefulness without other dogs barking.

Dolly
Breed: Miniature Poodle
Age: 3 years (approx.)
Intake: Dolly was found in home after a welfare check. Owner died in sleep, two days before.
1 other dog on site. Do not appear bonded.
No further information.

I gasped at the revelation. Poor Dolly had lost her owner unexpectedly and was alone for a few days until someone came in.

Wait a minute, what was that last part again? I reread the last sentence.

1 other dog on site.

Dolly had a sibling? I thought back to this morning at the shelter. Which kennel did Samantha pull her from? Was she alone in the kennel? I don't even *vaguely* remember a dog being with her, let alone any cold, hard facts to rely on.

"Virtual assistant: Set a reminder to ask Samantha about the other dog," I called out to my robot wiretap, as my mother referred to it.

"Note added. When would you like a reminder?"

At the robotic voice, Dolly's ears stood up, and she looked around to see where it was coming from. I reached over and pet her ears, soothing her thoughts as she looked very concerned.

"Remind me at 5:30 pm Friday." I laughed at Dolly's suspense. "It's okay, Dolly. That's my assistant." I found myself picking up on my mother's baby talk language. Dolly did feel calmer instantly.

We spent the rest of the evening dozing on the couch, and I snapped a picture of her for my social media. *"Life Update: Adopted a dog. Everyone, meet Dolly."* Surely my 57 connections would eat this up. And within minutes, I had 16 hearts.

As we prepared for bed, I realized I hadn't considered what would take place when I went to work tomorrow. I lived close enough that I came home for lunch anyway, so I would just see what happened and pray for the best.

"Dolly," I felt a little unsure of my words, considering she wouldn't know all of them, but I had a feeling she understood me. "I work tomorrow. Every weekday. But I will be home during lunch to check on you." I placed her bed on the floor beside mine, but far enough that if I got up, I wouldn't accidentally step on her.

"Goodnight, Dolly." I gave her head a few pets, and out of nowhere, I had tears running down my cheeks.

Dolly looked very concerned, and she licked my hand.

"Oh, thank you, Dolly." I was surprised at my own emotion but knew it was a combination of feeling overly overwhelmed and overtired.

I made a huge life decision today. I slept that night very lightly, waking up to every creek and bump, expecting Dolly to need me or outside or something I hadn't considered, but she slept quietly through the night.

By the time my alarm went off, I was barely drifting into slumber, and while it used to be difficult coaxing to get myself out of bed, I peeked over and saw Dolly standing at the bedroom door. I lunged out of bed and opened the door as fast as possible while she circled. I remembered I had the grass pad, so we tested it out. It worked beautifully, and not one of my neighbors needed to see me in my pink bathrobe– their *loss.*

I jetted into the shower, getting ready as quickly as possible so I could take Dolly outside a few more times before I left. She seemed easy so far, just desiring some quality rest from the looks of it, and she was snuggled back in her bed as I slid out the door.

Being an introvert amongst *extreme* extroverts at work was a daily battle. Every Monday morning, we would meet in the conference room, where the entire team would get briefed on our proceedings, case updates, and tasks for the week, so there was never any question about what needed to be accomplished.

One of my co-workers, Chaz Gorman, was very *slick.* He was your stereotypical, *sleazy* guy who would probably return to college just to be in a fraternity all over again. He always made it a point to sit next to me at these meetings, even going so far as to slide his chair as close as possible. It wasn't that he *wanted* me; rather because I *didn't* want him, that I was now the target of much-unwanted affection. He wore heavy amounts of cologne and had an ego the size of Australia.

I rarely spoke out in these meetings, and only if called upon, which, given my status as a paralegal, was uncommon for lawyers to ask my advice on a matter. But my strong suit was research, and lately, I'd been given more work because they felt I did the most thorough job out of the rest.

From the pages of Katie's dictionary:
Silence
Sīləns
Noun

The knowledge that anything you say can and will be used against you in a court of law.

We all shuffled into the conference room at 8:59, as our meetings would promptly start on the hour. I saw two empty seats near the door, rushing to grab one when I turned and saw Chaz make eye contact and give me a head nod. "Suzie?" I called over to the other newer paralegal who'd just transferred to our firm from our headquarters in Montana. "Why don't you sit with me in case we need to team up on anything?" The look on Chaz's face was livid. Suzie, who'd been standing next to Chaz, glanced over, and glared at him as she accepted my invitation. "That's a great idea, Katie."

Phew. One less creep to encounter today.

The head of our firm, Frank Fink, entered the room, and we all smiled and said good morning. If we were the solar system, Frank would be the sun. While the work culture could be toxic at times for me, being different on the scale of values, Frank was the reason I stayed and probably the reason everyone stayed. He was a kind, older man who you'd know would never come at you at 4:30 pm on a Friday with a surprise. If something was wrong, he didn't ice you out. And when you did good, he congratulated you immediately. There was no secretive narcissism in Frank, and nowadays, that is rare with a boss.

Frank cleared his throat. "Good morning, gang. Hope everyone had a stellar weekend. Me and the wife headed to the coast and did a little ice-cold surfing. My teeth are still chattering!"

Everyone let out a laugh, nodding in approval.

"I've realized we've had a lot of changes this year. Quite a few of you are new to our firm, and other than your names, we don't know anything about you. I'd like to change that today." My heart immediately began racing. This had never happened before. Our Monday briefings had always been just that— brief, to the point, and *work-related.*

"Let's go around the room, sharing whatever we want to, nothing we don't, and let's make it fun, guys!" His cheer was contagious for everyone *but me.*

"I'll start. You all *should* know I'm Frank. What you probably don't know is I collect snow globes— the glass kind. Before you get any ideas for my Christmas present, I only like to buy them myself!" Nervous laughter croaked from my throat. I had a mild sweat breakout along my hairline.

We went around the room, and I learned that Cynthia from Indiana was married with four kids under the age of ten. Surprising in the least, because she didn't wear a wedding ring and seemed to be always going out with *'the boys,'* as the office collectively called the group of male post-grads who worked here.

Darren was a first-generation college graduate and had been working on getting his parents immigrated here from Zimbabwe. Jackie shared that her favorite color was blue, and she and her husband hosted a poker game every Thursday for charity. Michaela commented about her love for snow globes as well, and a few people cringed. Jonathan talked about the weekend that he spent roasting a chicken and perfecting his sourdough bread recipe and walked around the room with a picture of perfectly crisp looking loaves.

Suzie was next, meaning I went directly after her and I still didn't know what I would say. Suzie stood up and introduced herself while simultaneously whipping out a picture of her calico cat. Suzie told us she was single and identified as a *'Crazy Cat Lady.'* People smirked and smiled, *the boys* whispering amongst themselves and laughing.

She sat back in her chair, her expression changed as if considering that she may have overshared information about herself. But I felt like anything I would say was an overshare. Frank nodded at me, giving me a verbal prompt as well. "Katie, you're up to bat. What did you do this weekend?"

Whew. He asked a direct question that I had a prepared response to.

"I adopted a dog."

The crowd went wild. Like my experience at the pet store, this revelation set off my co-workers in an endearing way I didn't know they were capable of. They all started bombarding me with the *usual* questions for my dog ownership; "*What breed and is it a boy or a girl?*" "*Where from?*" "*How old?*" "*Trained or naughty?*" "*Show us a picture!*" Several people backed that up, responding in whooping 'yeahs!'

I hammered out the answers as if I was reading off her adoption paperwork.

"Miniature poodle. Girl— named Dolly. We think she's about

three. Trained. She's getting *Bytes & Bark* kibble, *Surf & Turf* treats, and getting groomed at the pet store on the 29th." A few people nodded at the extra information.

I added a few more tidbits, expecting those questions to be next, and was surprised how that sparked another round. Meanwhile, I pulled out the picture I took of Dolly last night for my social media. Frank motioned to Jackie, his assistant, who retrieved a cord to hook into my phone. "Let's cast that on the big screen, shall we?"

I didn't expect anything less after revealing the news about Dolly, and once again, I felt more comfortable in my skin with my co-workers than I ever had before.

As Jackie handed me the cord to cast my phone on the screen, it must've had a software aneurysm because my phone swiped back a dozen photos and froze in place. I visibly panicked, stood, and said, "Jackie, wait a second." I put one finger up to stop her, but her back was to me as she and Frank were consumed with troubleshooting the projector.

"Just a second, Katie. I'm just as excited to see it as you are to share it. Aha!" Jackie swapped the cord placement, and you'd think in my lapse of brain function during a panic episode, I would've had the wherewithal to simply *unplug the cord from my phone.* No, sometimes it's just not that simple for my brain to comprehend.

In a flash, a photo of me getting ready for work while wearing that *hideous* shapeless vomit gray coat that I took to show my mother what heatless curls looked like while using the belt from your bathrobe, along with my exuding shame— captured the attention of the entire office.

Katies Biblical Application
..And if I perish, I perish. Esther 4:16

"Oops, Katie, I think– " Jackie now understood what I was trying to prevent.

Finally, I had the lightbulb go off, and I unplugged the phone.

"Was that a bathrobe belt in your hair, Katie?"

I didn't respond, and I understood immediately that Suzie was trying to squash any shame she felt by her oversharing by placing it on me.

Katie's Words of Law
Tort
Tôrt
A social "no-no", but not technically an illegal act of wrongdoing (with exceptions).

"It's called heatless curls, Suzie." Jonathan quipped back. "And with hair like Katie's, that is naturally frizzy, it's a great idea. My wife is a hairdresser, so I pick up on these things."

Gee, thanks, *Jonathan.*

Unplugging my phone magically *unfroze it,* and I selected the *correct* photo, plugging it back in.

The cuteness of Dolly's picture on the big screen made the entire room let out a chorus of 'oohs' and 'awes.'

"How did this come about?" Frank asked, still smiling ear to ear about Dolly. They all turned to me for her adoption story. I nodded, remembering I recounted this many times yesterday to strangers I could do it again now.

"We had the manager from Newtown Animal Shelter make a plea for adoption at our church yesterday." Suddenly I felt like I was having an out-of-body experience. I felt confident speaking as surely as Samantha in front of my co-workers.

"You see, the shelters are full. They have run out of options for their animals." The room turned solemn, some gasping around me. "It was what I had to do." That made me sound a little *high and mighty*, and I wasn't about that, so I added. "I wasn't sure about it. I was— I am still very nervous about dog ownership, but when I saw Dolly, I went for it."

The room *applauded.*

Frank stood. "Katie, thank you for sharing." He turned to the table. "Gang, why don't we focus some efforts on the Newtown Animal Shelter this week? We still haven't picked our non-profit for our annual giving drive." My jaw dropped. "And on that note— look, I love animals. How about this," Frank walked from the table, hands in his pockets, and looked out the floor-to-ceiling windows at the rainy weather outside.

"If you adopt a pet from a shelter or rescue— whatever it may be— " we all paused in absolute amazement, "— you get a 5-Day

PAW-ternity leave!"

We all laughed and clapped, cheering him on. He was pumping his fists in the air, receiving praise. "Jackie, write it up and pass it to HR. And while we are at it, why don't we turn our old conference room into a doggy daycare for our employees!"

At this moment, I may have blacked out from the ricochet effect of my actions. My face was stiff and numb from smiling. Everyone patted me on the back as the room shuffled out, still cheering.

Frank was doing a slow jog, high fiving everyone on the way out, and I overheard him yelling from the water cooler. "Who wants to go with me RIGHT NOW to Newtown!?" People started screaming, and Suzie chimed in. "Buster needs a friend!" The frat guys stopped their cheering to look at Suzie, who was up in arms, smiling. They looked at each other and then started cheering again when someone pulled out confetti poppers they *just happened* to have on hand.

I was standing now, though I didn't remember getting up from my seat in shock. I looked at this group of oddballs in amazement. What just happened? And what was it about dogs that brought everyone together?

I gave the group a few minutes to calm down before I pretended to collect all my materials for the meeting, but they were still impeccably organized, considering we hadn't done any business talk. When I hoofed back over to my cubicle, half of the crew was gone, no doubt having taken Frank up on his offer to visit Newtown.

I smiled and remembered my prayer from yesterday to help the pets. Looking around once more, I noticed the people who were absent now were some of the ones who rattled me the *most.*

"The Lord works in mysterious ways," I whispered, beaming.

Five minutes into my lunch hour, I started collecting my things ready to leave when I checked my social media. *42 Notifications.* What now? I only had 57 connections. I clicked on the tab and was flooded with comments and reactions, half of which were my mother, who was replying to every comment herself, *thanking them* for their kind words regarding my new dog.

Then the text came in.

Hi Katie, this is Samantha. I'm absolutely floored. We had eleven pets find homes this morning, and they said you sent them. Your boss Frank even donated $1,000. Are you my guardian angel?

My heart was warmed. She sent a snap a moment later, and opening it up, I saw it was a photo of cringey Chaz holding a Persian Cat with the caption,

Soul mates (paws emoji) (white heart emoji).

Another text immediately followed.

That guy just asked me out. What do you think? (laughing

emoji).

I wanted to reply with a big warning sign, but then I realized she must've thought he was a cheeseball, or she wouldn't have had the laughing face. Objectively, I didn't know him that well. My suspicions told me he didn't have much going on in his personal life either. He seemed to go for any woman that would look in his direction.

Oh really! I don't know him that well. Can't form an opinion either way.

I knew that was a lame cop-out, but I didn't want to be *complicit* in whatever happened between them. You need to be so careful these days, at least, that's what my mother had told me from the day I was born. I certainly didn't want to *recommend* anyone go on a date together. For all I knew, either of them could be a serial killer; or worse– the type of person who stands the moment the airplane lands.

Katie's Words of Law
Accessory
Ăk-sĕs'ə-rē
Noun

Telling someone they look good before they leave the house when in fact, they do not.

CHAPTER 5
A DOG'S NEED FOR SEASONAL SPORTSWEAR

I hurried home to check on Dolly, and when I raced up the steps, I peered into the small window next to my door. She was sitting up in her bed, alert. Did she hear me coming? I opened the door and greeted her. Her energy levels had gone up tremendously since yesterday, and she raced over to me, wagging her tail. I felt a twinge in my heart to be greeted so enthusiastically. I took her out to her grass pad once again while I heated up my soup in the microwave. She quickly did her thing and then wanted to come back inside, where she retrieved a toy from the collection we purchased and shoved it as far as it would go in her mouth. I laughed and reached for it, but she ran off, not wanting me to take it. "I was going to give it back!" I hollered over to her, where she was now tearing into it under the futon.

Every time I peeked over at her while I ate my soup, she started wagging her tail, but her focus did not leave the toy. It was a toy shaped like a birthday present, with a little bow on top, all made of a plush material. Inside it was a squeaker that she loved to activate. I found the noise to be pleasant and *cute. She was cute.*

Everything she'd done was cute. I looked at her in wonder. "How hard could this really be?" She looks back at me, not feeling my sense of overwhelming anxiety, wagging away.

When I returned to work, the rest of the staff reappeared, all smiles and looking exhausted. I knew the feeling well. It was how Dolly and I both felt yesterday. Jenna, one of our accountants, came by my desk not a moment after I sat down. "How is Dolly settling in? Is she experiencing any anxiety or acting standoffish?"

I never considered she might be, but now thinking about it, why wouldn't she? A major change in surroundings like that would be jolting to anyone *or anything, for that matter.*

I considered a set of house plants I'd had for years. They got adequate sun, water, and nutrients from a regular schedule of fertilizer. But I took a temp job right out of college and was thrust into a very negative work environment and absolutely hated the work. That first week of my being there, all my plants died. Once I was able to manage a change of scenery, some of the plants recovered but it took years for them to bloom again.

"So far, we are meshing well. She was a tad low on energy yesterday, but we also had a lot of errands to do after I adopted her."

Jenna nodded. She explained how her husband was an animal behaviorist, mostly contracted by zoos and specialized facilities. "That's perfectly normal. Give her time. Don't be surprised if she becomes much more loving and active as the weeks go by. She needs plenty of time and patience to adjust to her new mom." Jenna smiled and gave my shoulder a squeeze, starting to walk away.

Hearing the title made me throw my hands up and laugh in defeat. "That's me. I'm a dog mom!"

Talking with Jenna felt sincere, and instead of going back to her workstation as the conversation came to its natural close, I felt Jenna linger.

"So, you mentioned something about church?" Jenna's eyes were hard on me.

"Yeah, that's where I heard about the pets." I didn't know what she was asking about, yet now I found myself automatically using the *Dolly shield of protection* to provide an emergency exit from the conversation.

"What kind of church do you go to?"

Ahh. No matter how I felt about my own insecurities, every night I prayed that if the Lord needed to use me as a vessel, He could do so. I might not always be as effective as I hoped, but I'd never stop trying. Here it goes. "A non-denominational Christian church. Do you go to church?" I swatted the ball back in her court.

"No, but I, well, I feel drawn to the *idea.*" Jenna whispered now, and for once I felt my voice grow louder with each breath. "Do you have any questions about it?" I'd never felt so bold.

"Well, I'm not sure if it's a question," she sheepishly laughed, but there was no mirth in her eyes. I'm no therapist, but I could see she was troubled. "I've got this…heaviness, you know? From my past. I've read that God will forgive me. But I can't believe it because of the *things I've done.*"

She was talking with her hands and really emphasized *points.* I nodded in complete understanding. I wondered what I should say. I prayed for the right words to come to me at that very moment. Jenna's eyes were stuck on me, waiting, and I didn't want to disappoint her.

"We all fall short of the glory of God. No one is worthy as we are. We are a product of a fallen, lost world. But," I was now offering words of hope, "We can be born again." I reached out and held her hand. She was looking down now and I saw tears well in her eyes.

"I've done some terrible, *unspeakable* things." She spoke like she was cursing under her breath.

"We all have. And Jesus' gift is free. You just need to accept it."

Jenna seemed to ponder that idea momentarily. "But don't I have to straighten up my life first? Honestly, I'm struggling with inner demons."

"God is the one who helps you do that. Look at it this way; when we come to Christ, we are all imperfect sinners. I was completely broken and living a life I wouldn't even recognize if you showed me today. But when we repent of our ways, the ways of this world," I looked down at her hand, "we then ask God to save us, and He is the one who fights those inner demons. We get to call on Him for everything– pain, anxiety, *temptations,* " Jenna nodded at the last one. "And, of course, praise and just getting to know Him. He wants to know us and we want to know Him. He loves you more than you can comprehend."

Jenna abruptly stood up, releasing my hand to hug me. I didn't worry about the eyes on us. Surely others must be wondering, but it didn't matter what anyone thought. Jenna pulled from me, but her eyes stayed locked on mine.

"We would love to have you join us at church," I said. "You'd fit right in with the rest of us," Jenna laughed. "I mean it. I'll save you a seat next to me."

While I couldn't imagine someone as beautifully outgoing as Jenna needing to have a seat reserved to calm any social anxieties, it was still a new environment for her.

"Really? Thank you, Katie. Here," Pulling out her phone, "Can you text me the details? Time and location. I'll be there."

She handed me her phone, ready to add a contact number for *'Katie from work.'* I punched in my details, handing her back her phone, and she swiftly sent me a text, my phone buzzing from my purse.

"That's me. I appreciate it, Katie. I may or may not be attending alone. I need to discuss it with my husband and see if he wants to join. But I will see you then." I pulled out my phone.

It's Jenna!

"Got it." I motioned to my phone, and she nodded. She turned and walked off.

Katie's Biblical Application
"Always be prepared to give an answer to everyone who asks you to give the reason for the hope that you have." 1 Peter 3:15

Frank was nowhere to be seen until about 3 pm, when he waltzed in with a black lab-type dog on a blue leash. "Everyone," he was laughing so hard he could barely get the words out. His wife Angelica was with him. She came by the office sometimes for lunches or staff birthday parties, and we all loved her. "This is Frank Junior, 'Junior' for short. And before you start in," he chuckled at some of the guys, "I didn't name him. Angelica did!" We all laughed.

"We've been wanting a dog for a while, since Bubba passed away." Angelica nodded. I remembered him taking a few days off after his golden retriever passed away from cancer last year. "Couldn't think of a better time to do it than today, with my staffers, who are really my friends with me!"

It was a very heartwarming moment. Frank then let Junior off his leash, where he proceeded to stick his head in everyone's *private areas.* Frank, seeing the mistake, tried to catch him, but Junior saw him coming and picked up speed. We were all roaring with laughter, Frank and Angelica included.

Junior was eventually captured when Suzie got a handle on his collar and waved Frank over. The guilty look on Junior's face was adorable. He wasn't ready to get caught, there were still people he needed to "greet." Angelica took the leash and said goodbye to everyone, giving me a wave and mouthing 'thank you.' Frank waved them off, announcing to the group that Junior was about to go get a full checkup at the vet. My heart skipped a beat.

Why hadn't anyone told me to do that?

I recalled Samantha giving me information about the veterinarian at which I'd receive a discount. I will call tonight and get an appointment for Dolly.

The rest of the day was mostly uneventful compared to the morning. There was still some snickering and a few "woofs" in the hallways— people stopping by with their proof of 'paw-ternity leave,' but it was a tiring day from all the excitement. I considered my new week's leave and considered the best time to take it. But something told me to wait until she got into the vet in case she needed extra care for any reason. And for no reason, I suddenly felt worried.

"Dear Jesus,

My mind is once again in overdrive. Please send me your supernatural peace, as now I'm feeling fear of the unknown. I will care for this precious creature you sent me.

In your name,

Amen."

Finally, the workday drew to an end and I got home as quickly as I could without speeding. I had the same greeting for Dolly, but this time she was napping again and when she saw me, she rolled on her back and did a big stretch. It was precious and I took that as a sign I should scratch her tummy. She loved it.

"Did you have a good day?" The baby talk ensued. We were getting along so well. I was feeling mildly overwhelmed with the new responsibility, but it was proving to be rewarding.

"I'll be right back, *sweetie*." I jumped up to make the phone call to the vet, scattering through the small pile of notes from yesterday. I found the card she gave me. I punched the numbers in my phone. They answered on the second ring, and I let out a sigh of relief.

"Parker Ridge Veterinarians, how can I help you?" The woman had a Jersey accent.

"Hi there. My name is Katie Fitzgerald and I adopted a dog yesterday from Newtown— "

"Congratulations, Katie." The woman cut me off. "I suppose you're calling to get an appointment from Dr. Wylons, yes?"

I love it when people make it easy for me. "Yes, I am! Thank you."

"Okay, let me see what he has. Please hold while I check."

Abruptly, the sound of jazzy-spa music came on. It was very close to a pop song I'd heard before but also remarkably unplaceable. I was just getting the hang of the methodical dance I'd choreographed for it when she came back on.

"Okay, hun. How about tomorrow at 11:30 am?" I could hear her furiously typing on the other end of the phone. I couldn't imagine what she was keying in, considering I hadn't even made an appointment yet, and I let the question distract me.

"Well, I would need to check with work, but– " I remembered the new *paw-ternity leave*, plus our liberal policy for time off. Besides, I hadn't taken more than three days off in the few years I'd worked there. I had *plenty* of vacation days, and thanks to our lack of briefing this morning, I technically hadn't been assigned any specific work. "You know what, that'll do fine. Thank you."

"Okay, Katie. Come ten minutes early to fill out the paperwork. Do you have pet insurance? If not, I can help you with that."

Pet insurance? I laughed at the visual of a dog with a briefcase selling insurance, but it made *so much sense.* "I don't, yet. That would be great if you can. Thank you."

"Come twenty minutes early, then. My name is Patty. I'll get you all situated. Thanks, dear." Click. I set down the phone. I loved nothing more than when other people anticipated what I needed, especially when I didn't know I needed it– like Samantha. I looked over at Dolly, who was inviting me to play with her as she squeaked her toy. I went over to her, sharing the news.

"Tomorrow, you will be getting an exam just to be sure you feel your best."

My mind flashed back to a photo my mother sent me years ago when she first took Edward to the vet. He was wearing a full-faced muzzle, with the caption, *Edward loves his new doctor!* She had said, "I told them this wasn't necessary, but Dr. Lakeson insisted after Edward did a little stampede on him when he walked in the room.

He's such a misunderstood little guy. But it really makes him look like a *bad boy.* I think I'll get momma's tough guy that spiked collar, after all."

I picked Dolly up and held her with one arm, carrying her around the house. I think I really liked Samantha. She was the type of person I needed in my social life. It was a little out of my character, but I decided to return her earlier text with a phone call.

"Hi Samantha, it's Katie."

She seemed a little caught off guard, but not in a bad way.

"Hi Katie! How is everything going with Dolly?"

I realized now that she probably thought there was an issue that might only be resolved by my *returning* Dolly.

"Oh, everything is wonderful. You were right. She's exactly what I needed. I can see that now."

Samantha let out a sigh of relief. "Thank you, Katie. You don't know how happy that makes me to hear it. And I really do thank you for everyone you've sent to us and your church. You'll be happy to know we have adopted twenty-six pets in the last 24 hours! That means open kennels, so we can officially accept more pets. For the first time in a year, we have more going out than coming in!"

I remembered this woman was crying in her car just a day ago, and I told her she was making a difference. My prayers had been answered.

"Dear Jesus,

Thank you!
In your name,
Amen"

Samantha sounded busy in the background as the bell on the shelter's front door rang. "I've just had some more carriers delivered from a donor!" She excitedly exclaimed.

"Well, I won't keep you, Samantha. I just wanted to say I will see you on Friday."

Samantha paused. "Oh yes, about that, Katie. You see, we've had such an influx of adopters this week— that class will have a few more people than I originally thought. Of course, I will still be here, and I promise I will have your seat reserved!"

Was it painfully obvious how socially awkward I was that she felt the need to say that? Regardless, I was relieved to hear it.

"That's wonderful! Thank you for reserving my seat. I'll be there with bells on." The first time I used that phrase and wasn't being sarcastic. I should get a T-shirt to commemorate the moment.

We hung up, and I texted Frank about missing work tomorrow because of Dolly's appointment.

He texted back almost immediately, agreeing I needed to take the day off, and said I should just take the rest of the week, plus next Monday, since I worked today and it's a new benefit and *rule.* I didn't want to argue with him, and his use of emojis in the text seemed so joyful that I just gladly accepted.

Well, I wouldn't want to break the rules. Thank you (dog emoji).

He replied.

Thx, see u next week (dog emoji) (dr emoji) (tennis ball emoji) (thumbs up emoji) (dog emoji).

Still holding Dolly, I whispered in her ear. "Guess what? I have the next seven days off!"

She looked up at me with wide eyes, tilting her head as if saying, *'Now what?'*

I replied, "That's a great question, Dolly. Let's ask my virtual assistant for the answer."

"Virtual assistant," I had yet to come up with a name for my robotic voice to answer to, "What's a good activity to do with dogs?"

"Activities with dogs: see dog park. There are two within your preferred radius of three miles. I've sent the details to your phone."

Buzz buzz.

"Okay, Dolly. It looks like there is a *small dog park* right up the road! Should we go explore that now?"

I started to notice that she reacted cute every time I asked her a question. She would cock her head, wiggle, and slightly wag her tail. I looked outside— not raining, but a little overcast. I went to her bag of things that I still hadn't organized yet, which was out of my nature as I was usually very neat and tidy. I found the thicker pink sweater we had purchased yesterday. It took me several minutes to figure out the harness went on first, *then* the sweater, with the loop for her leash having a built-in hole in the sweater. Dolly was very patient, and I apologized to her for the delay, laughing at my ignorance of how to dress a dog.

Once she was in the getup, I snapped a quick picture of her because she looked so tiny with her brown curls almost static against the sweater. I sent it to my mother who immediately replied.

Lolly Doll looks pretty in pink (dog emoji) (pink bow emoji) (heart emoji).

Before I could reply, actually— before I could blink, three more texts came through from my helicopter mother.

Where are you going?
Give me an address.
Isn't it getting dark soon?

From the Pages of Katie's Dictionary:
Sleuth
slooth
Noun
(Insert photo of Katie's mother here.)

It was 5:27 pm.

We are going to the Bark Park at 613 Ave W. Sun will set at

7:13, according to my weather app. I'll be sure to call the police on any suspicious bags left unmanned, but they may just be (poop emoji).

She video-called me. I answered it to find the screen zoomed in on the bridge of her glasses.

"Mom, hold the phone away from your face, please. I can't see you."

"Oh, sorry, hold on." She pulled the phone outward, and I saw that she was outside in a lawn chair. It was sunny and flowery around her. "I just got a notification that your package was delivered already! I just ordered it yesterday. So cool! Anyway—since you're going out, Dolly's going to need to wear the rain boots I sent. Also, let me know what she thinks about her knitted hats."

I peeked out my door, and it wasn't sitting on my step yet. "It must be in the front office, but they close at five. I'm sure they will bring it up tomorrow." I turned the camera to Dolly. "She can't wait to see her new clothes. I don't want to cut you off, but we were just leaving."

"I better get back to my case anyway. We just got new details." She would say, "*we*" as if she was *actually* involved in solving a crime. "Have fun, you two! Don't talk to strangers and text me when you get there and again when you get home. I'll be tracking your location regardless. Bye-bye!" She hung up.

I really wished I could ban her from the mystery channels.

I loaded up a small backpack with one of Dolly's cookies, the foldable water bowl I saw at the checkout stand yesterday, and some waste bags and a water bottle. My stomach growled, and I realized I had forgotten about dinner, so I grabbed a small bag of almonds and a few wrapped chocolates and settled on getting something *convenient* afterward.

Picking up Dolly, we waltzed to the car as I whispered in her ear that we were off on an adventure. I saw she was not shaking in the evening coolness, and it seemed the sweater was doing its job.

The Bark Park was less than a mile from our apartment, but I was surprised that it was behind a small, wooded area. There was a large parking lot with a handful of cars.

If my mother only knew I was about to be traipsing through the woods.

But it was still daylight, and I could see a young family walking further ahead on the path, so Dolly and I embarked down the wooded lane.

It opened up into a huge clearing with a large, fenced area marked "Off Leash", and a smaller fenced area marked "Under 20lbs," and a built-in agility course. There were several people there of all ages with dogs of all sizes. I was surprised to see only one Dolly-sized dog who was currently alone in the small pen, so I quickly walked over and placed Dolly inside, keeping her leash in my hand in case that dog wasn't friendly or not interested. The other dog, a small white, frizzy-haired mutt with a head like the Chihuahua we met at the pet store, but a larger, plump body with skinny legs. It looked like its proportions were drawn by a toddler, and I couldn't hold back my laughter when it walked over to Dolly because its hind legs *wiggled.*

"That's Prince Henry," a woman called over to me from the benches. "He's friendly, don't worry. Not a mean bone in his body." She was referring to my clenched fist on Dolly's leash when I realized even my body was hunched in anticipation.

"Oh, okay. This is my first dog. Just got her yesterday." I called back to the woman.

Several people looked over at me and nodded, smiling, throwing out words like "congrats" and "nice."

Dolly and Prince Henry acknowledged each other briefly. Dolly seemed more interested in the grass Henry was standing on than him, but they both started to play after a minute, and it did seem harmless. I unlatched her leash and awkwardly walked to the benches marked "Pawrents." I sat beside Prince Henry's mom for a while. Neither of us said a word until I became very curious about her dog. "What breed is Prince Henry?"

The woman cackled. "I call him a torpedo. It certainly is the shape of his body!" She laughed, and I stood to examine his shape from a distance, seeing it was an accurate description. I started laughing a little *too* hard, and she just shrugged and smiled, saying, "I know, it's crazy."

After a few minutes, I began to feel bad for laughing at this little creature who couldn't control the shape of his body, so I tried to scale back my laughter, only for her to pull up a picture of when he was a puppy.

"He was born fat," she explained, which made me giggle again. Looking at this puppy picture of a sad little face, wiry hair going every which way, and a nearly naked body sitting in a pen, I realized he too had been at the animal shelter, and my laughter subsided at the sobering reality of the pets who needed homes.

"Dolly is from Newtown," I told the woman, pointing at her as she was now playing a rousing game of chicken with Prince Henry.

The woman nodded, smiling. "Adopting is the only way for me." She pulled out a small photograph that was in her purse next to her.

"This is Cora. She was dumped by her "*family*"at the animal shelter when she was twelve because they *bought a puppy.* "The woman made air quotes with her fingers when referring to the dog's previous owners. In the picture, there was a precious older dog with a white face and big brown eyes. She was surrounded by blankets and toys and had a chew bone sticking out of her mouth. "After my husband left me for a younger woman, I heard about Cora, who'd been through the same thing, and knew I had to get her. We helped each other heal." The woman put the picture back in her purse. It appeared she had a designated spot for it. "I'll never stop missing her, but she improved my life."

CHAPTER 6
TAKING CREDIT FOR MY PET'S APPEARANCE

Prince Henry started trotting away from Dolly and found something to roll in. "Henry, no! You naughty boy!" The woman jumped up and ran after him, laughing. She stepped into the pen and picked him up, giving him a once-over to see if he smelled.

"That's our cue," she walked back with Prince Henry and took her purse. "Someone needs a B-A-T-H!" Prince Henry's eyes immediately went wild, and he squirmed, nearly falling out of her arms. "Oh, I forgot, he knows how to spell!"

She started walking away when she looked down at Dolly. "Oh, I know you!" She called out to me. "She was here earlier— with your husband?" The look on my face must've been cross, as she immediately backtracked. "Or brother?" She smiled to break the stale moment.

Hollering back, I fumbled my words. "I'm lonely." Oh no, "I mean— I'm alone. Ugh! I'm SINGLE!" I nearly screamed when I realized how embarrassing my slip-up was, with all the other people turning to listen to this exchange, and I hadn't even answered her question. Even Prince Henry was completely still, eyes locked on me.

She nodded, understanding. "She must have a doppelganger in the neighborhood. Take care," she picked up her pace and quickly disappeared into the trees.

My face was hot from my Freudian screwup, and I beelined to pick up Dolly, leave, and never return to this park. I remembered there was another park in the area and vowed I wouldn't make a fool of myself at that one. To prolong the pain, when I hopped into the pen to catch Dolly, she took off thinking we were playing.

Remembering Jenna's words about Dolly's adjustment period, I didn't want to discourage the play time. I worried it would hurt our relationship if I acted rashly, so I started whispering to her to reason. "If you let me catch you, we can go to the other park and play all night. We could *live there* if that's what it takes. I'll buy a tent. We really, *really* must leave this one." I was motioning to the ground as if she would know I meant business. She slowed down, wagging her tail, and I ran over to catch her. It was then that I stepped into something special.

I heard snickering from the Pawrents benches, and I wasn't sure I could sink any lower, but I knew it was always that moment when you feel lowest that you need to stop, pause, and reflect. To which I did. I could wash the shoes. I would never see any of these people again. Dolly was having fun. Everything was alright. Breathe. Breathe.

BOOM.

Something hit my head at high speed, but it was tiny and light and didn't hurt. A miniature, bright green frisbee fell to the ground. In my humiliation, I pretended it didn't happen– any of it. The dog poo, the flying saucer to my noggin, the people laughing at me. This was what introverts had nightmares about, and I was sure I would for the rest of my days.

"Excuse me, miss?" a male voice called.

I stood still, thinking that if I didn't move, I'd become invisible, and he would walk away.

"I'm sorry about the frisbee. Yikes, I have a terrible aim." He let out a low laugh, and soon enough, the rest of the dog park patrons were busting up.

I started to dry heave in what felt like crying, but it turned into a voracious laugh, and Dolly, very concerned, ran over to me and I picked her up. She started licking my face, and I felt better. Still laughing, I turned around to see the man who was speaking.

I couldn't have prepared for this moment if I'd been given a year's notice.

Yes, *of course, he was handsome*– the odds of him not being in this very instance were *low*. He had scruffy hair and green eyes. It looked like he had just come from work. He was wearing scrub pants and a V-neck. I tried not to look him up and down, but I did hone in on his hands and noticed a lack of a wedding ring. I let out a sigh, having a complete argument inside my mind. There was no way *he* was single. All the cute guys I'd met in the last decade were either taken, committed (both asylums and priesthood), or identified as male witches. He must've just forgotten to put his wedding ring back on after the gym where his personal trainer wife was giving dance classes in her time off from being a supermodel.

But the biggest shock of all was when a small boy around ten years old walked over with what could have been Dolly's twin. I noticed this the whole time the man was looking at Dolly– I was looking at this dog– and we both looked quizzingly at each other.

The little boy piped up. "Woah! You have the same dog as my uncle!"

The resemblance was *uncanny.* My mind drifted off to the note in Dolly's intake: *1 other dog on site.*

"It appears we do, buddy." He patted his nephew on the head. "What are the chances of that?" He let out another small laugh, reaching down to pick up the dog from his nephew's arms.

"Hi, I'm Eli, and this is Carter." He held out his ringless hand, meeting my free one that wasn't holding Dolly. I robotically shook his hand but still hadn't said anything in reply. He turned to Dolly and reached out his hand for her paw, which, just like at the pet store, she accepted the shake, daintily putting her paw in his palm.

"And what's your name?" His voice got a little higher, appropriate for dog-speak but still manly– all while revealing a dazzling smile.

"Um…this is Dolly." Finally, the attention was off me, and I could stumble through my words again. But hearing me speak, he tilted his head and stared back. "And you are?"

Now I was getting weirded out. Why was a married man interested in my first name? Of course— unless he *wasn't* married— but how could that be?

Katie's Words of Law
Innocent Until Proven Guilty

Give the man a chance to finish introducing himself before the wild suspicions begin.

"Katie."

He smiled and nodded his head. "Hi, Katie." He just stood there, smiling at me, and considering me with some sort of *wonder.* He straightened his body, crossing his arms as if he was waiting for *me* to make conversation about our matching dogs. He ran his fingers through Carter's fuzzy curls. Carter let out a small yawn as he looked around us. No, Eli wasn't about to budge. He was making this *hard* for me. The ball was in my court.

"I adopted Dolly yesterday from Newtown." It worked.

"You did?" Those green eyes widened.

I was used to smiles and joy whenever I said this, so I was a little caught off guard by his reaction.

"Yes— I did." Now questions pressed on my mind. "Where did you get Carter?"

"Newtown."

Okay, well, I realized it *was* a big animal shelter in our

neighborhood so— that didn't mean this was Dolly's sibling, right? Or…?

He let out a laugh. "I got Carter a few years ago when he was just a baby." He paused. "Should we see if they know each other?"

Now that was a great idea. I nodded, and we leaned down to set them on the grass. Carter closed the distance between them immediately, and they sniffed each other. He bounded around Dolly in a quick loop, looked at her, crouched down on his front legs, and let out the smallest but mightiest-for-his-size bark. We both laughed.

"It appears they do." I closed my eyes as I uttered another lame comment. Must I only speak when I must painfully point out the obvious? Could I be a *little* more mysterious?

"Well, Katie, since our dogs are acquaintances, and it's likely they are probably litter mates…that means it would be an injustice to them for us not to have play dates." He smiled, looking like he felt pleased with himself for such a smooth response.

I was elated to hear him basically asking *me* out and was halfway into a nod, ready to reply something witty about being a paralegal and taking a stand against injustice, when a beautiful woman in pink running shorts jogged over to us. Her perfectly tanned legs made me look nuclear with how pale I was in comparison.

"Eli, there you are! Are you ready to go?" She held up her hands, flashing a *huge* diamond ring.

So, he wasn't married, but *clearly,* he was spoken for. It was all in my head, after all.

Feeling a shiver from Dolly, as if she was reacting to the situation, I said, "I'm sure we will see you around. Bye-bye, Carter," so the woman would know I wasn't hitting on *him.*

I turned to walk away and heard the woman say something about the dogs being *identical.* "Wowzers— twin doggies!" She seemed kind as if she wanted me to reply so she could hear about the dogs, but I had no energy left.

I was halfway through awkwardly stepping out of the small dog pen when I remembered what my shoe was covered in— the exact shoe I was leading with and had in their perfect line of vision as I lifted my leg over the short fence. But the most embarrassing part about this afternoon was happening live: the squish from my shoe loudly echoing with each step for everyone on the Pawrents benches, and now Eli and his presumed fiancé to hear. I wondered if Dolly was as ashamed of me as I was.

The quick walk through the woods holding Dolly was just a long-winded prayer for my shame.

I felt Dolly's short legs tighten on my arm as we went down a set of wide steps into the parking area. Loading her up in the car, she hopped into her carrier and did a quick spin around just like the times before. But this time, she was wagging her tail when she looked back at me.

"Did you have fun, Dolly?" I put my hands on my hips, smiling at her for an answer, and tilted my head. She started to wag harder, and then the best thing happened: she barked in reply.

I closed her door, and we zipped home. The sun was setting fast now, and I heard my phone buzzing. It was probably my mother letting me know she was tracking my location and that I missed my turn. The old me would've glanced at it at a stop sign. But I had precious cargo now, so my mother could wait until I got home.

I'd forgotten my mild starvation by the time we pulled into my parking spot. I'd have to make do with something I already had, but at this point, anything I could find was better than leaving the house again. When we got in, Dolly went straight to her water bowl and was lapping it up. I found a box of macaroni and cheese from my pantry and decided this was a day that only cheesy carbs could cure.

While the water boiled on the stove, I heard another buzz from my phone.

"Just a second, mom!" I called out as if she could hear me.

But it wasn't my mother. It was Samantha texting me.

Hey, girl. You will never guess who I just got off the phone with. Eli, which I am presuming you've already met. LOL! Tommy remembers him adopting Carter a few years back and said he's cool. Anyway...he asked me for your phone number. Just wanted to check with you before I pass it along. Let me know what happens with Eli (heart eyes emoji) (dog emoji) (twins emoji).

Wait just a minute. *He called her?* For my phone number? Maybe– oh my. Either he sincerely just wanted the dogs to meet, and it was never a romantic thing or– or–

I decided to reply to Samantha immediately.

Hello there! Yes, we did meet briefly at the dog park. Sure, you may pass my phone number along. He mentioned the dogs' wanting playdates. Think he is married or engaged though, so it's just about the dogs. (dog emoji)

My water was at a roaring boil, so I quickly threw down my phone on the table to tend to it, slowly adding in my macaroni.

"Virtual assistant: play soft music."

A lovely instrumental came on quietly in the background. I peeked over the pony wall in my kitchen to where Dolly's bowls had been set up on the backside and saw she'd moved on from her water to her kibble. Her little crunch noises were adorable too as she took a few kibbles and chewed proudly, mouth open.

Watching this little well-behaved sweetheart enjoy her food in her new apartment wearing her new sweater made my heart skip.

"Dear Jesus,
Thank you for this unexpected adventure with a dog. You sure do know what you're doing.
In your name,
Amen"

I really enjoying Dolly's company. She was the perfect little friend for me.

My phone buzzed again. Thinking it was Samantha, I reached over, already smiling. I was wrong again. It was Eli.

Hey! This is Eli from the Bark Park (tennis ball emoji). You took off before I could get your number. Samantha passed it along to me, but said she got your permission first. Does that mean you *will* see us for a playdate? Carter sure would enjoy it!

I set the phone face down on my counter. It was almost time to drain the macaroni, and I started to have a hot flash. This handsome guy with a matching dog wanted a platonic relationship with me. What should I do? There was only one person to consult: My mother.

Dolly and I got settled on the couch, and I removed her sweater and harness, grabbing my big bowl of macaroni, and dialing my mother for a video call. She answered on the first ring.

"Well, there you are!" She sounded alarmed, but she was smiling. "There's my girl! How are you?"

"I'm fine—"

She cut me off. "Yes, I can see that, Katie. I was talking to Dolly."

She asked Dolly a few more questions and got a head tilt in response. "I was reading online that poodles are one of the smartest dog breeds around. She can understand me, you know."

I was laughing already. "No doubt she can, mom." I paused. "Well, I have a mystery that I need an armchair detective to help me solve."

Her eyes widened, and I knew she was excited. She changed from silly to serious. "Give me the facts of the case."

"Well, Dolly came from a home where her owner died. Nothing mysterious about that. Anyway— "

My mother's eyes were wild. She looked at me stone cold.

"What was the cause of death?"

"Old age." She nodded, looking relieved. "Okay, so what else?" This is what she loved doing

"There were *two* dogs in the house."

My mother pulled her head back fast. "Two dogs? But not bonded?"

I nodded. "Not bonded."

She let out a gasp. "Okay…so who got the other dog?"

"I'm going to ask about it on Friday at my pet owner's class."

She nodded. "Well, there's no harm in asking. Okay, so what's the rest of the story?"

"We just met one of Dolly's presumed litter mates' owners. His name is Eli. And he just texted me."

Her jaw dropped.

"So let me get this straight. Dolly has a *sibling* that was adopted by a good-looking stranger, and now you're getting married?"

"Not quite." I think even Dolly rolled her eyes on that one. "He said he got the dog named Carter when he was a puppy. Dolly seemed to enjoy playing with Carter for the few minutes that passed. If it wasn't for the woman standing next to Eli– that, and, well I stepped in some– "

Predictably, she honed in. "What woman?" Her forehead was scrunched together, and she looked riled.

"My best guess, fiancé? Not clear. They seemed chummy. He was also there with his nephew."

We both caught on at the same time. "Sister?" She asked.

Yes, that had to have been it! No wonder he was so boldly asking a woman for a playdate with his dog. That had to have been a relative.

"In that case," I flipped the phone over to text.

"Hey! Where did the video go?" My mom protested, even though she'd just been staring at a static screen of Dolly staring back at her.

"I need to text him back," I said it proudly, and I knew she could hear my smile. "Just hold on a second. I can't do this without Jesus!" I closed my eyes for a quick prayer and felt the peace of the Holy Spirit wash over me.

"Dear Jesus,

Please forgive my rude behavior at the dog park towards Eli's sister.

I pray I will not be so quick to judge again.

Please guard my mouth so I don't appear... Desperate. Please don't let me feel desperate, either. I trust You and You're timing for my love life.

...
And please let that have been his sister.
In your name,
Amen"

When I commenced my prayer, I turned back to the video.

"Yes, you do need to reply! What are you saying? Read it to me. But start with his text. From the beginning! What was said?"

I explained the entire meeting at the Bark Park, starting with the frisbee. She was in a laughing fit when I got to the squeaky shoe.

"How does this happen only to you?" It was hilarious, and now that I saw that it was *probably* his sister, an innocent misunderstanding, I realized I acted a little rude.

"Katie," my mom's tone sobered. "Don't compare anyone to Paul. He was a wonderful man. And there are more out there. Instead of looking for him in everyone who talks to you, listen to who *they* are."

"This coming from the supersleuth that assumes *everyone* is an ax-wielding lunatic? Okay." I smiled. But I knew she was right. I had wanted to find a partner, though I hated admitting it— it was *bad,* but every now and then, when I had even the mildest interest in someone, I felt that no one compared.

"He would want you to be happy." My mother hit it home with the timely remark. I nodded. She was right.

"Okay, back to my text. This is what I'm thinking— "

Hey, Eli. Nice to hear from you. We would love to have a playdate. I'm off from work all week if you two are around. (twins emoji) (dog emoji)
Katie

From the Pages of Katie's Dictionary:
emoji
ē-ˈmō-jē

noun

    The language of those born after 1990; variability of meaning depends on the user, therefore impossible to decipher.

"What's up with all of the emojis?" My mother questioned my texting until I explained my reasoning behind it. The dogs *were* twins, right?

"Can dogs be twins?" She fought back.

"Okay, this is getting ridiculous. Before we start to argue about how many angels can stand on the head of a pin, can I please have permission to hit 'send' here?"

I hit the button immediately before she responded and switched back to the video.

Shrugging her shoulders but smiling when she saw Dolly return to the screen, "Well you don't need my permission. I just think I would've worded it a little differently."

I could always count on my mother to send me that little bit of doubt after I'd done something irreversible, like getting bangs at the mall hair salon.

"Oh, I know *you* would have asked him for his social security number for a quick background check."

She nodded her head in approval. "Now that— *I like that.* Can you add that in there? You can never be too careful these days."

My phone buzzed and I swapped it back over to text.

"Read it to me in real time, Katie!" My mother hollered.

"Okay let me proofread it first," I mumbled.

How about the Bark Park tomorrow at 2? I'm working a double shift, so I get a 90-minute lunch hour.

My mother didn't miss a beat. "Ask him what he does for a living!"

I laughed at that one.

"I will tomorrow. He was wearing scrubs today, so it must be something in the medical field."

"Or he just dresses terribly."

We cackled together for a while longer before she said the quiet part out loud. "Okay, the obligatory, *I've got a busy life,* time has passed, you need to get back to him."

We decided to keep it short and sweet.

Sure. See you then.

And to the joy of my mother, I didn't use any emoji's.

"Tomorrow is Dolly's checkup. So, I'll be going straight to the Bark Park, most likely."

My mother smiled. "Wear muck boots."

After we hung up, I read back through Eli's texts. I *was* excited for the meetup and to see how we all interacted with each other. I closed my eyes, the soft music still playing from the speaker, and Dolly still nestled on my lap on top of the cozy blanket. Eli had nice eyes, and I liked his spitfire personality. I felt we had chemistry, though I'd like to think I preferred someone who didn't challenge me. I knew deep down that's exactly what I *needed*–someone to bring me out of my shell. My personality was fun-loving and even *silly* at times. There were just very few people I'd ever feel comfortable being myself around.

My mind swatted back to Paul in a Manhattan minute. My mother hadn't brought him up in a while, but it wasn't as if I hadn't brought him up myself. I could still feel the weight of my engagement ring from the day I heard that message on my answering machine.

"Hi Katie, it's Paul. I'm calling from my dad's phone. Look, we've been in a wreck in his plane." His breathing was heavy, and his mouth sounded like it was full of sand. "I'm hurt." I could hear mumbling in the background. "I just wanted you to know I love you and I really want to marry you, Katie. I dream about our life together and... I will see you again."

"End of messages. Press 1 to save. Press 2 to delete. Press 3 to play again."

It all happened so fast. Paul and his uncle died from their injuries sustained from a small, fixed-wing airplane crash. His father, who'd been the third person on board, survived but was in a coma for three years. Then, one day, just like that, he *woke up.*

"It's like the plot for a movie," people who knew would always comment. Except for the part where his brother died. And his son, who happened to be my fiancé. And my early chance in life for marital bliss.

But years had slipped by. I was a different person then. It was just as I became a Christian and was learning to feel the love of my Savior. Paul was a remarkable, loving soul. I took comfort in the fact that he believed in the Lord, as I was, since he led me to it and I was attending Paul's church. The last service I attended there was his funeral. I couldn't handle the points and whispers from everyone who didn't know me but knew I was his fiancé.

It was about a year later that I moved a few states away for my current job, but everyone knew it was to get a fresh start— to not be the sad case of the woman whose fiancé died— to now get the chance to be anyone I wanted to be.

There was relief in this move; not knowing anyone, not knowing any *places.* It meant there weren't painful memories attached to the most mundane activities— that I could go to the corner market just up the street and pick out a loaf of bread without being able to place him there, standing in the checkout line, grabbing me a single rose from the bucket at the register.

Grief was like that for me. I'd been very attached to Paul, of course. We were engaged. But it wouldn't let me go. It had its claws in me. Moving was my only solution, and I was relieved that I didn't face opposition from my mother to do so.

"I totally get it, Katie. You'd better find a futon, though, because I'm going to visit you way too often." She hugged me, and while we were embracing, I saw the engagement pictures of Paul and me framed on her mantle. I wasn't the only one who lost Paul, and I couldn't ask her to take them down.

"Let's go get your car serviced and check the tires before your big move." I knew I would miss the friendship I had with her, but truthfully, we spoke so often on the phone and video chatted it was like we were never apart.

CHAPTER **7**
DOGGONE GOOD TIME

After I'd been here a year, my mother had casually probed if there was anyone cute at my work— or if I'd met anyone at the new church I'd been attending. I gushed out to her, "Yes! Her name is Judy and she's 89."

My mother laughed. "I'm very happy to hear you're making friends, Katie."

I knew by the tone in her voice she wanted to ask if I was going to start dating. People from back home would sometimes message me out of the blue on social media and bluntly ask the same thing. At first, I thought I was just a spectacle for them all to see, and they wanted Act 2 of the young widow. I ignored them all until eventually, they stopped messaging me completely.

Until I got Dolly.

That night, when I checked my messages, I had three from people I hadn't spoken to since Paul died.

Oh my word! YOU got a DOG? I'm so happy for you!

Dolly's so cute (cute sad emoji)

Wow cute pup, girl. I am so excited n' hope U bring her back when U visit.

When I visit? "Who said I'm visiting?" I had my reply typed out but didn't hit send because it wouldn't have helped anything.

Then I thought about it. Would I ever be able to visit again? I supposed I could. I'd been here for quite a long time and my mother had yet to visit. It wasn't that she didn't want to, but she had a tough work schedule and since she started helping her local dog rescue, it seemed like every month she had another foster dog to care for.

It was only a day's drive; with Dolly now, it might be a little longer. But she seemed to like the car. I wondered if there was a better way for her to travel. I hopped on the pet superstore website and typed in a few words. "Dog car" revealed hundreds of results for car seats of all types. I was elated to see the bucket style seat that elevated the pup to be able to see out the window.

Buy Now.

"Dolly, how about a road trip?"

She smiled at me with her brown eyes, but her sleepiness returned, and she nestled back to her slumber. I could hear little baby snores coming from her and knew I better not move an inch. Thinking that, I was immediately reminded of how uncomfortable this couch was and searched for a better one.

"Comfort Deluxe Stain Resistant Cloud Couch" came up high

on my list on the furniture website. The color was perfect— an earthy greenish beige that fit perfectly into the background, and I could accessorize with fun pillows and blankets. The shipping was fast. It will be here next week. The price was a tad high, but looking at Dolly in her peaceful dreamland, I hit the button anyway.

Add to cart.

I texted my mother a picture of the new couch, and she immediately called.

"What's that about?"

"No more futon after next week. We will just have to come visit you!"

My mother was elated. "Really? That's the best news I've heard all day! Hold on a second." I could hear her screen door opening. Her neighbors must have all been out in their yards because she hollered out to them.

"Katie and my new grand dog are coming to visit!" I was laughing at her when I heard a few voices I recognized in the background.

"That's a good question, Fred, let me ask them." Shifting her attention back to me, she asked, "Katie, is Dolly good around other dogs? Fred has two shih tzu's." I knew for a fact she was, remembering the wiry Prince Henry and, of course, Carter.

"Yes, very good with others." I was proud. My mother was rambling off to the rest of her neighborhood when I informed her we were going to bed soon.

"Okay, Katie. This is just great to hear. Let me know when you decide the dates and I'll make certain I am free from any obligations. Oh— just try not to come on the 18th next month. That's when our case goes to the grand jury."

I could never get over how she called anything she was following, *our case.*

"That shouldn't be a problem. I'm off for the next seven days on Paw-ternity leave, and since it's just a day trip, we were toying with the idea of popping over for a few nights."

"Oh my! In that case— I better go— the house is *unrecognizable*—I haven't cleaned since you left!"

"Well, maybe we could go to the coast for a night? I really miss that salty breeze and the little restaurant on the cliff. Do you think they allow dogs?"

"I know for a fact they do. Susan and Little Susan went there a few months ago. I'm getting low on my saltwater taffy stash anyway! That sounds great."

I felt the adrenaline pumping through my body as we made more exciting plans. "Well, if we are going to the beach town, I'd love to rent one of those cruiser bikes! I bet Dolly's carrier will fit in the back basket if they are still the same tricycle-style ones."

I could hear my mother shuffling around, with things falling over. "What are you doing?"

"I told you, I'm power cleaning. I have years' worth of things lying everywhere. I don't want Dolly to think I'm a hoarder."

"Did you hear my idea about us renting tricycle cruiser bikes?"

"What was that? Tricycles?" She was barely listening. "I may be mentally ill, but I don't like to look like it." I heard her start the washing machine.

"What? How does a tricycle make you look mentally ill?"

"Oh, did I say that? I mean, go for it, Katie. Rent the bike, I'll walk beside you."

" "
...
" "
...

We both sat in silence for a moment before I had an outburst of laughter. "Okay then, I'll let you go prepare. Goodnight."

She repeated it back and hung up. The sound rustled Dolly from her nap, and I seized the moment to carry her to her bed and get ready for mine. I tucked her in her orthopedic cushions and covered her with a blanket. She did a little stretch and roll, landing on her back with her head perfectly using the side of the bed as a pillow. It was cute.

"Dolly, you are such a little cutie!" I was starting to make less sense with my words, but that was the *fun* of it.

She closed her eyes and I tiptoed to my bathroom. After my nighttime skincare regime, I brushed my teeth and put my hair up in a silk cover to prevent further frizz and breakage. With the humidity here, I needed all the help I could get. *"At least until you find a husband,"* Judy's voice rang through my mind. It was her anecdote anytime I told her I was watching my figure or needing to get my hair done. I loved her sense of humor.

That night we both slept soundly, which I desperately needed after the night before. I was out the second my head hit the pillow and didn't wake up until my alarm went off the next morning.

"Oh no…" I meant to turn off the alarm, since I was able to sleep in today. For a moment I forgot Dolly probably needed to go to the bathroom, and I hit snooze. Sitting up abruptly, my eyes went to her bed, where she was still sitting, halfway under the blanket, but her head was up as if to say, 'Good morning.'

I slid out of the bed, stretching and petting her simultaneously.

"Shall we take you potty?" I whispered. She must've known the command because she filed out of her bed, out of my room and I followed her to my patio, where I slid open the door and she quickly used her grass pad. It was raining out, and I cringed seeing her shiver, but she ran back inside and did a hilarious full-body shake, a small mist coming from her body.

"Good girl, Dolly!" Wow, was every dog this easy? I had a feeling they weren't. My stomach rumbled.

"Time for break-ky!" The moment I said it, my hand covered my mouth in shock. Since my career path nearly led me into *English Literature,* I was horrified at my grammar. But Dolly was thrilled at the excitement and started doing little half twirls around the living room. I poured her kibble, and she pranced right over, the little delicious crunch noises a feast for my ears.

As I ate my vanilla crisp cereal and strawberry yogurt, I planned for the day. Today was vet day. My mind was ignoring the play *date* later, because for all I knew, it was strictly platonic and probably something that happened all the time in the dog world. My mind fired back, 'Do you really think litter-mates parents meet all that often?' It was a good thing only Jesus could hear my thoughts.

I reached for my devotional book and read today's timely study titled 'Hope for the Future.' Its core takeaway was that God had written all our days in His book. There was nothing that had or will happen that He didn't know about. Therefore, we shouldn't worry about anything; just follow Him, and He will make our paths straight.

"Dear Jesus,

I pray for your will in my life. I trust that no matter what, You are with me and there is nothing to fear or worry about. I cast my anxieties on you, Lord, just as you said in 1 Peter 5:7, "Cast all your anxiety on him because he cares for you."

In your name,

Amen"

The moment I ended my prayer, I heard a squeaky toy activate, and I laughed at Dolly's timing. "Oh, is it time to play now?" The joy overflowed from me, and I felt the Holy Spirit wash over me. The last few days were proving that life with a dog was very enjoyable and not something to fear.

"This is fun, Dolly. Now let's see if you can fetch?"

I softly tossed a toy a few inches from her, and she took the bait, pouncing on it and giving it a big chew before shoving it as far as it could go into her mouth. She ran off with it, hiding under the futon, and the toy would squeak every few seconds, a signal she was still playing and having a great time.

"Okay, Dolly. You get that squeaker!"

It was time for my shower and to get ready for the day. My heart skipped a beat thinking about what I would wear since it was raining. That gray raincoat I bought at a super sale last year couldn't be worn again. The color, or lack thereof, drained every bit of life from my hair and cheeks and didn't do any justice to my face. While showering, an idea came to me. Last week I saw a pink raincoat by a brand I recognized in the department store window. I wondered if it was still there.

Putting my hair up in a towel, I traipsed out to the living room in my plush bathrobe.

"Virtual assistant: Is the RainGearX Pink Slicker in stock at Norlands in a size… Medium?"

"Logging into your Norlands account." The robotic voice paused. *"They have the merchandise you requested. Shall I set up a curbside pickup at the earliest time available?"* I let out a sigh of relief.

"Yes. Thank you." I realized I didn't have to thank my robot, but *manners mattered.*

"What a relief to know I won't look dead," I told Dolly as I dressed in a black turtleneck and skinny jeans with thick socks and pulled the black muck boots out of the back of my closet, running them over to the door mat. I ran back to my closet, quickly doing my makeup routine, blow drying my hair, and using an anti-frizz serum liberally. I styled it into a half-updo, securing it with a few pins. This wasn't a gala. This was a rainy day at the dog park, where there would be plenty of landmines to step in, I reminded myself.

But there was still something missing. Hesitantly opening the jewelry box that sat on the shelf, I picked out a pair of pink jewel earrings and put on my rose-gold watch. A little fancy for the Bark Park I decided, but I didn't care. It made me feel polished.

Dolly perked up when I waltzed back into the living area, as if she agreed, *you look good.*

"Your pickup is scheduled for 10:45 am. I've sent the details to your email."

The robot voice made Dolly's ears pick up slightly this time, but it made me jump since I wasn't expecting it. "Thanks!" I called out. That gave me exactly enough time to get to the vet early for the pet insurance sign-up.

I looked at my watch. We still had about ten minutes till we had to leave, and I went through Dolly's bin of accessories to get her ready for the day. I remembered my mother sending that package. I peeked out the door, and sure enough, it was on the porch.

"Yay, fun mail, Dolly!" I tore open the box, pulling out all the darling outfits my mother showed me, plus a few more, to my surprise. The small dog closet needed to be assembled, and the hangers came separately wrapped in clear plastic. "I know what we are doing tonight," Laughing at the giant assortment of items, I snapped a picture to send to my mother. "Thank you for the wardrobe. Love, Dolly." Dolly stood beside the things. The pile was bigger than she was.

I found the raincoat that I recalled her saying something about and paused when I saw it was a beautiful shade of rose– *very* similar to the coat I had just committed to from Norlands. Hmm… I laughed nervously.

"Could it work?" I asked Dolly. "Well, too late now!" It took me a few minutes to get her harness loop through the raincoat, and I did find the little rain boots my mother sent, but I decided I wouldn't subject Dolly to those *yet.* I tossed them in the small bag I used last night at the park, along with a few more snacks and her water bottle and bowl.

We loaded up in the car and drove over to Norlands. To my delight, the traffic was unusually quiet this time of day, and we made it across town in no time. I slid into the designated spot for curbside and clicked on the link my virtual assistant emailed to signal I had arrived.

Not a moment later, a fit, tanned blonde woman came out holding a large Norlands bag. She headed straight to me. It was the woman from the Bark Park that I *assumed* was Eli's fiancé. Even under the overcast sky, her ring sparkled from a distance.

Her long legs glided over to me, and I awkwardly opened my front door, waving hello to her.

"Katie Fitzgerald?" She hadn't looked back to me yet, still reading the receipt. "I have one 'Perfectly Pink Rain Slicker' in a size Medium. Is that correct?" Her name tag reading *Audrey* matched her blue eyes as she looked up at me and made the connection. "Oh, it's you! I know you," She smiled coyly.

"Yes, that's my order." I hoped she didn't know I was meeting Eli later and bought a fancy new coat for the occasion.

"My brother Eli said you guys were meeting today."

I felt my body deflating at the confirmation. *They were siblings. Thank you, Jesus!* But the shock and horror that came next nearly crippled me. "Did you buy this for the occasion?" She chuckled.

My face reddened, and the confidence of the morning was waning fast.

"Oh, that? No, I mean– " I shook my head, trying to backtrack. Why did it have to be *her* bringing this out to me? I have shopped here at Norlands countless times and not once did I remember her.

"I'm just kidding, Katie. *I hope you did because* it will look beautiful on you." Her laughter stopped and she sincerely smiled. "I hope you two have fun with the dogs today. I made Eli promise to send us pictures tonight of them playing! We all love Carter. Especially my fiancé. It's funny how men just gush over little dogs." She shrugged and grinned. "Thank you for shopping at Norlands. I hope I see you again VERY soon, Katie!" She jogged off.

My heart drilled as I slid back in the driver's seat, quickly reversing and getting us out of dodge. Once we hit the freeway, I felt calm again. *She hoped I bought it to see her brother?* How sweet of her, I thought. My mind was going every which way, but it was okay. I was okay.

We reached the vet with minutes to spare, and I spied a pet

relief area. "Do you need to go, Dolly?" She stood in her cage, and I reached into the Norlands bag, retrieving the new coat. It was as beautiful as I remembered in the window and would fit perfectly over my heavy sweaters in cooler weather. It had a nice lining to it, which added warmth and comfort.

I pulled off the tags and proudly went to retrieve Dolly. "Yep, we are twins, alright."

The coats matched nearly *identically.* I wondered if this had been done before or if it meant I was a lunatic. We went to the grassy area and lingered for a few minutes. My insecurity about wearing a matching color to my dog was growing by the millisecond, but we were out of time to dilly-dally and had to face the music.

We approached the glass doors of the vet office, and they slid open automatically. Dolly wasn't sure about the big scary noise they made, so I scooped her up and walked to the counter.

The woman with the Jersey accent greeted us, her eyes feasting on what she saw before her. "Well, hello, girls! Don't you both look adorable today?" She smiled but there was no laughter, just sincerity. "Can I get your name, hun?" Her long, perfectly polished red acrylic nails were already typing a novel before I spoke.

"Katie Fitzgerald with Dolly."

A lightbulb went off in her mind as she put her finger in the air, saying, 'just a second.' She rolled her chair over to the other side of the U-shaped reception area and grabbed a clipboard with a sticky note reading *Katie.* "This is for you to fill out. Once approved, the insurance is $19 a month, and this is what it covers." She pointed to the list of everything under the sun I didn't know could happen to a dog, along with a few things it didn't cover, like annual dental cleanings.

"Do we really need an annual dental?" I whispered to her, not wanting to seem like I wanted to neglect my duties.

"It's just what's recommended, hun. It prevents all sorts of ailments, which if you think about it, makes total sense right?"

I nodded and went to the seating area, where I filled out the paperwork while Dolly waited patiently in my lap.

The questions were vague. *Pet Name. Gender. Age (approx.). Breed. Known Health Issues. Neutered (Y/N).*

"How's it going over there, hun?" The Jersey woman was petite, and I couldn't see her unless I stood up, so I just hollered back since I was the only customer in the office.

"It's about ready, but I need to find out a few of these answers from the vet before I can turn it in."

"Of course. Let me see if he's ready for you girls. You both look so pretty in pink." She winked at me, and I felt my face redden. Maybe it wasn't so abnormal after all to match your dog?

"Hiya. I have your 11:30 here. Yep. Okay, I'll send them back." Click.

"Dr. Wylons will see you in room three. It's just right over there," she pointed to a door off to the side with a giant 3 on it made from paw print fabric.

"Okay, thank you." I nodded and took Dolly into the exam room.

Curiously, the lights were off. I turned them on to see another person sitting in the chair, holding a cat, and both appeared to be asleep. I was so startled that I might have let out a whimper. Perhaps it was only a whimper to me, but everyone else heard a blood-curdling scream.

Patty screamed back and rushed over from her desk. I poked my head back out and asked if she meant another room. She peeked inside and let out a sigh.

"Oh, I completely forgot about them. Katie, go to room four, please." She slid back to her desk, and if I didn't know any better— which I didn't— I'd swear she was wearing tap shoes. There was no sneaking around for her, was there? Her flamboyance was starting to make sense. Before I left, I'd have to ask her about her dancing. After all, I was somewhat of an expert on the subject, having taken Tap 1 when I was five, only to get stage fright during my solo recital when they had me tapping my right shoe to the beat of a Prince song. Hardly seemed appropriate now. That song was better suited for the aerobics class I took when I was seven.

In room four, the door was open, so I walked into the sterile atmosphere and found no surprise guests. It felt like the lighting was a little too bright, the paint was the wrong color, and the scent was very clean but mixed with wet dogs. I didn't love it, so I couldn't imagine Dolly felt comfortable. As if on cue, she started trembling slightly. Instead of putting her up on the table, I decided I'd wait till the doctor came in and gave instructions.

I'd always hated hospital settings. If they'd swap out all the lighting with something a little more *flattering*, it'd be one thing. It was bad enough when you were on a hospital bed, wearing a very thin veil that was a poor facade for a body covering— everything was exposed, and your pores looked 10x the size. Every freckle was darker, every spot bigger, and no matter what you were in there for, the lighting always made it look worse than it was.

And it appeared the rooms here were just as confusing as at the hospital. At least this office was all on one level. The last thing you wanted to do was get the room numbers confused with the floor and wing numbers. I attempted to visit my mother once after her routine liposuction and I didn't realize how large the building was.

"She's in room 223E. Right down the hall, make a left and then she will be on your right."

"Great, thank you!" I walked down the hall, realizing she didn't tell me *which direction* down the hall, but I *boldly* assumed she would correct me if I went the wrong way.

When I finally made it to 233B, the curtain was pulled around the bed. "Hi, I'm here! I brought donuts like you asked." I heard a groan behind the curtain. "Are you decent?" I yanked it back before she could answer.

But she wasn't decent, and it wasn't my mother. *And it wasn't a "she".* This poor guy had quite a few things *wrong,* and I decided he deserved the donuts more than mom did. He seemed very thankful when I left them on his table.

As I turned to leave, he was making deep, guttural noises and blinking his eyes rapidly. I immediately knew what he was trying to ask. 'Yes, they *are* gluten-free."

CHAPTER 8
THEY TAKE A DOG'S TEMPERATURE HOW?

I checked my watch out of habit. We sat there for about another minute when I explained to Dolly, "Doctors are notoriously late to meet their patients. This is perfectly normal." She looked around fearfully with big eyes. I stared at the back door to the room where the doctor would come in, waiting for the door handle to turn. I checked my watch. 11:31. Relax, I thought to myself. You still had *hours* before your date. Er— Dolly's *playdate*.

Finally, around 11:33, the doorknob started to turn, and in walked— wait a minute— this can't be the doctor Samantha told me about. He's *way too young.* He's— my age. Things were looking up. He walked in with a clipboard and a very frazzled hairdo. "Hi... Katie?" He looked over to Dolly, then to me. "Or are YOU Dolly?" We both laughed. "Wait. YOU must be Katie. I am Dr. Wylons. It's a pleasure to meet you." He held out his hand to me, and I awkwardly shifted Dolly so I could quickly meet his hand.

"I was expecting— "

He cut me off. "My father?" He smiled ear to ear. "As of Monday, he's retired. So, you're stuck with me," he winked. "You can call me Taylor." He spoke smoothly.

Imagine my horror as I felt my cheeks redden in reaction to his *flirtation.*

"Dear Jesus,
Please let me leave here unscathed from this embarrassment and don't let him notice my face is as red as a tomato.
In your name,
Amen
P.S. - If he is flirting with me, I pray that I am confident about that before returning any gestures."

Just then, Dolly barked back. It was the perfect *save* and let me take a breath for a moment. He started laughing and put his hands on his hips. I already knew from doing that at home that she would bark again, which she did.

"Well, either she wants me, or she wants someone else!" He loved Dolly's personality, and he walked closer to us, reaching for her. "May I?" He looked into my eyes with his perfect blues.

"Of course," I didn't even blink when I gave him my precious cargo.

It's like when you go through airport security, you don't question anything. *"Take off your shoes, belt, and coat."*

To which you reply, *"Of course, here you go."* But it's just the beginning. *"Take off your wig, Ma'am."*

"This isn't a wig, it's my hair."

…

"That's your hair? But it looks like the hair on my kid's Barbie after they washed it in the kiddie pool."

…

"It's just so… frizzy."

…

"It's my hair," I choke out.

"Move along, Ma'am."

"Nice to meet you, Dolly. Let's see how you are doing." Taylor began a hands-on exam, feeling her spine. "We are just going to do a nose-to-tail check first."

I liked that he explained what he was doing while working through it.

"My receptionist noted that Dolly was adopted from Newtown. I think that's great." He smiled. It wasn't a question, so I just nodded back. He had a very confident aura about him. He put his hand out to Dolly and said, "Shake!" and she put her paw in his hand. "Good girl," he kneeled to inspect her paws. I was impressed at the *thorough* care she was getting.

He had his stethoscope out and listened to her breathing, then her stomach. "Everything sounds good so far." He locked in on me. "Weight?" I robotically answered, my mind shifting to the nurses asking me at the start of every checkup.

"147." He burst into laughter. "Thank you." He picked up Dolly from the metal counter and set her onto a tabletop scale. The scale read *'5.0.'*

"A perfect five." He looked pleased and wrote that down on his chart. Then, he pulled out his flashlight and held her head, but she didn't seem to like that.

"Katie, do you mind holding her while I inspect her eyes? I think she wants her mom for this one."

Mom. I suppose that's me. "Sure." I stood up and retrieved her, but with the giant counter between us and my being only 5'4", I realized that one of us had to lean over quite a bit because he wasn't much taller than I was. I put my elbows on the counter and dramatically pushed my upper body forward so he could comfortably check her when he simply walked *around the counter* and stood beside me.

"Oh, you can do that, huh?" I whispered, now sliding down from the metal table, flashbacks of the horrible slides in elementary school that gave you both whiplash, hearing damage from the deafening noise, and the need for tetanus shots.

He smiled and informed me that his dad was taller. "My dad is six foot seven," waving his hands at the height of the table. "I have my suspicions I was switched at birth, but then again, my mother is four foot ten. I'll be getting these tables lowered." He shined his flashlight in Dolly's eyes, teeth, and ears. He was inspecting her ears for more than a minute. "Any anxiety issues?"

"Who doesn't?" I said, jokingly, but he turned and gave me a very concerned look. "Is she having any trouble at home?"

"No, no. She's a perfect angel so far. I mean, I just got her Sunday, but I work with a woman whose *husband* is a pet behaviorologist?" I knew that wasn't the right word but kept rambling, "And she gave me the signs to look out for."

"The pet behaviorist?" He was half listening, but his attention was in the right place since he was still inspecting her ears.

"The wife of one."

He clicked off his flashlight. "Oh, that's great, Katie. Keep an eye on it.

He then had Dolly walk up and down the counter, using his arms to make sure she didn't fall off the sides. "Her gait is perfect as well. She's a very healthy pup." He wrote something down in his notes. "I'd estimate she's about two or three."

I was going to ask about teeth cleaning when I saw the thermometer pulled from a drawer. "This is the least favorite part for all of my patients, understandably." He laughed as he took her temperature.

"Is it just you and Dolly?" His question came sideways at me, just as the thermometer turned the same direction, but he maintained eye contact during the temperature taking. I couldn't pretend *it* wasn't happening, but I was pleased by his question just as much. I decided then that he *wasn't unattractive;* he was interesting to look at, in a bookish, stocky, *different* way. He looked like he rode a bicycle to work with one pant leg tucked into his sock, but it didn't tarnish his boyish charm. That's what it was: he was sort of, in a distantly familiar way... *charming.*

"Yes, I am single," I said with a smile. He pulled out the thermometer, nodding at the temperature. This was all working out so well for me, first I adopted a dog, *now I met a veterinarian?*

He let out a laugh. "I'm sorry, I— I meant, are there any other pets at home?"

I felt my cheeks start to redden again. "Just Dolly." I hated getting ahead of myself.

"Dear Jesus,
Please, please give me the wisdom to know the difference between flirting and veterinary medicine.

…
Please.
In your name,
Amen"

He tossed his wavy hair to the side as he felt her tummy area. "Everything looks good with Dolly. Keep an eye on her ear canals— they look good, but if I were you, I'd make a grooming appointment soon so she can have them cleaned."

I was happy to report that she'd be getting groomed tomorrow. He nodded.

"It appears she's already been spayed by this small incision here." He pointed to it, which I came closer, and saw with my own eyes. "That's great news. I was wondering about that." I remembered my clipboard, picked it up, and started filling in some of the blanks.

5 lbs. 2-3 years old. Spayed.

When I looked back up, he was looking at me, his hands once again on his hips, indicating he was done with his exam. "I like your matching raincoats." He wasn't moving, just honed in on me with an intense gaze.

"Oh, thank you, it was an accident and now it's too late for either one of us to change," I smirked, now feeling better after having two reinforcements about our outfits. "So now what? For Dolly. I admit I'm a little overwhelmed by all of this, you see I wasn't anticipating pet ownership and now I would appreciate any insight you can provide. Do we need anything? Can you recommend supplements, special food or...?" The longer I went on without him saying anything, the more I lost my train of thought and was feeling a little surprised by his brazen gaze still on me.

"How about dinner? Last I checked, we all needed food."

I was floored.

"I'm free tonight if you are?" He picked Dolly up and brought her back over to my arms. Dolly wasn't shaking and didn't seem to mind him.

Once I read something in a magazine at the doctor's office waiting room about dogs knowing who was *good* and who was *bad,* instinctively.

My mind went back to my– *Our playdate*– with Eli, who said he had 90 minutes, so that would give me plenty of time to prepare for a *date.*

"I am available tonight. Where would you like to meet?" I said this knowing it wouldn't– it *couldn't* be my apartment. My mother would have a field day if a stranger knew where I lived. Once, in response to her worrying about someone driving me home (the date I refused my bathroom to), I asked her, "What about the mailman? What about my neighbors? They all know where *I live.*" To which she replied, "It's always someone the victim knows, Katie. Wow. Don't tell me you are that naive."

He didn't miss a beat. "How about Decarlo's on 19th and Fremont?"

Okay, a *fancy* place. Luckily, those Mary Janes were in my closet, just *gathering dust.*

"That will be fine." I realized I didn't know what time, but thankfully, he looked at his watch and was apparently a mind reader. I hoped not.

"How about at six?"

I nodded and said something that didn't even *remotely* come out right. I wanted to say, "Sounds good," but then decided, "See you then," and it came out unimaginable.

"See you good." He looked at me, puzzled, and laughed.

Then, to my horror, he repeated it. "See you good, Katie."

I walked out of the room feeling stunned, as if I'd been the one who had my temperature taken *rectally,* and silently slipped up to the woman at the desk. There was a man in the lobby redoing the outside window. Instead of reading *Michael Wylons, DVM* like it did when I walked in, it was being updated to *Taylor Wylons DVM.* The woman at the desk, who I remembered as Patty, stood up and smiled at me, and I felt it was a personal question when she asked, *"How did Dr. Wylons do today?"*

Either the walls were *just that thin,* or she was this friendly to everyone. I felt myself busting up with giggles, and I whispered that we were going on a date tonight. I wasn't halfway through the sentence when I regretted it, though, because the look on her face proved *she didn't hear a thing.* Rather, she was clearly *horrified* to hear it. She sat back down and nodded to me.

"I know, he's a *little* dreamboat." Was all she said. Does that mean— does she have feelings for him? What have I gotten myself into? I didn't know what to do. "What's the damage for today?" I held out my credit card that had been in my front pocket, along with my car keys. I was dying to get those out and leave.

"With your adoption discount, it's $59 today for the exam." She took the card and swiped it, both of us standing in silence the entire time. Finally, after looking like she might erupt, she told me what was bothering her.

"He went out with my sister last year. He never called her again and she was very upset. It was just the one date, to the batting cages, but she felt a strong connection." She shrugged. "Be careful with that one."

Phew. The air thinned out immediately and I felt so relieved it wasn't *her* that went out with him.

I took my card and receipt and daringly made eye contact with her again. She was back to smiling. "Thank you, Katie." I nodded and smiled, and Dolly and I got out of there as fast as we could.

"Can you believe what just happened, Dolly? You probably think I get all kinds of gentleman callers!" Dolly just looked up at me. "You did great. Now we are off to the Bark Park!

There was still a little bit of time before I was to meet Eli, so we drove to the parking lot, and I texted my mother that we were there, waiting for a stranger in the woods. Then, to really get her going, I turned off my phone. I waited three minutes and turned it back on. 13 texts and a voicemail. I called her back.

"Hi, I'm fine. I was just kidding with you," I stammered out before she could even start. "Now that I have your attention…" I started the conversation. She wasn't happy with me, but she let me talk for once, and I explained about the vet and, most importantly, about my date tonight.

"Describe to me once more what he looks like? Are you attracted to a man who rides a unicycle?"

"No, I never said he rides a unicycle. He *looks* like he rides a bicycle with one pant leg tucked into a sock. He's a little… eccentric."

"Eccentric? You know who else was described that way?" She hammered, and I knew what was coming– a long-winded list of reasons why this guy was bad news.

"I don't want to know, mother."

She huffed a little but dropped it. Her voice went higher. "Aren't you meeting Eli soon?"

"In eleven minutes, yes. I am probably going to go sit on the benches in five minutes and wait for him there."

"Good. He won't see what kind of car you drive that way." I glanced around the parking lot. I was the only one here. "Yeah, that's a great point." Her paranoia came at the cost of my patience sometimes, but I found it was easier to just agree, even if I wasn't always walking around with pepper spray in my hands, ready to target anyone who spoke to me, she could at least imagine I was. It was how she showed love.

"I'm only going to ask once. Do you still have that tool for your keychain that could work as a self-defense weapon?" I knew it was coming. Laughing, "Yes, mother! Okay, gotta go. A white unmarked van with tin foil covered windows just pulled up next to me. He's motioning for me to get out of my car so I can help him, he looks injured. Talk to you later."

I hung up. She apparently knew I was joking this time, because it had been 25 seconds, and I hadn't heard back.

I gathered up Dolly and we made our way through the wooded area, feeling the dew of the day coating my shoes. We stopped every few yards and I let Dolly sniff things. She was highly intrigued by a little moss-covered stone when I heard a car door shut nearby.

"Hello, ladies!" Eli hollered from the top of the short trail. I looked back at him, and my heart sank. Carter was tugging and making leaps and bounds to get to us, Eli breaking out in a jog to keep up with the leash.

"Hey, Eli. Hi, Carter!" I tried to appear aloof, mysterious, stoic– but I worried I was coming off as rude, uninterested, and *strange.* "How are you guys doing today?" I added a little foreign pep in my voice, and it sounded half-normal.

"We are doing awesome, aren't we buddy?" He bent down and gave Carter a pet. "And Dolly?" He reached his hand over to her, and she momentarily looked up from her mossy stone to give a slight sniff, before returning immediately to it.

"Who's ready to play?" He reached into his pocket and retrieved a bright orange squeaky toy, activating the noise, which sent Carter into a frenzy. Dolly looked up with wide eyes at the noise, too, which was adorable. Her little tail gave a slight wag when Eli squeaked it again.

We shuffled over to the Bark Park area and put them into the small dog pen, removing their leashes. I was pleased to see one other person there, an older woman who was talking loudly on her cell phone while absently tossing a frisbee for her retriever. The dog kept catching it mid-air. It was very entertaining to see.

"Oh, watch out, Katie! Frisbee incoming. Are you feeling PTSD?"

I learned quickly that he was a jokester, which I didn't mind. I was laughing before we even sat down.

"I'm fine. You might be liable for my injuries, though." I shot over a smile at him so he knew I was joking, to which he gave a noncommittal comeback like, "Okay, let me know then."

"So, what do you do for work?" I asked him, noticing his scrub pants again. He was either in the medical field or just a poor dresser, as my mother pointed out.

"I work for a large podiatrist clinic as their X-ray technician. Pretty interesting stuff, the foot." He motioned to his foot, smiling.

"Oh really? Tell me more about that." I replied, sounding a little less enthused than I'd hoped, recalling a book I read once about winning people over. *Ask them questions about themselves,* which was always my cop-out anyway, considering I didn't enjoy talking about myself.

"I really enjoy it. I'm always moving and meeting new people. They are there because they have pain or a major issue, and I get to brighten their day a little with my jokes and conversation. I couldn't sit behind a desk all day without socializing. That's a job for *anti-socials.*

He was literally the *opposite* of me.

"Enough about me," he said. "What about you? Where do you work?"

Where? We are giving locations already? I shut out my mother's voice in my head which prompted me to run. I took a deep breath. He's a normal guy. Can't I be normal too?

"I'm a paralegal." Good, normal answer to a *normal* question that I had *just* asked him.

"Wow, I knew you seemed intelligent." He winked at me, and I blushed like mad.

"Haha, I guess so?" What an *unintelligent response.* Better jazz it up. "Yeah, I'm an antisocial who sits at a desk all day, researching old case laws to get our murderer clients off the hook."

I smiled but as soon as I realized my joke didn't *slap,* my eyes went flat. "I'm just kidding. We do family law— no violent crimes. Just custody, mostly." *Long pause.* "Sometimes it involves pets." He looked like his hair had been blown back and he started laughing.

"These days, that doesn't surprise me one bit. If my wife ran off with the milkman and wanted to take Carter with her, I think I'd bankrupt myself trying to stop it!"

I wasn't sure if that was a reference to something or just a joke, so I nervously laughed until he continued.

"Tell me everything there is to know about you."

Oh, wait. There's the dreaded prompt that I couldn't answer without ticking off my dear 89-year-old friend. But I decided to be up-front and honest rather than mislead him with my own discomfort and spend the rest of my life training to hike Kilimanjaro and running marathons on Christmas mornings because I may have mentioned that I love the outdoors— as in, *photographs of the outdoors—movies taking place outdoors—songs written about the outdoors.* Not crawling through mud on my hands and knees, hiding my tears through the guise of "family bonding" when really all I wanted to do was distance myself from this family.

Not that something so extreme ever happened to me personally, but I had a classmate in college who was even more bookish and introverted than I was. We teamed up a few times on projects, and she confessed to me one night that the star player of the Rugby team had taken a strong liking to her, and she reciprocated the feelings, but she was worried he would expect athletic ability from her that she didn't care for or have the talent for.

A year later, I saw their wedding announcement on social media. They were wed on a beach in Hawaii, which was convenient because their honeymoon would be spent doing an Ironman Triathlon together. But not just them– *his entire family.* And I wasn't saying that people can't change, enjoy exercise, and be bookish introverts, but it was just an odd pairing.

"Maybe he's trying to kill her. That happens on a lot more honeymoons than you think, Katie." My mom's first reaction when I told her the news of her nuptials.

Eli cocked his eyebrow as if to say, 'Well?'

I would give it to him straight. "I love reading, jigsaw puzzles, and Jesus. My social circle consists of my mother, who's lovingly overbearing and an armchair detective, and my 89-year-old friend Judy, whom I see every Sunday for brunch after church. My perfect night is staying in, making popcorn, and watching some lame made-for-tv movie, then going to bed early. And I've always wanted to try one of those places where you paint ceramic pottery. It also seems I am painfully introverted at times."

He smiled and nodded slowly, his mouth agape, but nothing came out. Though it looked like he was trying to say something. *Anything.* Maybe he needed the Heimlich.

"Wow." He let out a laugh at the amount of information thrown at him. "That's great. You are very *interesting,* Katie."

I am? Well, that's good. But I didn't believe him because now I felt like Susan in our Monday morning meeting yesterday. *Lame.*

I stole a glance at him while he was looking at the dogs. His green jacket made his eyes light up like a Douglas Fir tree. His hair looked a little more *groomed* today, and he smelled like soap. He was quite appealing to the eye, and glancing back at the dogs, they were getting along swimmingly. *It felt right.*

"They sure do like that squeaker toy you brought," I broke the silence by pointing out the obvious.

Dolly and Carter each had turns with it in a game I wanted to know the rules of. They would each squeak it a few times, let the other steal it, and then back again. At one point they both had their mouths on it at once, but when the other would squeak it, the toy would inflate more, causing one to let go.

"I know it. I found this great new pet store downtown off 11th street. I should take you ladies there sometime. They have an epic squeaker toy section!"

Making plans? Very good sign, I thought.

"That sounds great. It seems like Dolly really likes squeaky toys!"

Eli grinned. "Oh, they are Carter's *life.* He goes through them so fast. I'm always running out to pick one up at the store. The good thing is I've found that nearly everywhere except the gas station sells them."

"So, you're telling me, Carter's had you on late night squeaker toy runs? To the point that you checked the gas station?" I started busting up laughing at the thought. "What's the difference between a dog and a baby? Because I can't figure it out anymore!" We both cracked up, and it felt so nice to laugh with someone.

Eli went on to tell me about when he first got Carter and how he felt a little out of place having such a small dog. "I went to the shelter and asked for a Lab, a German Shepherd, you know— something with size. I pictured us camping, hiking— my dog fishing with his bare teeth. But I quickly found out that the shelter here doesn't give you what you want, but what you *need.*"

"Yes! That's how it went down with us, too. They just handed her to me and told me where to sign!"

We were in stitches laughing as he told the rest of his story.

"So, there I am, walking out of Newtown with Carter, who was just 12 weeks old at the time, so he was too tiny for even a leash, but we made do. I was feeling a little hesitant, I'll be honest— "

I interjected, "Same."

Eli nodded, "It's scary when you feel like you didn't have a say in the matter on even which pet. There was another dog there that I'd seen when I walked in, but the staff insisted on Carter being my guy. And they were right. I just didn't see it till a few days had passed and this hilarious little man personality came bursting through!"

"Dolly seems very sweet and feminine so far." I smiled. She was, as far as I knew, an easygoing gal.

"She is adorable. And all those things I wanted in a dog?

Carter has them. Except for fishing with his teeth, but he is known for trying. It's just that his eyes are bigger than his mouth!"

We chatted a bit more about Newtown and the workings of adoption, when I told him the story of Samantha coming to my church, which he thought that was a great idea.

"Which church do you go to?"

"Three Maples."

He nodded, having heard of it.

"What about you, what do you guys do for fun?" I couldn't wait to hear about him.

"I like to go for walks, check out new coffee shops, and I really love to travel. Last year I went to Machu Picchu for five days with a college buddy of mine. This year we are planning on going to Alaska in July to visit Denali." He had stars in his eyes when he spoke of it, going on about it being the highest peak in North America. But suddenly the conversation turned solemn. "I had a brother who died when he was just a teenager. It was his dream to travel and see the world, not mine. But when he died, I promised I would make the most of my days. I found a list of his dream trips and every year I've tried to do at least one. I couldn't start until I was out of college and working, so I haven't made it that far down the list, yet."

I nodded, drinking it in. Despite my best judgment, I let a secret of mine slip.

"I lost someone, too." The air stood still. I never wanted to lead with grief and loss, but having it is significant. It becomes a part of you, threaded in your DNA. While I didn't want to share, I realized I wanted to *connect* with Eli. And we did, on that level. He didn't ask who, and I didn't share, but he lightly put his hand on mine for a moment. It was the universal "I'm sorry for your loss" gesture, and in return, I put my hand on top of his, so it was sandwiched for a second. His hand felt very masculine, aligning perfectly with my own. It made my palms tingle like they would start sweating profusely.

Then I let go, suddenly worried that I had clenched his hand a little *too hard,* never wanting to let it go. He pulled his hand away.

No, I didn't want him to fear that he was never getting his hand back, like a vending machine fiasco.

He hadn't directly inquired about my loss since I let it slip about my grief, but I didn't want our play date to end like this. I regretted saying anything at all and wished I could just start over.

"What I said before… about losing someone?" He turned to face me as I spoke. "It was a long time ago. I'm past it now." And then the word vomit encroached in my throat. I tried to swallow it, but my mind had a tricky way with words sometimes, and like my announcement at work yesterday, I sometimes had an out-of-body feeling where I'd become someone else. Someone *confident. Fearless. Outspoken. Without fear of repercussions.* You know, the opposite of *who I really was.*

"It was my fiancé. But I'm ready to find a new one." I tried to stop the words from jumping out, but they did. The worst part? The tone of my voice. I was trying to sound dainty, delicate, and *feminine,* but my throat went dry, and I sounded like a black widow who chain-smoked cigars laced with helium. *Why, oh why, Lord must I come off so… desperate?*

"I mean, I've let go from the loss. I will never forget him, but it was a long time ago."

To my relief, Eli nodded and lingered. "Thank you for sharing that with me. I was engaged once as well." The oversharing had begun and I was here for it.

"It was about seven years ago. We met in college but didn't start dating until senior year. We got engaged quickly, right after graduation, but two days later she showed up at my doorstep with a letter explaining why she couldn't marry me."

"Did you read it?"

"You are the first person to ask me that." He gave me a look like I'd never seen. It was surprise and sadness. "I put the letter away for almost a year. And then one day, I decided to read it. She said she couldn't marry someone outside of her faith. She hoped I'd convert to her religion but wanted it to be genuine. She wanted me to want it for myself, not just a relationship prerequisite. I was interested, and I took a few classes at her church as an 'intro to the Bible' sort of thing. I did feel pressure. But ultimately, it was so important to her that she couldn't wait around for it. I totally understood."

I agreed with her, wholeheartedly. But now I had to know.

"What religion is she?"

"Christian." My heart dropped.

While I was open-minded to anyone because we all start somewhere, I *prayed* to find a Christian man I could learn from and grow with. I looked at the ground and moved a few rocks around with my muck boots. The dogs were tiring; nearly an hour had passed somehow with these glum topics, and I, too, was feeling tired.

"To have someone end things over a belief system really opened my eyes." Eli, to my surprise, continued. "The timing of reading the letter was weird. I told you I waited a year? Well, that evening, I had a college friend call— the one I travel with, he told me he'd just been '*saved.*' I didn't know what that meant until he explained this newfound *grace.* He asked— he begged me to go with him that night to a college-aged group at his church, and I agreed."

My heart was pounding. I was hooked on his words and the more I listened, the more I hoped it had the result I so deeply wished for him. For me.

"I never stopped going. Now, I am the leader of that group, bringing college-aged kids closer to the word of God." Fireworks went off in the distant portions of my mind. "Do you want to hear the craziest part?"

I wasn't sure I did. I got what I came here for: an unspoiled crush on a handsome guy.

"My old fiancé… Carolyn," What does she have to do with this, I wondered… "She's just gotten back in touch with me."

"Absolutely bonkers," meaning my *luck,* or lack thereof with men. I felt defeated. Tired. Empty. Here was someone who could very well be my perfect guy, but I remembered my prayers. Could God be showing me the doors are not all open here? Yes. And no matter how hard it was to move on from these situations, I trusted His timing, His will, and His design for my life— not mine. It was good to remember that if it were up to me, I'd have been married off at 14 to the lead singer of a boy band. And not every relationship has to be romantic. I took a deep breath, and decided to enjoy this for whatever it was and just relax.

He looked at his watch. Accepting that this was ending, I looked at mine.

"Are you working today?" He asked, showing genuine interest.

"I'm taking time off. 'Paw-ternity leave.' It's a new benefit at work."

He started laughing.

"Sounds like a great place to work."

It really was, I thought to myself. Despite some of my co-workers being a little too *party* for me, it was a great, positive atmosphere.

"I should get going. Still must make lunch and all that."

Lightning clapped nearby, and we both jumped at the noise. It was time to make an escape at this new revelation about his old fiancé being back in town. I mumbled something and went to grab Dolly, who appeared frightened at the noise. She dropped the squeaky toy and was trembling. "It's okay, let's get home."

Eli did the same with Carter, swooping him up from the pen and walking bow-legged out, watching where he stepped. He *saw* my shoe yesterday! Just then I heard a *squish*.

"Oh, dang it! You are rubbing off on me, Katie!" He laughed hysterically at the goo all over the bottom of his tennis shoe.

"Go get yourself some muck boots. I learned that fast yesterday!" We were both laughing as we walked to our cars, twin dogs in tow. "Hey, I forgot the squeaky toy." He looked concerned as he stared down at Carter. "It's his favorite. I better go back for it."

"I'll go with you. I need the exercise from my *desk job.*"

He laughed in agreement, joking that he couldn't imagine that. But then he looked serious. "It's important to love what we do. And do what God calls us for."

"I agree." I felt the chatter coming easily now, flowing out of me carelessly. I was comfortable with him. Maybe it was after I slid into the friend zone, or at least put myself there when he confessed about his old flame contacting him. If I was honest with myself, *I needed friends.* The fellowship of fellow believers was important to me. I had Judy and my mother. That was the end of it. I might have gotten Jenna from work, but now I also had Eli. I had no problem with a platonic friendship for our *dogs' sake,* as he pointed out yesterday, being the reason behind his asking. I had hoped very much for more, but this was enough because I was trusting God and his timing for my life. Love included.

Eli retrieved the squeaker and met me back at the edge of the path to the parking area. He squeezed it one last time for Carter, who he now held like a football. He showed him that he had it, then put it back in his pocket.

We spoke lightheartedly and waltzed to our cars. "I had fun today. We should meet up again sometime!" Eli said, speaking mainly to Dolly.

"Totally! It was fun. You have *our* number." Putting Dolly back in the lead with that one, the focus comfortably shifted back to her. "See you around."

He waved and got Carter loaded in his hatchback as I got Dolly situated for the short drive home. I left the parking lot first, with him behind me. *Don't drive like an idiot.* I'm not sure why, but whenever someone I *knew* was behind me, I'd start slowing way too early, wait too long at a green, or accidentally drive over some wet paint, making a trail of breadcrumbs all the way back to my parking space.

CHAPTER 9
IT'S A SMALL WOOF AFTERALL

Leaving the first intersection, I couldn't help but notice he made the same left turn as I did. *Surely, he must live in the area.* The next turn was two blocks later, and then a right, which he slowly followed. *Not unusual, half the town lives in the suburbs.* Then a quick left turn and I was in my apartment complex, *and so was he.*

All the years spent growing up with my mother led me straight to this moment. I nearly stopped, but decided I'd throw off the killer by making a wrong turn. I'd go the *long way* around my complex. My right hand instinctively wrapped around my keychain weapon as I took another left when I should've gone right.

Four bright orange traffic cones and a flag were blocking the road not even three feet in front of me. The woman that worked in the front office, Janine, had been standing outside talking to a construction worker as another man held a jackhammer, staring blankly at me. Janine saw me and put her finger up to the man as she ran over to my window.

"Katie, is everything alright? We have this blocked off for now due to the road damage here. Can you go the other way?"

I nodded. "Yes, I'm fine, I was just uh– " Then it hit me– the perfect excuse. "I wanted to come see you to add Dolly to my lease." I pointed to the back seat of the pet carrier.

Janine smiled. "Oh, of course! Why don't you call and remind me in, say, an hour? I'll find the paperwork and get it ready for you."

"That's great. Thank you, Janine." I started to back up, checking my rearview mirror. No one is behind me. I turned onto my lane, where three buildings were made in the shape of a U and another three sat to the left. I lived in the third one on the right. I pulled into my spot, quickly grabbing Dolly, ready to run for my door. I didn't see him out here, but I did see a few of the neighbor ladies who were retired and always, *dependably,* people-watching.

I was halfway to the stairs leading up to my apartment when I heard a familiar laugh. "Don't tell me you're *following me?*"

It was Eli, standing a few cars down from my own parking spot. I gave him a quizzical look. "YOU live *here?*" I was shocked, but it came off like these apartments were *too good* for him. I glanced back at the neighbor ladies, who, at some point, pulled out a bag of chips and were watching us like it was the series finale of *Days of our Lives.*

Eli nodded, looking around. "Last time I checked, yeah. I'm over there in 301." I felt prompted to say my unit when he motioned to his apartment, but I held back. "What are the chances?" He looked at me, stunned.

"There's what, a hundred thousand people in our area? About 500 apartment complexes. A few dog parks per county and countless dogs. I'd say it's weird." He looked shocked at my hammering out of numbers, but we did just have a little too much in common for never having seen each other before.

He stood there for a minute longer and my tenuous grip on everything in my arms failed. I started dropping a few things, and when I went to catch them, I'd spilled the entire contents of my purse on the ground. I'd grabbed Dolly at high speed along with my keys, bag, and water bottle so we could hightail it inside without the serial killer spotting us, but now he was galloping over to us, Carter on the leash trailing behind him. He grabbed my keys and handed them to me, as I stuffed them in my purse, along with the contents of everything that had spilled.

My lipstick, sunscreen and cell phone were on the ground along with a wide array— to my horror— of *feminine products of all shapes and sizes*. Why did I have so many? Was I planning on stocking a bathroom vending machine? I tried to grab the fistfuls of those first, cramming them in my purse before he saw, but I could tell by his expression he was suppressing laughter.

"Dear Jesus,
Please don't let Eli think I'm like the woman from the Bible who bled for 12 years.
In your name,
Amen"

Once everything was back inside my purse and out of his sight,

I stood up, and Eli grabbed my water bottle. "Can I help you carry this to your door?"

My hands weren't full to the brim, but I relented. I glanced over my shoulder. The neighborhood watch group was still fully engaged in *whatever it was* that was going on here.

"Sure, that would be fine."

He picked up Carter, who looked visibly tired from all the playing, and we walked over to my steps. "I can take it from here," I said, taking the loop of the water bottle lid by my finger, only then remembering my keys at the bottom of my purse. Judging by Eli's look, he was remembering the same thing.

"Would you like me to wait until you get inside?" He was smirking but I knew I'd rather him not see me juggling at the top of the steps. "That's alright. You better go eat lunch before you return to work."

"Thanks, Katie. I took an extra shift from another clinic that we work with since they are down a tech. I don't mind since Alaska is very expensive." He smiled wide, revealing his beautiful white teeth that were perfectly *imperfect,* a few crooked but they added to his charm. Charm? I just remembered my date tonight. And the words came up in my throat once more.

"Well, I'd better go get ready for my date tonight."

Eli's eyes widened. "Oh, *alright.* Do you have a boyfriend?" He was suddenly *very* interested in my love life for having entanglements of his own.

"No. It just happened. I took Dolly to get a checkup and the doctor asked me out."

"Which vet do you go to?" Now things are getting interesting. I heard one of my neighbors start talking only to be hushed loudly by another who was listening in to our conversation.

"Dr. Wylons… Jr. He just took over his dad's practice."

Eli nodded. "That's where Carter goes. I haven't met Junior yet." He crossed his arms, now speaking defiantly.

I nodded along, letting the conversation take its natural course.

"He's very– eccentric." I don't know why I described him that way to Eli, but the damage was done. He visibly lightened, laughing a little.

"Yeah, that doesn't surprise me. His dad is the nuttiest part of a fruit cake." He let out a howl at his joke, and now I felt insecure about going on a date with a wacko's son.

"Well good luck with Carolyn," I added that in, reminding him that my dating wasn't really his business anyway, though immediately regretting it.

He nodded, smile fading. "See you around, Katie."

Eli walked away, Carter peeking over his shoulder at us before vanishing behind the building. I took to the steps, stopping on the first one and slowly rummaging through my purse while hoisting the water bottle between my knees. Feeling the jingle in my fingertips, I reshuffled all my contents and put the oversized water bottle inside my purse, draping it over my arm. We took the stairs one at a time, and I quickened my pace. As I slid the key into my doorknob, a woman called out to me.

"Have fun on your date tonight." I froze, turning back.

"Thanks, Marge." I gave her a head nod. If anything, Marge would be a very reliable witness for my 20/20 special.

I shut the door behind us and resisted the urge to slump onto my couch and stay there forever.

Katie's Biblical Application

"Give me two months to roam the hills and weep with my friends, because I will never marry." Judges 11:37

I was wrestling with the anguish of Eli being unavailable in my mind while also trying to reserve some hope for my date tonight. Dolly and I both were exhausted from the day's events. I filled her bowl with kibble since she must've worked up an appetite. *I know I had.* I decided to pre-eat so I wouldn't be ravenous at dinner tonight and could focus less on whether I had spinach in my teeth and more on if I felt something flapping in my nostril.

I took out my leftover macaroni and cheese and reheated it, knowing once it had gone cold, it never returned to its creamy glory, but I just needed something. Dolly had taken a long drink and was at her kibble, sniffing it out when I sat down at the table. Pieces from my jigsaw puzzle stuck to my bowl and arms as I rested them between bites.

"Dear Jesus,

Thank You for this food. Thank You for today; the unexpected meetings: I pray Your will comes from it. And I will accept whatever that may be.

In your name,

Amen."

I felt the words pour out of me. I opened my eyes and looked at Dolly, now taking one piece of kibble at a time and chewing widely for me to see.

"She's such a funny little thing."

My mind trailed to Eli, and I wondered if he was saying the same prayer about finding his future spouse. But my mind stayed on Eli well after that thought passed. He was... Different. I liked something about him. Of course, he was attractive, but it wasn't even that. There was something *deeper* about him. I felt intrigued by him. Not to mention our coincidences. But none of it mattered, he was getting back *in touch* with his ex-fiancé.

But when I looked at Eli, there was something else. He looked familiar to me in some way.

My mind went back to my prayer. I took a few bites of my food, instantly feeling recharged, but I felt I needed a refresh before my date. I decided to take my time and find the perfect outfit to wear, re-style my hair, and lounge a bit. Remembering it was a nicer restaurant where people went for engagements, birthdays, and *prom,* I started browsing through my small wardrobe.

I knew about the scale of the place after I'd been to it one time for my coworker Collin's big promotion to partner, when he invited the whole office out. While everyone ordered cocktails and wine, I ordered a lemonade and immediately 3 people asked me for a ride home, not even waiting for a reply before they slammed their drinks in unison. *How lovely,* I had thought.

At that moment, a young couple walked in, the girl wearing a corsage and a pale pink ball gown. The boy was in a tuxedo that looked like it was 2 sizes too small. "Must be prom," Collin hollered out, already slurring. The rest of the group started *oohing* and *awwing* some recalling their prom experiences.

"I remember my prom! The best night of my school career. The ladies and I all went together for a girl's night." Jamie recalled with joy.

"Prom was epic. I had two dates." Chaz already had his hands up to accept the victory cheers from the guys, but only a few high-fived him.

"Let me guess: your sister *and* your cousin?" Darren's comeback left us all laughing hysterically.

When the group calmed down, I sat on a bar stool that overlooked the restaurant. The prom couple put their orders in with the waitress, and a moment later she brought out two red fizzy drinks with cherries. I still remembered the details of my prom date like it was yesterday.

Our moms were friends, and, following their direction, he asked me to go with him. I wasn't about to say no, as it was the only invitation I received, and I decided I wanted to be there rather than skip it and always… *wonder* just what kind of teenage nightmare I had missed out on

He picked me up in his mom's minivan, and I tried not to notice his hair was shagged like a mullet. Let's face it– it wasn't *like* anything– a spade's a spade. My date had a mullet.

From the Pages of Katie's Dictionary:
mullet
mŭl′ĭt
noun
Business in the front, societal collapse in the back.

Prom officially started at 7 pm, so he decided we would have dinner at 5:30. That's a little too much time, isn't it? I was worried we'd have too much extra time to spare. I took my time at dinner, but we still finished up an hour later. To my horror, he wanted to go directly to the prom, which was downtown, and we ended up sitting outside on the bench waiting for the doors to open. The camera crew was already there, and they started with us, forever documenting the fact that I was the *first to arrive* at my senior prom with my date wearing the mullet.

Once inside, there were a few dances we awkwardly swayed to, keeping more than a bible's distance between us. We were just friends, and we both knew it. Neither of us wanted to appear like it could be otherwise. After a little while, they announced Prom King and Queen– two people I only knew from passing in the halls. Well, the year was ending. This part of my life was ending, and I was ready to leave this all behind— high school and prom. I asked my date if he was ready to leave. I was back home by 9:00, yet somehow, my feet still hurt, my makeup was failing, and the light curl in my hair was all but a memory.

"Have any good prom stories?" Jenna whispered to me, breaking my trance, and I saw how obviously I'd been staring at the high schoolers.

"Not one. You?"

Jenna excitedly nodded. She couldn't wait to tell me how she was a professional dancer about to be signed on by a basketball team, so prom was just another place for her to show her moves.

"I had a custom dress made with pants underneath and I did a few handsprings. Now that I think about it, I was a little cocky back then. But that's what landed me a spot cheerleading for the Rangers." She shrugged and took a sip of her drink.

"Tell me more about the basketball team." I kept the conversation on her, but I was genuinely interested in how this former *NBA Cheerleader* ended up at our boutique law firm.

"I found out I was pregnant with Mark, my oldest. Got married quickly after that and the rest is history." She smiled, but it was waning at the hooting and hollering from our coworkers. "I'm ready to get back to my guys. How about we call a cab for these drunkards and flee the scene?" It was the best idea I'd heard in ages.

Now that Jenna had asked me about church, the pieces of her life were starting to come together. I decided I would genuinely like to get to know her and vowed to text her later.

Back to my wardrobe. I wondered if I had *anything* that wasn't what Judy would describe as drab, that I didn't already wear today? After some trifling through the back of my closet, that was a mix of *out of season* and *out of style,* I found a few things I'd forgotten about. I picked out a black knee-length skirt, and a satin-finish green top, since it was my best color, next to pink. But since I would be carrying my pink rain jacket, I didn't want to overdo it. I paired the outfit with dark hosiery and midi black boots that zipped on the side. Putting my hair up in hot rollers, I realized I couldn't stop thinking about Eli. I wondered who Carolyn was. I wanted to know more about Eli. It was all just too much. So, while my hair cooled, I went to the laptop computer and typed in what I knew.

"Eli x-ray technician podiatrist Newtown" I clicked search. A picture came up from the Newtown News. From the thumbnail it looked like him in the background. I clicked on it.

"James McArty Podiatrist Wins Award"

James McArty, owner of 'Footnotes' Podiatry Clinic has won a local achievement for business excellence. Silas Harold, Mayor of Newtown presented McArty with the Local Pioneers award on Thursday for maintaining the highest ratings of Podiatry Clinics in the state.

Pictured from the left: Jessica Lyles, Administration. Beth McArty, wife of James. James McArty. Eli Skatey, X-ray technician. Monica Morley- Physician's assistant.

Skatey? As in, *Katie Skatey?* I shook my head and let out a howl. Dolly looked up. Well, it was a good thing he wasn't available or if he was, and we got married… What a hilarious name! I blushed at the thought when I pictured us standing at the altar. What is wrong with me? He's *taken.* Right?

I pulled open my social media and typed in his name. *Eli Skatey.* Only three results came back. I knew when my name was searched, *hundreds* of women with my identity returned.

The first picture was of an older man, zoomed in heavily and taken from the angle of his chin. This unflattering picture wasn't helping, I wanted to tell him. The second profile didn't have a picture at all but referenced their location in the United Kingdom. I clicked on the last one of a landscape, opening it up larger to see. Machu Picchu. This was him. I knew it. Looking around the profile, it didn't show too much information that was public, except his location, Newtown, and his age: 29. I scrolled down to his friends list.

379 Friends. I clicked on the list, typing in the name Carolyn in the search bar. *1 result.*

Carolyn Jane. Her profile picture was of two different women, so I was upset that I wouldn't know which one she was, but it didn't matter. They were both beautiful, more so than I. They each had long, thick hair, one darker, one lighter. Tanned, tall, and fit versus my short, pale, and average build. While I maintained a *somewhat* slim figure– I knew I couldn't compete with these ladies. *No wonder he asked her to marry him,* whichever one she was. I took a deep breath and shut the computer.

Dolly was just getting comfortable in her bed when I covered her up with a blanket. She was tuckered out, which pleased me since I would be leaving tonight. Then I remembered Taylor. One more trip to my laptop; the screen was still up, and I typed in his name. *Taylor Wylons.*

A profile page came up, Dr. Taylor Wylons DVM. This was him, no mystery about that. Though I was surprised he had his professional abbreviations on his personal page. I clicked on it to see what I was getting myself into, suddenly feeling less enthused than I should. Did I even remember what he looked like? Eli seemed to make my mind forget the rest.

Taylor, I mean, Dr. Taylor seemed confident, borderline *full of himself* while I was with him this morning. I was hesitant to even feel that way because I still wanted something to work out very soon for me, but I was hoping I would feel otherwise after viewing him online. I scrolled for a while; then I realized after looking at his profile, I really didn't learn anything about who he was as a person. Everything was public, which was nice, but the only thing he shared was veterinarian articles. Only one picture of himself, too, standing next to a very tall older man with the same *large nose,* so I was assuming it was Wylons senior.

This photo, however, had *comments.*

Marcy Lundvall: 'Looking great as usual.'
Nicholette Mandery: 'Long time no talk, friend.'
Frank Howard: 'Jackie says hello to you both.'

I clicked on the top two comments, investigating their profiles briefly. With what little information was displayed, they appeared to be a great fit for my co-workers. Both liked to have fun, maybe a *little too much,* dancing on tables, fun. These women would think I was a *square.*

He either likes party girls or doesn't, I thought. But then I remembered something: *it doesn't matter what he likes.* God will send me love. I know He will. I just need to be patient.

I went back to my vanity and pulled out my hot rollers. "Oh no!" I rolled them a little too tight, and now I had small ringlets. I ran to the bathroom and put some water on my hairbrush, trying to undo the damage. Thankfully, it started to loosen up, but I couldn't see around wearing a ponytail tonight, lest I wanted to look like Shirley Temple.

My phone buzzed from the kitchen. "Just a second!" I hollered out as if it could hear me. I ran to the phone, and it was Judy. I answered excitedly. "Well, hello, girly!" She laughed on the other end. "Hi there. How are you?" Her voice was chipper, always making me feel like I was basking in sunlight. "I'm doing great. Are we still on for tomorrow night?"

"That's why I was calling, dear. Pastor Bill and his wife Julie have asked me to help at the Wednesday night married couples bible study. The gal who normally does the coffee cart is out of town. Well, it's no surprise they come calling on me. Everyone knows I make the best coffee around. I told them I have a hot social calendar, and I'd need to check with you first."

"Oh, that's no problem at all! Should we reschedule or just figure it out after church on Sunday? I can't wait for you to meet my dog."

"How about you call me in a few days, and we can figure out a time. I don't want to impose on your bonding."

I laughed and agreed to call. "That works for me. Say, you want to hear something a little wild? I have a date tonight with Dolly's veterinarian."

It sounded like Judy dropped to her knees. "Praise the Lord! He led you to this man! It is all working out for the good of Him, my dear. In that case, tell me everything."

I went on to tell her about Dr. Taylor and my analysis of his social media. "Everything at this point is from the point of view my mother instilled in me so keep that in mind— stranger danger."

Judy laughed. "I remember you telling me she's a bit of a crime sleuth."

"Yes, very much so, and paranoid to boot! So that's all I know about him. He asked me out and shocked my senses— I didn't see it coming at all. But, in his defense, how often do you think he sees two ladies in matching pink coats?"

"It was over for him the moment you walked through the door."

Now that I'd told her all about Taylor, I felt something building up inside of me. *Pressure to like him.* I hated that feeling so I knew it was time to tell her the other part.

"Now, let me tell you about someone else."

Judy gasped. "What do you mean? You've met another man?"

"Yes. His name is Eli, and we met at the dog park. The most unbelievable part? We think he owns one of Dolly's littermates."

"Hold on, dear. I need to sit down for this one. You know I can't stand and listen at the same time."

I hammered on. "I mean we don't know for a *fact* they are littermates, but they are *identical* in size, shape, hair– He is a boy, that's the only difference. His name is Carter."

"A boy and a girl. So, what's next? Is he single?"

"Carter? I think so." I teased Judy and she laughed. I knew very well *who* she was referring to.

"Well, I assumed he was single, because he invited us for a playdate. And I ordered a new jacket for curbside pickup, and you wouldn't believe it, but it was his *sister* that brought it out to me, and she was encouraging me I thought."

Would his *sister* know the details of his love life, though? I wondered.

"Very good signs, indeed." Judy was hooked on my story. I was sad to give her the next update, for her and myself.

"But then told me his ex-fiancé just got back in touch with him." I sounded more defeated than I meant to.

"That doesn't mean anything, dear. I've just gotten back in touch with Marlon Brando by turning on the television. Doesn't mean we are in a relationship."

"That's a good point. But he seemed… Happy about it."

"Go enjoy your date. Let's let Eli think about things for a day and see if he gets in contact."

She always had the best advice. I looked up at the time. Somehow, I'd been on the phone for nearly an hour.

"Thank you, Judy! I better go get ready. Wish me luck!"

"I expect a full report when I hear from you next time. Buh-bye, sweetie." *Click.*

To my relief, my hair loosened up quite a bit more during the phone call. I managed to wear a half-up style, like what I'd been wearing earlier in the day, but just a little dressier.

I looked in the mirror at my finished look. Pairing it with a blazer, I was ready to work at H&R Block. I needed something to jazz me up a little, keep things fresh and age appropriate. I rummaged through my jewelry box and found some rose gold dangle earrings. They polished my look, but it still didn't look *trendy.*

I returned to my closet and found a pair of pleather pants I'd bought last fall. I made the purchase in honor of my tween days when I was obsessed with a television show heroine who wore the style. I remember the pair back then I begged my mother for when I was just a chubby-cheeked twelve-year-old.

She relented and let me try a pair on, and I instantly felt like a superhero, just like the woman on television. Except when the zipper broke the next day, and I had what my mother refers to as my "second nervous breakdown" in her chart of my life that she displays to all her guests like a crime map so they can figure out what went wrong with Katie's love life; I promised my baby-fat self

I would one day own a better pair.

So, when I saw these on sale, I laughed, but I knew what I had to do. I tried them on and surprisingly, they weren't tight and had quite a bit of room. In the dressing room, I gave each leg a "HI-YA!" karate chop just to test them out. As quiet a person I may be, I did not then and will never care what my fellow shoppers think of me.

I changed into pants and felt much more comfortable. They didn't have the shine of the teal liquid leather jacket I wore all through sixth grade, but I was pleased with the finish. I slipped on a pair of black ankle boots and felt much *cooler.*

Spinning in the living room, I let Dolly take the sight in.

"Do you approve, my sweet?"

She yawned and I covered up her tiny body with a blanket, tucking it in around the edges so she was securely wrapped up. She looked so cozy that I suddenly felt tired too.

"How about a short nap?" I picked up her bed and set it next to me on the couch.

"Virtual assistant: when does my new couch arrive?

"Estimated arrival for Order #548372 is next Tuesday."

"Woohoo! It shipped sooner than we thought, Dolly. Isn't that great?" She looked up at me, still not sure about the robotic voice, and immediately put her head back down. She was tuckered out.

I set my phone alarm for thirty minutes from now, which would give me exactly twenty-five to make the drive to the restaurant which was across town. It was no use, though, something made me feel jittery the instant I closed my eyes. Yes, I was a tad nervous about the date, but why? It is either going to be good or bad. Why worry about it? My alarm went off all too quickly and I got Dolly's bed back on the floor, double-checked her food and water and took her to her grass pad one more time before leaving. Now, I was rushing, which I don't like to do, but boy, did it make me feel *alive*.

"Virtual assistant, play soft music on low."

I scratched Dolly's head, grabbed my new pink coat, and ran out the door, shoes banging loudly on each step. Marge and her friend were no longer outside, but her blinds were open as her apartment window faced my door. I could see her looking out. I should introduce her to my mother if she visits. They would get along royally.

CHAPTER 10
BARKING UP THE WRONG TREE

When I was at my car door, I heard a voice call out. "Have fun tonight."

I was expecting it to be Marge, but the voice was *male.* I looked up to see Eli.

"I thought you had to work late?" I couldn't hide the look on my face and realized I was now questioning him like I was the detective.

He nodded, "I was supposed to. But when we got home, Carter had a bit of a limp." I looked down at Eli's feet, Carter was sitting on his hind legs on his leash.

"Is he okay now?" He looked normal to me.

"Yep, right after I called in to say I couldn't come back, he straightened out again." Eli shrugged and laughed.

Feeling the weight of the car keys in my hand, I was being pulled in two different directions. "I better get going, I'm running a few minutes late."

"I imagine you've never been late in your life." He smiled at me.

"Well, I don't like to be, that's for sure."

He was still staring at me, but now slyly analyzing my outfit.

"You look nice." A respectful comment that I wasn't sure how to take, but appreciated, nonetheless.

"Thank you. What are you up to tonight?" I'm already late, what's a few more questions?

"We're just making it a boy's night in. Got to catch up on our favorite show. I have a new true crime documentary."

I burst out laughing. "Don't tell me you're into that, too!?" I chuckled in disbelief.

Eli was surprised. "Into what? True crime? Yeah, I like the show alright. I try not to focus on true crime things, but some are just interesting. Bringing justice to the families and all."

"You and my mother would be best friends." I smiled ear to ear.

"That's good to know." He winked. *Winked!* I felt my cheeks reddening and he gave me the out.

"Have a nice time, Katie." He turned away, Carter's little steps running ahead of him before they disappeared behind the large wall of hedges that separated our buildings. I could hear his feet climbing the steps.

The drive to the restaurant was shorter than I remembered, or it might have been I felt like I was floating on moonbeams. I pulled into a parking spot close to the door. I was only one minute late, and I ran inside.

The hostess smiled at me and asked to take my coat the moment I stepped up to her podium. She came behind me and slid it off my shoulders. "What a beautiful outfit," her voice was sincere.

"Thank you." I smiled back. It was a boost of confidence before my date. "I'm Katie Fitzgerald, meeting Taylor Wylons."

"Taylor is waiting for you." *Taylor.* Not Mr. Wylons. First-name basis. How many dates did he bring here?

She escorted me to a table in the lounge. Taylor was looking over his shoulder at the stage. A band was just assembling. "Here you go," the hostess pulled out my chair for me to sit. Taylor stood.

"Katie! You look beautiful." He said it so quickly, I wasn't sure he'd even seen me yet.

"Thank you."

The hostess walked away. Taylor took a sip of his wine.

"Would you like a glass?" He motioned to his drink.

"No, thank you. I don't drink." Great, starting off the evening with that *bombshell revelation.* It was so uncommon for people not to drink by choice that even when I heard it, I assumed they were in recovery or in one of those long-haired freaky people cults.

Thankfully, he didn't ask, but me being me, I felt I needed to elaborate. "I just never really have."

He smiled. "You are every parent's dream come true."

A singer came out on stage, and I was instantly distracted. It was a young man who had shaggy black hair that reminded me of my post-high school romantic interest in a musician. My friend introduced us, and he was very charming in an old-fashioned way—

opened doors, walked on the outside of the sidewalk. Things teenagers don't seem to do anymore. It wasn't until I saw him in concert a week later that I realized he was a cross-dresser. He told me he only wore women's clothing on stage, to which I wanted to believe him. Just a few days later, my mother and I invited him over for dinner. After he left, we noticed a red blouse she had hanging on the clothesline was missing.

Someone started playing the saxophone. "Do you like jazz?"

"I'm not sure. I've never really heard it."

"This is a great place to get exposed to it. Very classy acts." Taylor was pleased with the tunes. "So, Katie. Tell me about yourself." He took another sip of his wine, emptying the glass. He reached for the bottle to refill it.

"Well, I'm a paralegal. I moved here a few years ago and I like it. The rain gets a little old, but– " The waitress came over and Taylor, who had appeared to be listening to me, stood.

"There she is!" He reached out to hug her, which lasted an uncomfortably long time. "How are you, Clarissa?" He was still touching her shoulders as they were at arm's length, utterly oblivious to my presence.

"Doing better now that you're here!" *Gag me.* Did Taylor invite me on a date, or am I just a third wheel on theirs?

Clarissa gave him a long-winded story about her recent *adventure* in the Caribbean, giving extra details about what she and her supermodel friends *wore* while on modeling contracts. I glanced back over at her, as I had been staring ahead at the singer who reminded me oh so much of my teenage dream. Yeah, she's a model, alright, but most importantly, Dr. Handsy is still touching her arms.

"You know that tattoo I have on my lower back?" Clarissa motioned to her backside, turning slightly to jog his memory.

He closed his eyes and smiled. "Of course, the tiger. How could I forget? I recall picking it out for you!"

That was it, I'd had enough of this. I excused myself for the bathroom. "I'll be right back," I shouted into the abyss as certainly they couldn't hear me, but the singer nodded back to me. Since we were the only ones sitting in the lounge, and with Taylor and Clarissa embracing, I was his only audience.

I made it into the bathroom and looked in the mirror. "What are you going to do?" I asked myself. I was all dressed up– would it be disappointing to leave? Yes. But if I stayed, would I feel even more so? Another yes. Sigh.

Walking back out to the hostess podium, she looked confused. "Can I help you, Katie?" But all it took was once glance over her shoulder to the lounge and we both saw them together, still.

She rolled her eyes. "I'm sorry."

"It's alright." I couldn't believe it, but I felt a tad *slighted* emotionally. Tears welled in my eyes, but I was already feeling a little fragile lately.

"Here, let me help you with your coat." She held it out for me sweetly, pulling it on and then came around me and zipped me up. She was old enough to be my mother, and she took on that role, just when I needed it most.

She leaned in, whispering. "He's here with a new woman every week, but never twice. Clarissa… Well, she's married."

I nodded. It was clear I'd dodged a bullet.

Yuck. I couldn't believe I went out with this guy. And worse, Eli thought this was the type of guy I liked!

I exited the restaurant and got to my car, expecting him to run out any second to apologize, but he didn't. I put the key in the ignition– checking– he's still not running outside. I pulled out of the parking lot, looking back in my rearview mirror. What a dud. Time to find a new veterinarian.

Dolly seemed surprised to see me, as her tail wagged wildly under the blanket.

"Hi Dolly, I'm home! That was a terrible date. I wouldn't even call it a date." I picked her up and felt her warm kisses on my face. I kicked off my shoes and kissed her cheek.

"I should've just stayed home with you to begin with."

I carried her around while I rummaged through my dresser, picking out the perfect pair of pajamas. They were soft purple flannel pants set with a purple cotton shirt. I then had to put on my purple socks because it's important to always be put together. You never know when there will be an emergency outside and you'll be seen on the ten o'clock news.

'Hello, this is Rhonda Meyers reporting from KA4U News. I'm here at the Brooklane Apartment Complex where resident Marge

Wilcox witnessed a suspicious vehicle roaming the area. Good thing she called the police, because it turned out to be the infamous 'Garbage Can Strangler,' known for attacking several people, and resulting in many injuries. No deaths reported, and now that he's behind bars, residents can breathe a little easier tonight knowing he's not hiding behind the dumpsters that line most alleyways here in Kelly Park.

'Katie, you were just telling me you knew Marge and that this heroic behavior is nothing out of the ordinary." She put the mic in my face.

'That's right, Rhonda. Marge knows more about myself than I do. Last week she left a bottle of stain remover on my stairs; it was as if she knew I spilled spaghetti sauce on my beige carpet."

'A true hero, indeed. Back to you, Chip."

My phone buzzed. Probably Taylor, but I still rushed to look. I felt… Used. I craved vindication.

But it wasn't Taylor. It was Samantha from the animal shelter.

We are still on for Thursday, right? I was thinking we could get dinner before. There's a cafe a few miles down the road that allows dogs. (dog emoji) (salad emoji) (dog bone emoji).

Well, that was an easy question.

I'd love to. Send me the details and we will be there! (dog

emoji)

My social calendar was filling up *fast.* I put Dolly on the couch with a blanket and went rummaging through my kitchen drawer.

"It's in here somewhere," I reassured myself while searching.

"Aha!" I found the day planner. It was from a time in my life when I had more hope for my social life but much less activity. I opened it up and filled out the dates. We had a grooming appointment, a new pet owner's class, and now dinner with a friend. I filled in the couch arrival day and a reminder to call Judy and schedule a time for me to take Dolly over.

I knew my virtual assistant could remind me, but sometimes it helped me to see everything written down on paper. My week was still mostly open, so I started looking online for dog-friendly activities in the area.

"Dolly, there's a 'Paws and Paint' happening at the Art Walk on Thursday morning! Does that sound fun?" She wagged her tail. I would have preferred to stay home but it was no longer about me. I had this little furry creature who liked socializing and deep down, I felt like I was enjoying it too.

My appetite was lost after the evening's *date*, but I still felt like drowning my sorrows in an oversized serving of something. I put a bag of popcorn in the microwave and hit the button. Dolly's ears perked up when she heard the popping, only to run out of her bed and paw at my legs when I poured the bag into a bowl.

"Oh, does someone like popcorn?" I didn't see how a bite could hurt, so I gave her a piece and she tore it out of my hand and ran off under the couch where she enjoyed it. I followed her, suddenly concerned she could choke on a kernel.

It wasn't like we had a vet we could call.

Getting on my hands and knees, I peered under the couch where she was excitedly crunching away on the small puff, leaving nothing behind.

"All is well, then." Relieved, I vowed to be extra careful with what I gave her and decided I'd look up a list of things that were and weren't safe.

Right when I picked up my phone for a quick search, it buzzed. *New Message from Taylor.*

My heart quickened. What could he possibly say an hour later? *You went to the bathroom a while ago. Are you okay in there? Do I need to call for help?*

"HI! 911? My date went to the restroom at DeCarlo's, and I've just sent Clarissa in to check on her—yes, from the Swimsuit Special Edition—I know, she's really something. 5'11 and, I think, around 110 pounds. Well, she's naturally a brunette but the blonde just makes her tan pop. Oh yes, anyway, where were we? Oh, my date has FALLEN IN!"

I'm sorry you decided to leave.

Excuse me? So, is it my fault in his eyes?

He was full of himself if he thought I was even going to respond to this narcissism.

I tossed my phone onto the coffee table and grabbed the remote, settling in with Dolly on the couch with my big bowl of popcorn.

"What should we watch?"

The rain picked up, and I grabbed the second blanket from its bin beside my couch. We were so comfortable and relaxed. I felt contentment wash over me.

There's no place I'd rather be than here.

We found a thriller to watch about a con man who stole library cards and checked out horribly embarrassing titles in their names but never returned them. Then he created a card for himself where he would personally request all the books he already had, alerting the library staff that the books had gone missing, which put heat on the victims.

I dozed off for a few minutes, waking up to his first victim yelling.

"No, I did NOT check out *The History of Butts by Seymour Legg*," one woman pleaded from the podium in court. Dang, there was a jury and everything.

"Dolly, remind me to check my library checkout history."

It was a poor plot, but I was tired and only realized I fell asleep when my phone woke me up two hours later.

Reminder: groomer appointment tomorrow.

How could I forget? It was nearly 9 pm.

"Should we call it a night, Dolly?"

I opened the sliding glass door to her grass pad, and she went out quickly, did her thing, and ran back in. I was lucky that I had a corner unit with a large tree, so I had two big windows in my living room and since we were upstairs, it had vaulted ceilings. But occasionally, the tree branch would scratch on my window and scare me silly.

My first apartment in my hometown had a similar tree. That's why I picked this unit. It felt like home— just hundreds of miles away. I remembered the first days I lived alone. There was a sense of intrigue, wonder, and *suspense.* My mother reminded me every moment that suspense was not necessarily a good thing. But that time in my life felt exciting— full of possibility, as if, at any moment, the perfect man would fall out of the sky and land on my doorstep and meeting him would never require my leaving the house or attending uncomfortable social situations.

I thought of a classmate I'd sat next to during school for years and never spoke to until we were paired together on an assignment our senior year.

We might have been strangers, but our first conversation rapidly went to the subject of dating, where she disclosed she'd been on several dates from a popular online matchmaking service. Then she had excitedly told me she was going out with a man that very night, and that she hoped he was her future husband. But the more we discussed it, I learned that she hadn't met him yet and that this was the twentieth first date she'd gone on in the last year.

I never made the connection between myself and that woman until just now. In my twenties, I just raised my eyebrows at her but never thought about her *motive*. Her longing for marriage made sense to me. Her desire for union gripped my heart, too. I *assumed* I'd be married one day. But what if I didn't? Would I be unhappy? Or would I be serial dating strangers online?

I picked up Dolly and hugged her tight, realizing I was wrong for raising an eyebrow at that classmate. *I was wrong to judge her at all.*

I tucked Dolly into bed, and I found once again, the contentment washing over me. I was happy in my life. Dolly started yawning.

"Dear Jesus,
Thank you for this day.
Please forgive me for judging that woman all those years ago.
I never understood her longing for love until now.
I trust in your timing, Lord. And if it's your will that I do not find a husband, I am okay with that, too, because you have my days planned out in your book. I want the path you've chosen for me.
In your name,
Amen"

I clicked off the light. "Goodnight."

I was still smiling as I lay in the darkened room, thinking about

Dolly's little yawns.

The next morning, we slept in until 9. I didn't realize how tired I was. I sat up, instantly worried that Dolly would be standing at the door again, but was relieved to see she, too, was still in bed.

I slid out of the sheets and took her out to her grass pad.

"Groomers today, Dolly. Are you ready?"

She tilted her head. It was a beautiful, clear day out.

"Should we get extra messy before the groomer? Should we go to the Bark Park?" She wagged her tail. "Park?" She started jumping around. *My girl loves the park.*

We had a lazy breakfast, and I took my time showering and getting dressed in some 'running around' clothes, as my mother used to call them: loose fitting but still showing some resemblance of a figure.

I also called her to tell her about my date, or lack thereof.

"He sounds like a pervert." She was upset that he had *any* of my personal information. "What exactly does his office have on you? Your home address!?"

"Calm down. I'm sure he's not looking to be on Dateline. He's just bought the practice from his father, who was very well loved in the community." I realized that fact would do little to quench this fire.

"Oh great, so we know *nothing* about this guy! What's his name? I'll ask my people."

"*Your people?* Who on earth— okay you know what? Never mind. If he shows up here— which he won't— I'll file a report with the Better Business Bureau!"

"Fine. Whatever." She sighed. Though she was a raging mother bear, she also knew my limits. "What are you and Dolly doing today?"

"We are going to the Bark Park and then she has a grooming appointment this evening."

"How are you wanting her to be styled?" I didn't even know what she meant.

"What do you mean, how? They are going to bathe her, trim nails, those kinds of things. Right?"

"Yes, but you can choose *how* you want her hair. Do you want her to look like a little lioness? Or a little bear cub? All one length? How about pigtails? Have you considered bow colors to match her collar?

"Whoa whoa whoa!" I hadn't had enough coffee for these kinds of decisions yet. I looked over at Dolly as she investigated the coffee table with the bowl of stale popcorn sitting on top. I fell asleep before I could eat it.

"I think bows sound cute. I'll let them decide."

My mother paused. "Let *them* decide what she looks like? Do that and regret it!" Her tone told me she was feeling very protective over Dolly already.

"Okay, fine. Send me some ideas that you approve of. I better get my day started now."

"I've already added several options for her to her Pinterest board. I'll send you the link."

We hung up and I took my time brushing my hair out. The curls had flattened in all the wrong places, but I managed to style it with a few clips and finished with an anti-humidity spray since I knew I couldn't trust the weather here.

I lathered up my face with a brightening scrub, then liberally applied sunscreen, and a swipe of light blush to each of my cheeks once it dried. I threw on a tinted lip balm, putting the tube in my pocket for later. Studying my face in the mirror, I looked bright and well-rested.

Grabbing the muck boots from the tiled floor in my laundry closet, I placed them by the door to slip on before we left.

"Dolly, what would you like to wear today?" I went through the clothing my mother had sent and found every outfit had a loop for her harness. "It's not raining, how about something cute?"

I pulled out the school uniform dupe and laughed again. It was the same plaid pattern that I had to wear every Chapel Day for the years I attended. Not a hideous green, but not that great either. This outfit had a tiny tie sewed on and a white collared shirt, but the whole thing went on as one piece.

Once on her, I couldn't take it off. *She was a mini-me now.*

"This is what you'll wear once you're old enough to attend private school." By the look on her face, she didn't find it nearly as funny as I did. But once I slipped on my boots, she knew we were going somewhere, and that little curly tail started to wag.

We stepped outside and breathed in the humid air. It was sunny today, which felt amazing after so many consecutive days of *dread.* But it must have rained early this morning because the concrete was wet, and I could feel my hair starting to rise.

Once past the wall of hedges, I glanced toward Eli's apartment, expecting him to be there. He wasn't, but I *wished he was.* He's not available, Katie. My mind swatted any further notions, and I reminded myself of the Lord's timing. *"There is nothing to worry about. Gods got this,"* Judy told me once, about nine months ago when I was fretting over another birthday and still being single.

Loading Dolly into the car reminded me too, I was no longer *alone.*

CHAPTER 11
PROFESSIONAL DOG FOOD TASTER

We arrived at the Bark Park, and my heart skipped a beat when I saw Eli's hatchback in the parking lot. I felt nervous, glancing at my reflection in the car mirror, horrified at my overgrown eyebrows and large pores. Why was the car reflection so much harsher than any other? I had plenty of natural light in my bathroom, but I was still shocked whenever I caught a glimpse in the visor mirror.

He might think I was following him. I recalled he had a mind for crime shows, and if it were my mother that I kept running into, she too would feel that she was being stalked.

I shook the ideas out of my mind. This was a public place, and I had the day off. It wasn't my fault that we showed up at the same time. I unloaded Dolly, and we made our way up the path.

It was both a relief and a disappointment when I didn't see Eli on the benches when we arrived. There were two dogs in the pen, smaller than Dolly but rambunctious as could be, and they pounced when they saw her enter. She playfully barked, and a woman called out from the bench. "Mickey, you better behave!" I nodded at her as

I sat down on the other side of the bench.

"That's Mickey and Minnie. They are only 12 weeks old and just full of it day and night." She looked over at me with dark circles under her eyes. "We also adopted a cat at the same time, she's even younger. It's the moment we fall asleep she decides it's time to run errands for hours on end. I have no idea what she does in the living room, but it sounds like she's fastened a baseball bat to her tail with all the banging."

We both laughed at her exhaustion. "They are just so cute though. I can replace the broken parts." She shrugged.

The broken parts. I had first-hand experience of a pet helping heal the broken parts of my heart while God finished up the rest.

"It sounds like you have your hands full."

"I've never had so much fun, to be honest. What's that quote, 'Not until we are bored, do we really find ourselves?' I was just in a rut in my life when a friend suggested I adopt. Obviously, she was surprised I came home with three pets! But once I was there, I realized I had a lot of love to give. I'd even take another one."

We both looked to the wooded area as voices emerged. It was Eli and *another woman* I immediately recognized from the social media profile. She was stunning. She had long dark hair with bright blonde chunky streaks. A natural tan to her creamy complexion. Full lips and dark almond eyes. Eli locked eyes on me and didn't break the connection until their walk led right to the bench I was sitting on. Carter jumped up, remembering me, and wanting to be petted. Dolly barked at the sight, although I wasn't sure if it was Eli or

Carter.

"Hi, Carter." I scratched behind his ears, and he wagged his tail rapidly.

"Katie. I didn't know you'd be here today. You should've texted me." Eli acted like he'd been caught *red-handed.*

"It was a spur-of-the-moment decision. I have the week off." My mother would fume if she heard me reveal my work schedule to a stranger. Well, I supposed he wasn't quite a stranger anymore.

"Hi there. I'm Katie. and that's Dolly." I held my hand out to the woman who was now awkwardly third-wheeling our conversation. I knew too well how that felt.

"Carolyn. Nice to meet you, Katie." She looked over at Dolly, making the connection of the twin dogs.

"Oh my!"

I went to get Dolly out of the pen as I needed a physical buffer from the romantic connection between Eli and Carolyn.

"They are identical!" Thank you, Magellan, we hadn't noticed. Sigh. My back was to them still while I gathered my thoughts.

"Dear Jesus,

Please forgive me for being such a jerk. I ask for Your peace to wash over me and guard my heart, mind, and mouth for behaving in such a way.

In your name,

Amen"

Holding Dolly, I considered the escape route of just walking down the path and leaving, but I remembered my purse was sitting on the bench. *I didn't like that purse anyway. I could cancel the cards, get a new phone. Be back in business by the end of the day.* Kind of hard to do without my car keys, however.

I spun around on my heels, a smile plastered across my face. I also squinted my eyes, so it looked genuine; but no doubt about it— I looked like a psychopath.

Sitting back down on the bench, Dolly on my lap, I looked at Eli and Carolyn. Why were they still here? Shouldn't they have been out in a flowery field barefoot and getting married? Wow, *someone's jealous,* I argued with myself.

Carolyn turned to Eli, now wondering the same thing. "Ready to go?" They came together, I guess. Eli, to my surprise, *ignored* her.

"How was your date?"

Carolyn's eyes widened at the diss, but turned to me, expecting something interesting.

"I wouldn't call it a date." I rolled my eyes.

Wait. Did I speak too soon? Should I have hinted that it was *amazing?* The woman next to me on the bench readjusted her seat, now sitting with one leg under her, and half turned so she could best watch this drama unfold.

"I'm sorry to hear that." He smiled. I looked away fast, in fear of being charmed by his perfectly imperfect teeth.

"Well, we better head out." He finally turned to Carolyn and acknowledged her. She tucked her hair behind her ear, and something caught the sunlight on her hand. *Her left hand.*

> *"Dear Jesus,*
> *Give me strength.*
> *In your name,*
> *Amen"*

They. Are. Engaged? Already? I mean I can see why— what a beautiful couple and they have *history.* Big time. They'd been engaged before; already knew they wanted to spend their lives together. What's once more?

I looked over at Eli whose expression made me think he caught me acknowledging the ring. He looked at it too, then back at me. He pursed his lips to comment on something, but Carolyn interrupted. "It was really nice meeting you." She was sweet, but to the point. Carolyn flipped her hair and crossed her arms. "Let's go." She commanded Eli, who nodded in response.

They walked off, and the woman next to me whistled. "Well, that sure was something. She was beautiful, I mean, really— is she a model? I think I've seen her on a billboard. But he couldn't take his eyes off *you.*"

"Really?" I was happy to converse with this woman who had a different perspective as a spectator. She was like the Marge of Bark Park.

"Really. He is interested in you."

"But they are getting married." I covered my face with my hand, the other holding Dolly.

"Not when he's looking at you like that."

I relished the thought, dreaming up this whole scenario where he confessed his feelings for me after just one short afternoon spent together.

"Dolly, what's that noise?" Her ears perk up, telling me she hears it, too. "Is that music?" I open the front door of our apartment. It's a little louder, but it's coming from the other side of my unit. Cautiously opening the sliding door, I sliver out to step on the small corner that isn't covered with Dolly's grass pad. "Oh, my word. It's Eli!" Hollering over to Dolly, who leaps and runs over, jumping into my arms as I lean down to catch her. We are wearing matching pink ball gowns with long silk gloves and our hair is in perfect updos— the classic beehive no less. Dolly's has small pink bow accents.

I gasp. It's Eli holding a boombox over his head like he's about to toss it into a dumpster. The song choice couldn't be worse for the moment, but my creativity must be really running dry if the last song I heard on the radio is what defaults in my daytime fantasy. "Katie, I know we've only known each other for 48 hours, but I like you. I've left that hag, Carolyn. I know she's a fitness model but looks and physical fitness don't matter to me at all. I prefer my women to be more bookish and knowledgeable about the letter of the law. You never know when that will come in handy these days. Come down here, please, and agree to marry me." The catchy song played on about having faith over fear.

The music was right about one thing. I needed to have faith that God was in control of this situation. Eli was the first *normal* guy I'd liked in a long time. Sure, there had been some abnormal ones in there, too, such as the professional dog food taster guy. We never met— we only chatted for a while online. It wasn't his job that was odd, because it totally made sense that dog food needed a human tester to make sure it was edible. It was his complete dedication to winning the world record for wearing the most layers of clothing day-to-day. You'd think such a record would have tiers, like all at once, but it was a bit of a competitive category, so they broke it down.

We did have plans to meet once, and it was purely a blind date as neither of us had a profile picture. I made it to the coffee shop early to canvas things out, and I gave him a general description of myself, and he did the same in return. But he never showed up.

There was a weird guy that kept trying to talk to me, but my inner twelve-year-old *'Stranger Danger'* lessons lived strong, and I ignored him. It couldn't have been a weirder coincidence that the man had been wearing layers upon layers of clothes to the point he was stuck in the booth, but my date said he had sandy hair, and that guy would be described as a blonde.

Now that I think about it, I wish I'd gotten his phone number. I would have liked a good food recommendation for Dolly.

"Well, I better get going." The woman at the bench stood, clapping her hands at her dogs. "Mickey, Minnie, time to go!" They ignored her and kept running around like crazy. She turned back at me. "They keep me young," she said, laughing. When she started to walk, I noticed her gait to be unsteady, she had a limp.

"Are you okay?" I asked, pointing to her leg.

"Oh, yeah, I'm alright. Car accident left permanent damage."

"I'm so sorry! How scary."

She slowly ambled into the pen, pausing before lifting her other leg. It was awkward for me to step in, the fence was maybe 18 inches high, but the grass was a little slippery even in today's sunny weather. I watched her carefully, feeling at any moment I might need to assist. The dogs gradually gathered around her, knowing it was time to go. She leaned down and scooped them up in one go and managed to get out of the pen again without stepping in anything.

"Maybe next time I see you, it will be you with the ring." She laughed at her words, thinking they must've sounded even more *unbelievable* than she imagined.

Yeah, right, I thought.

"Take care." I said, not even commenting on the ring.

I waited a few minutes before returning to the parking lot, not wanting any encounters with Eli or Carolyn on the way out.

"Are you ready to go, Dolly? We can go to another park!" She looked up at me with wide eyes. I thought she still had energy left to play, but there weren't any other small dogs around. I got up,

Dolly in tow, and we hoofed it all the way back to the parking lot. I was just getting my keys out when a red truck pulled up. I opened my car door, ready to jump inside if it was an attacker, but a man got out and went into his back seat and pulled out a dog. *A small dog.* He turned, facing me and I immediately recognized him as the man from the doggy bakery. I was nonchalantly fiddling with Dolly's harness, realizing he didn't know if I was coming or going. *I could just as easily pretend we had just arrived.* Suddenly, his dog started going nuts.

'Woo woo woo woo woo! Woo woo woo woo woo!'

"Whoa, Davey. What's wrong?" He asked his dog, then looked up in the direction the dog was barking, locking eyes with me. Dolly, too, was wiggling, but it was just her tail wagging.

"My dog seems to know yours," the handsome stranger spoke. "Is it okay if they sniff?"

He set his dog on the ground, holding the leash tight in case one became aggressive.

"Sure." I leaned down, still holding Dolly and not wanting her to get attacked in case his dog was upset. It was the barking that threw me off guard.

They both started wagging and the man's dog was being very gentle, so I set her down. I was the first to speak. "I just adopted her from Newtown on Sunday."

"I adopted Davey on Sunday." I've been down this path already with Eli, so I cut to the chase.

"Her intake forms noted another dog on the premises— her

owner died." The man had the look of a lightbulb turning on. "Yes. Davey too! Wow. So, they must have been roommates at their last home. Samantha said he came with another dog, but their old owner had just adopted him before they died, so the dogs weren't bonded. I'm Davey's third owner."

What were the chances of this? Pretty high, it seemed. *The Lord worked in mysterious ways.*

"Well, since they know each other," he started to ask me to join them when he looked back at my car. "Or are you just leaving?"

"No, she still wanted to play, but all the small dogs left so we were going to check out another park. We can go back here so they can play."

"Cool." He smiled and nodded, motioning for me to take the lead on the path.

Not so fast, potential ax murderer. Never turn your back on a stranger.

I swatted the compulsive chants out of my head, but I did feel hesitant. "I have to get something out of my car, we will meet you there in a minute."

Nice save. My mother would be proud.

I took a drink out of my water bottle and while I was at it, I refreshed my lip balm. I looked through the bag I packed and saw I still had the bag of cookies from the doggy bakery inside, so I decided I would share them with our new friends. We walked back over to the Bark Park, and I put Dolly in the pen. The man had Davey inside already and was pulling out small tennis balls of all colors and Davey barked excitedly. When he finally got hold of one, the man said 'drop it' but he wouldn't. He started laughing and looked a little embarrassed, "I swear he knew this command yesterday." He gave up the power struggle for the tennis ball and let Davey hold onto it, following me to the benches.

"I'm Micah, by the way." He showed off his sparkling teeth and smiled at me.

"Katie." Play it cool, I told myself. Yes, he was quite handsome, but that didn't mean anything. I had encountered plenty of handsome men with strange commonalities to my newly adopted dog this week. This was just the new norm.

"What a coincidence," he shook his head while looking at our two dogs chasing each other around. "I've seen stranger things happen." It was true, meeting Dolly's potential brother the last time we were here was high up on the list.

My mind went back to Eli, and I shut it down as fast as I could, changing the subject. "So, Micah, what do you do?" Right to the getting-to-know-each other part.

"I'm a fireman."

It was a very attractive line of work, I must admit. Rugged men only applied for that. "It's mostly saving kittens from trees, since we live in such a wet climate." He laughed to himself.

"So, is Davey a firedog? Or is that role reserved for only Dalmatians?" I really had no idea what I was talking about, but I knew I'd read something *somewhere* about it. I traipsed through my bag remembering the cookies we had to share.

"I got him as a therapy dog of sorts. I've just been promoted to a role that will help teach others about fire safety, and that means a lot of schools and young children. I thought I could take him as a way to get their attention."

If he would just target women's groups, he wouldn't need any help getting their attention, I thought. "What a great idea!"

He went on. "I found a dog fireman's costume online. Of course, I ordered it. I wasn't planning on getting a small dog, but as you know, they pick them out for you at Newtown."

I did know. "Yes, they just handed Dolly over to me, too." Now the mystery of the dog was solved. Micah noticed I had a blue bag in my hand.

"Is that from Pup Street Bakery?"

"Yes! Does Davey want one? I was just going to give Dolly one." I reached into the bag.

"Sure, that's nice of you. I know those aren't cheap." He laughed.

True, they were a small fortune at $3 apiece, but it was worth it for such intricate designs.

"I know. And I couldn't stop picking out designs." I held out my hand with the cookies and remembered the one I picked out that was slightly different from the rest. The *fireman's hat.*

"Well, this is one of those *stranger things happening* moments I was telling you about," I held out the cookie for him. His eyes grew wide, and he laughed, shaking his head. "That's amazing." He looked at the cookie and smiled. "Do you want to give it to Davey, or should

I?"

I handed it to him. "Go ahead." I got up and gave Dolly her little princess crown. She loved it, chewing happily as she did. I was so proud of her little crunching.

"She sure is a cute one," Micah gushed at Dolly, to which I agreed.

"I know, isn't she? So is Davey!"

"He's a little ham, that's for sure. Whoever had them before us sure knew how to pick 'em."

"That, they did." I smiled. There was possibly chemistry here, but I was really *trying* not to think too hard about it.

"So, tell me about you. What do you do, Katie?" He walked back to the bench after Davey was finished with his cookie and they began to play again.

"I'm a paralegal."

He nodded. "That's interesting. I was always intrigued by the letter of the law. My parents wished I'd become a lawyer, but I'm not really one for school."

"I totally know what you mean. School was so rough— being that broke and stressed in college— I don't know how I did it."

He agreed. "I took some classes for a while before I knew what I wanted to do— that's what led me to this position. I eventually got my degree in fire science, and while my parents were hoping I'd go on further, that was just all I could do. Money doesn't equal happiness, I told them."

"Right. Happiness is dogs!" I was surprised by my comment,

but felt it was the truth. I really had a special feeling for Dolly. There was no denying it, *I loved her.*

"It sure seems that way," he laughed.

We continued the conversation, chatting lightly back and forth for the next hour. It turned out he was one of those people who quoted movies a lot, and I had never been a big movie buff myself, so I kept getting lost. Then he'd see my confusion and explain the movie's plot, who said what, then tell me the background of the director and writer. It wasn't the *most* intriguing conversation, but I kept getting lost in his looks. I wasn't really listening anyway. However, the longer he went on, I started to feel my interest in him draining.

I tried changing the subject by bringing up a few books that I'd connected with, thinking that was something we *could* have in common, but he told me he didn't read.

"It's not that I can't read. I can!" he joked. "I just don't do that much reading, unless I have too."

So, I'd ask him if he liked puzzles. "Nah, that is something my grandma always has out. It's too messy and chaotic for me."

Maybe I should meet your grandmother, she sounds like fun.

"True Crime?" *At least he could get along with my mother.* "No way. The people that follow that stuff are really... Creepy." Ouch. Though I don't follow it myself, him thinking my mother was creepy kind of hurt.

"Church?"

"I've never been."

I didn't hold that one against him because if he'd never been exposed to it, I would love to share it with him. My mind returned to Eli's ex/current fiancé, originally leaving him because she wanted to marry a Christian man. I had the same feelings as her. I couldn't couple up without that belief being the core of our relationship, so without it, I felt things start to fizzle out here, and I swatted the thought of Eli from my mind.

It didn't have to be this way, though. As a Christian, it was my mission to share my faith with others and give them a message of hope. Who knew? Maybe he would turn out to be precisely the man I wanted. I decided to at least share the gospel with him to see if he was intrigued or just a flat-out non-believer.

But before I could dive further into the topic, he asked me a question.

"Are you single?"

I was intrigued at his question, but nearly instantaneously remembered he was probably asking because he was not.

"Yep." I had a flat tone and thin smirk on my face, looking straight ahead. I didn't dare ask him the same question, but he quickly replied.

"Me too." His response sent my mind on a rollercoaster.

'Good day, this is Katie with the Noon Newsbreak. Breaking news for this hour: We have a confirmed sighting of a single man at the Bark Park this afternoon. Sources say he is quite the movie dork, but God reminds me in every moment of my life how He has a

sense of humor. However, the team here at the Noon Newsbreak think I should just walk away right now, before finding out he's not only my neighbor, but he has been living under my kitchen sink for the last three years.'

I knew I should enjoy the direction of this conversation, and a week ago I would've been on top of the world. But right now, I only had one question in my mind: What would Eli think?

Why was my mind even going to Eli when I was sitting next to this gorgeous, single man who wanted to get to know me?

I went back to my original plan. "Do you believe in God?"

He smiled. "Nope." He extended his arm out behind him, nearly touching my body with it. If anyone were to walk over right now, they would assume we were together.

"Why not?" I looked down at my feet and pretended to adjust my shoe as I inconspicuously slid a little further down the bench.

"I don't know. I'm more of a sci-fi guy." He winked with his response as if the woman who was asking him *why* he didn't believe in God would be charmed by that.

"So, what does that mean?"

"I believe in evolution." He stiffened and pulled his arm back as the conversation grew a little more serious.

"Ahh. So, nothing plus nothing made everything?"

"Pretty much." He was smiling still, but he looked off into the distance as he answered my question.

"Where's the proof of that? I don't recall seeing any half-amphibious men walking around."

Although my childhood swimming teacher could nearly take on that very description.

"Well, it's just something I've studied and believe is the truth. I can't really give certain proof."

"So, it's a matter of faith."

He smiled and nodded. "Exactly!"

I looked back at the dogs. Dolly now had one of the little tennis balls she was moving around with her nose.

"What about this bench?" I knocked my fist on it. "Did it appear out of thin air, or does it have a creator?"

"My guess is it's manufactured by the same people who make the billboard benches at bus stops."

He didn't quite catch onto my drift there.

"Do you believe that someone made this simple metal bench, but there's no creator for the intricate design of human life?"

He didn't answer for a few minutes, but he looked at me with a shocked expression. So, I went on.

"Did you know that God formed you in the womb? He knows how many hairs are on your head. He has your entire life written in his book. And he loves you more than you can fathom."

"I don't know if I can believe that. If he loves me, why did my past happen the way it did? Why is there so much hurt and suffering around me?"

I wanted to reach out and take his hand, but I knew I couldn't do so platonically.

"Have you ever heard of Adam and Eve?"

Micah looked up at me again with a brilliant smile and nodded. *His teeth could bring world peace.*

"They lived in paradise and walked with God. I can't imagine how beautiful their life must have been at first. But you see, they were deceived and ultimately sinned against God. He told them they could eat anything except the fruit from the tree of Good and Evil, which they did, and now we live in a fallen world because of it.

"See, we all have free will. Adam and Eve had free will, and that's why they were able to commit the sin. You see what I mean? People aren't forced into living holy lives and as sad as it is, most choose a life of sin, even when they think they are good people."

"I'm a good person." Micah announced.

"And I'm sure you are. But not even one of us can live up to the glory of God. But there's good news— God sent His son to save us."

"Jesus, right?"

I nodded. "Yes! Jesus came to earth and sadly he was tortured and crucified. But he took on all our sin when he died so that we may be saved. We can't buy our own salvation or make it to heaven on our own. There's only one way— and that's to repent of our ways and accept Jesus Christ as our Savior. Doing so and we become born again."

"What happened to Jesus?"

I felt excited that Micah was engaging in this conversation, as not everyone showed genuine interest.

"Three days later, he rose again with a promise that he will be returning soon."

"Wow." Micah muttered under his breath.

"So, what do you think?" Suddenly a feeling of stage fright washed over me. Whenever I spoke to people so openly and boldly, I knew it was the Holy Spirit giving me strength to do so, and then my usual shyness returned.

"It's pretty interesting." Micah shrugged.

"Will you think about what we talked about?"

"About you being single?" He turned the charm back on and again gave me a million-dollar smile.

"Haha, good one." *Is that really the best comeback I had?*

"Yeah, I mean I admit I felt a little something when you told me that story."

"And it's not just a story. When I was born again in my 20's, I saw some real positive changes in my life. I started recognizing the deplorable behavior I was surrounding myself with, away from friends, relationships, and myself, of course. I began to lose the desire to do those things, but for a long time I struggled with a certain sin. But Jesus was tempted too. And I've learned to lean on him to get through it."

"So, what, do you have to go to church every Sunday?"

"You don't *have* to do anything, but finding the right church is a wonderful addition to your life."

My phone alarm went off. I nearly forgot about Dolly's grooming appointment. "I forgot we have an appointment to get to. I better go." I had exactly fifteen minutes to get there. I set the reminder, assuming I'd be home napping when it would alert me. If only I could see myself now, blowing off a gorgeous guy at the Bark Park instead of eating Bonbons and watching a low-budget flick. *My life is now a 'made for tv' movie.*

"Well, I had a really nice time talking today." He beamed. He seemed very sincere and *genuinely interested.* A feeling of dread washed over me. I hated to admit it, but we absolutely had *zilch in common,* besides our dogs.

The clouds rolled back in at once, and the temperature started to drop fast. "Another storm?" Micah said with disgust. I felt it too, it was so rarely nice here.

"Why do we live here again?" I laughed.

He turned to me, smiling, "I'm really glad you live here." He was laying it on thick.

I didn't respond, not wanting to welcome any further conversation or mislead him into thinking I was interested in him. *Poor Katie has a gorgeous firefighting admirer that she doesn't want.* I really needed to stop arguing with myself as I wasn't good at hiding my expressions.

He walked over and got Davey out of the pen, and I followed suit.

It was time to go home. "Come on, Dolly."

We walked to our vehicles as another group of dog owners crossed us on the path. All of us greeted the dogs, but not the owners, because *that's just how it worked* in the pet world.

"This is me," I motioned to my car and wasted no time loading

Dolly up. He waited for me to get into my car like a gentleman and even shut the door for me. I rolled down my window once I started up the engine.

"Can I get your number?" He had an uncertainty about his smile, as if he wasn't sure I would want him to have it. He was right.

I was once again reminded, *looks aren't everything.* Yes, he was handsome. Good gracious— he was gorgeous. But there was no foundation. Nothing pulled me to him like I felt with… Someone else. I hated this. I wished I could erase my feelings for Eli and transfer them to this hunk. But that's just not how it worked.

"I'm sorry. I'm running late. I'll see you around. You are welcome at Three Maples Church anytime. Service on Sunday starts at 9:30. I mean it, I'd love for you to come." I smiled *too* wide, trying to hide my anxiety and non-confrontational ways by showing all my teeth like I was wearing one of those whitening setups at the dentist.

He nodded, knowing I had just rejected him, but then he looked back with a glimmer of hope following my *invitation.*

CHAPTER 12
A PAWSITIVELY GOOD TIME

As I drove out of the parking lot, I picked up a mildly inappropriate speed once out on the highway. If someone had told me just a few days ago that I would be batting men off with a stick, I would've laughed in their face. *Look at me now.* At least I'd finally have something interesting to tell Judy.

We arrived at the pet superstore with seconds to spare for Dolly's grooming appointment. The grooming area had large floor-to-ceiling windows so parents could see the progress without going inside. We went in and were instantly greeted by a sweet freckle-faced girl. "Hi there. Do you have an appointment?" Her name tag read Liz.

"Yes, for Dolly."

She looked at their appointment book, finger scanning the page until she found it.

"Perfect! I will be taking care of Dolly today. Do you have any preferences for her style?"

My mother warned me this question would come up, and I

cringed remembering I never looked at her email.

"Could we just keep what she kind of already has?" She was cute as a button. I didn't see a need for a drastic change.

"Absolutely! And what colors does she like for her accents?"

"Pink," I answered quickly, though I had no idea what she meant by that. For all I knew I was going to pick up a dog dyed pink.

"Great. Do you want to come back in about 30 minutes? We won't be too long."

I don't know why, but I suddenly felt anxiety about leaving her with strangers.

"Sure," I said, choking back emotions. Get a grip, Katie! It's not like you're leaving the premises.

"Is there a waiting area?" I couldn't seem to locate a bench or chair.

"Unfortunately, not. Probably by design, to get you to shop!" She said with a laugh. It was the pet superstore, so I had no doubts I'd find a few things while I waited. I nodded and left, hollering out to Dolly. "I'll be back soon, sweetie." My voice cracked.

Walking over to the carts gave me a boost of rationality, and I was able to pull it together. I saw Mitchell walking out from the Fish department and I waved. He made a small gesture back, not remembering me in the least. *Fantastic, now you have imaginary friendships with the staff here.*

I pushed the cart over to the apparel department since it was closest to the grooming, looking in the window at Liz and Dolly as I walked by. First up, looked like bath time. Dolly was covered in little blue suds, and it was adorable. Liz was being very gentle with her, and Dolly didn't seem to mind as I saw a little yawn escape her.

Back to browsing. I found a sparkling collar that matched perfectly with the raincoat my mother sent. Then there was a tiny red check bandana that read *Mommy's Girl* in bright pink letters. I found several sets of two-piece leisure suits that reminded me of my own. *We could match.* Then I came upon a selection of doggy slippers, though I wasn't sure how they would work. I had a pair under close examination an inch from my face when a voice behind me startled me.

"Katie?" I turned to see the gorgeous Carolyn holding a bag of cat food.

Was I on *Candid Camera?* Or was the pet world really this small?

"Hi, Carolyn."

Her hands were wrapped tightly around the cat food— one covering the other, and I couldn't see her ring. At least she gave me that justice.

"I'm here picking up something for my elderly neighbor's kitty."

"That's very kind of you."

Not only was she gorgeous, but apparently, she was also a philanthropist. I had nothing else to say, but it seemed like she had something to say to me. She paused, changing her mind apparently, and turned away.

"Bye, then." She called out over her shoulder.

"Okay, then," I whispered back, and my eyes rolled, knowing she couldn't hear them and thankful she couldn't *see* them. Still holding the slippers, I absently tossed them in my cart. I was disgusted by my thoughts and feelings towards that woman and needed to stop immediately.

"Dear Jesus,
Please forgive me for being so, so jealous of this woman.
I don't want to be. I pray for a change of heart.
In your name,
Amen"

I took a deep breath. It seemed like an hour had passed, but my watch said it had been seven minutes. I turned to the toy aisle, looking both ways to prepare for another fiancé ambush.

Seconds later, Carolyn returned with a determined expression.

"I didn't mean to get in the way of anything between you and Eli." She looked remorseful.

Was it that obvious that I liked him?

"Don't worry about it." The words surprised me, but I was certain it was because of my recent prayer asking for help. Carolyn nodded, looking at the ground before walking away again.

My cart found its way into the Agility and Sports aisle, which was full of items you'd see on one of those famous dog shows that aired on holidays. The owners usually had to have some athletic ability, since they often ran alongside the dogs to keep them on course. I wondered what kind of words they used to encourage their dogs to keep going. Surely, it differed from what personal trainers said to us in gyms.

'You are going to have the most defined neck on the beach. Keep it going, and no one will recognize that muffin top of yours. One more and you'll be blasting those cankles away!'

I was halfway through reading about the installation and setup of the dog rope climb when the loudspeaker came on. "*Katie Fitzgerald, your pet is ready at the grooming station.*"

I wasn't expecting an announcement from the whole store that I was in here. I nervously scuttled my cart over to the big windows, assuming everyone I'd ever met would be shopping here at this very moment. I investigated the room where, sure enough, my little sweetie was sitting, paws crossed, waiting for me. Liz smiled as she opened the door for me. "I hope you like what I did today." It wasn't a question; however, Liz knew very well she was talented. I laughed in joy. Dolly looked adorable.

Dolly had two pink bows, one above each ear and the fur around her face had been trimmed up. Her ears were left slightly longer but shaped so that she looked like a fuzzy teddy bear. Her body was still full of curls, and her little black nails had been coated in pink polish. I gasped when I saw it. Never in a million years did I expect a dog to have better nails than me.

"It's pet safe– " Liz handed me a little tube labeled *Pawlish.*

"Can you please do mine now?" I held up my stubby nails, laughing. "Thank you so much, Liz. I especially love the little bandana." Dolly was sporting a crinkle-cut pink bandana that matched her bows and nails.

"I'm so glad you are happy."

"This is my first dog," I beamed excitedly. "How often should we come in for grooming?"

"About every five to six weeks, or more, if you want. If she just needs a refresh, or a Pawlish change, I'm happy to do it."

I pictured writing in my calendar, Dolly's nail appointment, and smiled.

She handed me the bill for $40. "Thank you so much, Liz. Here's forty and… a little something extra for you." I gave her a $50 bill and she nodded appreciatively.

"Congratulations on your new doggy. She was just an angel, but I'm sure you already knew that. It was a delight to groom her today."

I left the *salon* feeling proud of my girl.

"Should we go to the Doggy Bakery?"

She loved questions that involved the word, *go.* I almost forgot my cart full of things and pushed it one-handed to the front of the store, while still holding tight to Dolly as if someone might want to snatch her away. One of the cart's wheels was screeching loudly and stopping completely every few feet. Earlier the store had been playing soft music, so it hadn't been so noticeable, but this time Mitchell had just turned it off to make the announcement the store was closing.

"Good evening, *Furiends*," how anyone could say that with a straight face I'll never know, "we are closing in fifteen minutes. Please tell mom and dad to bring your final selections to the front of the store. And as always, have a *paw-fectly purr-fect day*."

Screech. Screech. Screech.

"Oh, someone's got the squeaky cart! I could hear you coming a mile away." Mitchell laughed and I felt my cheeks redden from embarrassment when I finally got the cart to his register. He saw Dolly and leaned down, so his head was at her eye level, still in my arms. "Oh, hello sweet thing. Did someone get all pretty and groom-ied? Did you get groom-y groomed? Do you like groomies? You look so pretty after your groomies."

Little surprised me anymore, but I did find it odd that Mitchell was now over by us, on his hands and knees talking to Dolly, since a line started to form behind us and nearly reached the treat aisle. But when I looked back at the people waiting, no one seemed to mind.

Dolly was enjoying the attention from Mitchell, and I put all my items on the conveyor belt. Mitchell finally returned to the register and inspected each item; commenting how cute she would be in this– those slippers will go perfect with that– and *oh my word, I didn't know we had these back in stock.* He was an absolute delight.

"Did you see we have the matching collar for this ball gown?" I'd half-forgotten I'd put the gown into my cart when he brought up the matching collar, but it was just too fun. "I didn't see it?" I hesitated to ask for it since I felt like a mosh pit might form behind me if I did. "Maybe I should get out of line first."

"No worries, let me get another cashier up here. You will die when you see it; it is covered in pink crystals."

"I'll take it!" I laughed and he made a call over his walkie-talkie. "Marissa, are you on?"

"Go for Marissa," a soft voice came on the radio.

"Can you send another checker or two? And please bring up that pink crystal collar to the front. We have an extra small fashionista here who can't miss out."

"Roger that."

Two cashiers emerged from the fish section and the line let out a sigh as it broke into two for them, leaving me alone at my register. They could sense I was going to be here for quite some time. As we waited for Marissa, I couldn't help but strike up a conversation.

"Do you have any pets? You are so good with them."

"I have four Pomeranians," he smiled and nodded, expecting my low whistle of shock. "I have my hands full. But it's so much fun," he beamed. "It started with just one, Billy Boy. An old girlfriend got one for Christmas one year, and she just wasn't a *dog person*—you know the type?" He whispered, as if not wanting to scare me away with such a thought. "I jumped at the chance when she offered him to me shortly after. Then a year ago, I heard there was a big puppy mill bust, and some of the dogs were being transported to Newtown.

I jumped at the chance, knowing they'd be some sort of small dog, but then I found out they were all Pomeranians. I walked out with three of them. I still can't believe it, but I have enough space and enough love to give them all. They are still learning how to 'dog' from Billy Boy, but they are doing amazing."

He was such a proud pet owner, and after having Dolly for several days, I knew why. It was rewarding.

"Here you go, Mitchell." Marissa handed him a collar that looked like it was made for royalty. It glistened and gleamed in the light; its pink crystals were all tones and shades, varying beautifully into the next. It looked like a crown. I winced when he had the tag to ring it up but was relieved it was still *relatively affordable.* Besides, *Dolly deserved it.*

"That will be $144.26. Oh, here's a picture of my clan." He pulled out his phone and held it out to me. Four fuzzy, frizzy, and lush *smiling* dogs looked back at me. Each one had on a miniature party hat and different color bow ties. They made me smile, feeling their warmth and cuteness. One was orange, one white, one black and a tan one.

"This is from Billy's fifth birthday party last year. Aren't they just beautiful?"

"Oh my. Yes! They are. Which one is Billy?"

"Jake is the orange one, Jeffrey is the tan, Kevin is the black one. My Billy Boy— my OG love— he's the white one. You don't see that color in the wild too much. He was from a breeder, though." He whispered the last part, again not wanting it to catch on. "Adopt, don't shop!" He sang it like it was his mantra.

A few people saw my credit card emerge, so they bravely got in line behind me.

"I'll be right with you." Mitchell called over to them.

I swiped my card, and he gave me a receipt. "Thank you for coming in today. I hope I see you ladies again soon!"

"Thank you, Mitchell. I'm Katie and this is Dolly."

"It's been a pleasure having you shopping with us today!" He orchestrated the line after we turned away. I was certain I wasn't the only one. Every customer must leave here feeling dazzled, excited, and *broke.*

"Next stop, bakery!" I tossed our shopping back in the front seat and loaded Dolly up in the back. "I know what we are doing tonight!" We had an entire wardrobe to put together and make use of those adorable hangers from my mother. We drove off to the bakery nearby. Pulling up to the front, no one was inside, and the lights were off.

"Oh dang, they are closed sweetie." I grabbed my phone and looked to see if there were any other locations.

"There's a doggy cafe on 11th street. Does that sound fun?" I looked at her in my rearview mirror. I was starving now that I mentioned it. My clothes were drab, since we'd just been running errands all day, but they weren't inappropriate for going out, were they? Okay, maybe the muck boots were a little much.

"Let's go home first and freshen up before the cafe." I sped home, pulling into the spot and grabbed my shopping bags. With

Dolly on her leash, I walked towards my apartment.

"Katie!" A voice called out.

When did I become so popular? If this kept up, I'd need to get one of those giant black umbrellas that celebrities used to hide from the paparazzi. Even if my new social life didn't hold, at least it would be good for my static electric hair.

It was my neighbor that bombarded me days ago with her quest for another dog. She was enthusiastically waving me over to her porch. "You gotta meet Mr. Twinkles!"

I laughed as we walked into a stranger's living room. As the door shut behind us, I heard my mother's voice in my head, but I swatted it away. A small dog with a torpedo-shaped body was wagging his tail with the same gumption as his new mother's waving. His hair was wiry and frizzy, shades lighter than the looks of his body. And he had a little bit— okay, a *lot* of underbite. He made me giggle just looking at him.

"He's adorable." The neighbor woman, who I didn't even know her name, approved.

"I know it. I wasn't aware that they just pair you up with pets there. I didn't get to choose?" She threw her hands up in the air. "But I couldn't be happier with this mug!"

She ran over to him, squeezing his cheeks with her hand. He leaned in and let her kiss his forehead. "Ever since my Bogart died, I've been so lonely."

I looked around her apartment. It was on a floor level, so it looked similar to mine but didn't have the vaulted ceilings. On every wall there were pictures of a little black dog in every scene imaginable: birthday parties eating a cake, dressed as one of Santa's reindeer, or eating a watermelon slice in the back of a red pickup truck. All photos looked professional. She noticed me looking and offered up her information.

"I'm a pet photographer. Here." She handed me a business card out of her card holder sitting on her dining room table.

Patricia Godwin
Pooch Plus Pet Photographer
On-Site and Studio

"If you ever want photos of your little princess." She gave Dolly a gentle pat on her head and Mr. Twinkles barked in protest.

"They told me he can be jealous." She laughed and picked him up. "There, are we all better now?"

"Well, we better get going. Thank you for the card! I will give you a call. And I'm Katie, this is Dolly. Congratulations on Mr. Twinkles."

"Thank you, Katie." She sat on her couch, letting us see our way out as I opened the door and left. I was just feet from my apartment steps, and we hurried our way up them, feeling like all the world was chasing after us.

I fed Dolly a little, just in case we didn't see anything good on the menu at the Doggy Cafe. *Blitz & Bones* was just one of multiple dog-friendly diners in the area. Who knew? I let Dolly take her time eating while I changed my outfit.

Choosing a light pink sweater that would go well with my new coat and black jeans, I slipped on some tan ankle boots. I put my hair half up, twisting some pieces to give it height and texture. And I figured the lights in any cafe were bright, so I accessorized with some sparkling earrings and my rose-gold watch that had little gem accents.

"Dolly, what would you like to wear?"

I emptied out the bag of everything I bought today at the pet store and didn't find anything that was good to wear to dinner. I returned to the box my mother sent, since I still hadn't put it away, and rummaged through. There was a perfect spring green pastel sweater with coral stripes and two pink and yellow flowers on it. "How about this?" She looked up at me but went back to her food. After she was done eating, we put her into the sweater and left.

"Time for one more adventure today."

We arrived at Blitz & Bones, and the place looked jam-packed from the outside. I had that twinge of anxiety when you think you're about to be turned away as I stood outside. But it looked like a large group was getting up to leave, so I went for it.

"Hello, ladies!" The exuberant host hollered out to us, causing every head to turn in our direction. "How many?" He already had his nose down in his reservation book.

"Just us." I wasn't sure if they counted Dolly as one since it's not like she'd be sitting in a chair. "Purrfect!" He rolled the 'r' and gave us a wink. "Would you like to follow me?"

He led us to a corner seat next to a window that overlooked a beautiful water feature outside. The sun was just beginning to set, but people were out walking their dogs and letting them play in the fountain. This diner was on the ground floor of a new condominium complex, which accounted for much of the hustle and bustle. But for a moment I thought it sounded fun to live above a diner catered to pet owners. Oh, how I'm changing before my eyes!

The diner was dimly lit; not the bright, sterile *unflattering* light I'd been expecting. Once we got situated, Dolly sat on my lap, I looked around in a quick survey of the place.

"We should invite Judy next time," I whispered to Dolly, not wanting anyone to see me having a conversation with my poodle. But upon my inspection, nearly *everyone* was talking to a dog.

A glitzy woman waltzed over to me, pushing up her black rimmed glasses with a bejeweled finger. It looked like heart crystals adorned each of her nails. "Hi girls. My name is Melanie and I'll be your server tonight. And what are your names?"

"Katie, and this is Dolly." I waved my hand under her head like I was Vanna White.

"So nice to meet you ladies. Have you been here before?"

I shook my head. "This is our first time."

Melanie squealed with delight. "That's wonderful! Welcome to *Blitz & Bones*. I do hope you enjoy it. Let me give you the lay of the land on how things work here. Order off the menu something that both you and your pup would like. We serve it to you on a plate and theirs will come in a doggy dish, so no bad habits start here." She winked.

"Everything is pet safe, even if she does accidentally get a bite of mom's food. And every Wednesday night we do a Bingo game that benefits animal rescue."

I panicked, realizing *today was Wednesday.*

"The game starts in about ten minutes, so you're just in time! Here's the menu and your Bingo card." She handed me a pink marker to dab the numbers off with. "Would you like a minute to look over the menu? Or can I answer any questions? I'd like to get your order in before the game starts if that's not going to rush you."

"What do you recommend?" I asked to buy myself more time.

"My favorite thing on our menu is the bacon egg quiche with the side salad." She pointed to the menu item. The description said it featured a mini egg crustless quiche for the 'pup-panion'.

"That sounds great. We will take that, thank you, Melanie."

"How about something to drink? We have a selection of spritzers, cocktails and mocktails here," she pointed to the drink section on the elaborate menu, "and we have beer or wine."

"I'll take a Moscow Maltese Mocktail, please."

"Great choice! I love grapefruit. And the ginger in that one is incredible. I'll be right back with it."

Melanie disappeared behind the curtain, and someone came out of the back room with a microphone and a master board for the game.

I felt a drop of sweat roll off my forehead. The last time I played bingo was at our office Christmas party. It took a near blackout card for Sasha, an intern, to alert the group I won the game.

"Katie, why didn't you tell us?" Frank had asked, his laughter turning into a slight frown. I didn't want to win because then I'd have to announce it *and* go to the front and collect my prize.

"I thought I'd give someone else a chance."

He was sweetened by my answer. "Katie, you are so kind. But fair is fair! Here you go– the grand prize!" He tore a tablecloth off a sideboard, revealing a giant gift package.

"A $200 gift certificate to The Fondue Pot, a flower bouquet of $150 value from Rose-Colored Glasses Florals, $75 rental credit for Norlands, so you can rent outfits for both you and your date, and of course, a party limo with full bar service to and fro. It's a complete night on the town, Katie!"

My co-workers started laughing hysterically.

"We all know how much Katie likes to go out!" Chaz spewed.

I like to go out, just not with *you*, I thought.

"Congratulations, Katie." Jenna patted my shoulder as she dropped the prize sheet and gift certificates before me. "You deserve it. Don't listen to those idiots." She whispered, rolling her eyes at the guys who were now wiping tears after they laughed so hard. Just what was so funny about it?

I looked at Jenna, who sat back in her chair only one seat away from me. Her bingo card was a near win– having one or two away from several possibilities. She had kids at home and wore a small wedding band. I quietly slid the prize over to her and smiled, getting up to grab my things. The party was over. I had already won the game. I said goodnight to Frank and his wife and left.

But now, this was different. No one in here cared who I was. Everyone in here was joined simply by the fact they were pet owners. In these parts, I was identified as the owner of my miniature poodle. It was the perfect hideout for introverts.

Melanie promptly returned with my drink. "Enjoy." She cheerfully smiled as she sat down a beautiful pink glass with a sparkling pick holding a lime garnish. I took a sip, the fizzy spices awakening my senses. If the food was as good as this drink, Dolly and I would be regulars here for sure.

Just not on Wednesdays.

CHAPTER **13**
CANINE CLOTHIER

"Good evening, everyPAWdy!" Laughter erupted as the hostess took over the microphone. "Who's ready for some BINGO?" He did a hip shimmy to his question while jingling a wand that looked like it was wrapped up in dog collars with bells on. People started clapping and cheering. Looking around the diner, I noticed how quite a few people were here without friends— just their doggy companion in tow.

"If this is your first time joining us tonight, welcome." He clapped and everyone, including myself, joined in.

"My name is Liam, and I own the Blitz & Bones Cafe," more people clapped at this revelation, "and I'll be administering the game tonight. My lovely wife Suzy is off rescuing more doggies tonight— so be sure to tune into our social media pages this week for information on the details. Okay, let's get right into it, shall we?" He looked down and read from a paper. "The Bingo card sales from tonight's game will benefit *For The Love of Paw Animal Rescue.* The first card, as always, is on us and taken from the proceeds of your drink tickets– so indulge guilt-free! No limit to how many cards you buy. There will be five games total, and if you so generously decide to donate your winnings instead, Blitz & Bones will match the donation." Everyone clapped again, and Liam raised his arms up, waving them into the air so we would clap even more.

"Last week, we raised $673 for *Senior Small's Sanctuary!!!*"

The crowd winded down from its cheering as he began to spin the bingo ball. "Now let me relive the days my mother put me in rhythmic dance as a child and let's get our BINGO ON!"

Now his moves made more sense. You could tell he was a talented dancer, even in his silliness for this game. But something about his graceful moves reminded me of my fear of *Flash Mobs.*

It was the reason I avoided the shopping mall altogether between November 1st and December 26th. Sure, I only witnessed a Flash Mob with my own eyes once, but it was the perfect storm of embarrassment. Hey, I enjoyed Christmas carols as much as anyone, but something about a group of civilians dressed like they just left a tap recital, *thrusting to the beat of 'Let It Snow', scarred me for life.*

I could tell everyone in the diner was serious about Bingo. Even the dogs were settling in, getting comfortable on the assortment of dog beds along the diner wall.

"Katie, would you like a bed for her?" Melanie whispered as I noticed everyone went silent so they could hear the numbers being called. Dolly looked like she was working up a yawn, so I agreed. "That would be wonderful. Thank you."

"First up: B9." A few people had cards covering their entire two-top table, hastily marking them off. I didn't have that number, taking a sigh.

She returned a moment later with a small donut shaped fluffy bed from the back. "Don't worry, we wash these between each dog, so you don't need to worry about fleas or dirt on your little princess."

Now that was service.

Our food arrived and it smelled heavenly. Melanie sat it next to the cards, making sure I had ample space for both. I nodded in appreciation. "Thank you, Melanie." One bite, and I was hooked. My hunger set in, and I was eating like no one was watching.

Liam spun the ball dramatically each time. "G6. *Like a G6.* "He sang the tune and did a snake-like dance while everyone laughed nervously, not wanting to miss a number on their cards. But his pace was good. While he didn't repeat himself more than once, he gave ample time to get the numbers marked on our cards. I had that number, and using the squishy pink ink, I marked the box.

This was fun.

"G39. O Thirty-NINE. As in my age for the last four years." He was one of those funny people that, no matter what he said, people giggled.

The game went on a few more calls until a red-haired woman stood with both arms in the air and whispered, "Bingo," as if halfway through, she changed her mind.

A few people clapped, and Melanie went around with a stack of cards. I finished my food while Dolly licked her bowl clean.

"How was your dinner?" Melanie smiled.

"Oh, it was amazing! Thank you for the recommendation."

"I'm glad you enjoyed it. Hopefully we will see more of you ladies here! Can I get you anything else?" She motioned to her cards.

"Yes, could I get a few more cards?"

Melanie nodded. Sure, they are a dollar a-piece. How many would you like?"

"Well, it's for charity after all. How about three?"

Melanie pulled them out of her apron and set them out in front of me.

"And what about another drink? The Shanghai Shar Pei Mocktail is my personal favorite."

"Yes, please!" I felt a little too eager, but after that delicious heavy meal, I needed something sugary to keep me alert.

She returned with a lemony grenadine drink that had a bright purple straw and cherries on top. It was deliciously smooth with a hint of toasted coconut. I loved this place.

"Okay Bingo round 2 starts now!" Liam called out, his fingers making a '2' that he immediately turned into a disco dance.

I ended up staying and played three more games and won the final round. When Liam called out that last number, "O29, as in, *oh my word, I'm 29 and still single,*" I surprised myself when I stood up and called out, "BINGO!"

I was proud, but it wasn't over the top like some of the winners. For the most part, this seemed like a group of fellow introverts.

"Congratulations! Come up here with your card to verify your winnings." I picked up Dolly and we waltzed up, confidently. A few people mumbled, '*aww*' when they saw her.

"Looks great. Here you go." Liam handed me the prize winnings which must have been around a hundred dollars from the feeling of it. I didn't know what to do next, so I whispered, "I'd like to donate this to the Paws."

Liam put his hands up to his chest. "Thank you so much. They will really appreciate it." He gave me a little slip about the pet rescue, and I went back to my seat and gathered my things.

"Thank you for coming in!" Melanie's voice rang as I walked out.

"We had a lovely time, Melanie. Thank you. We will be back."

It was getting late, and we were both yawning all the way home. Once inside our apartment, I kicked off my shoes and Dolly trotted to her water bowl. I went straight for my pajama drawer and found something extra comfortable and got ready for bed.

"That was fun, Dolly. I couldn't have gone without you." I know she didn't understand, but I hoped she felt that I appreciated her for opening my world up in unexpected ways.

Getting a second wind, I decided to deal with the mess around my living room before bed. Dolly had taken to her bed and went to sleep. I started gathering up my laundry and dishes that had been used and abandoned when I heard soft noises coming from Dolly's bed. I walked over. It appeared she was having a *nightmare.* Oh my, what could she be dreaming about that would be scary? Surely, she had a pampered life!

It reminded me of when I was a kid, and my mother had a nightmare so scary she screamed and woke herself up. My dad had always been a heavy sleeper, so much so that you'd wonder if he was even alive. You could pluck his nose hairs, and he wouldn't wake up. I am speaking from experience.

But this nightmare scream from my mother did wake him. He rolled over, not even half concerned. There were so many things he could've said or done. Was there a killer in the house? Had someone broken in and was stealing the contents of our underwear drawers? But no. My mother was disgusted to report that instead of lunging to protect his family just in case of a burglar, he said, "What? Did your shopping cart fall over during the blue-light special?"

I opened the directions for the doggy wardrobe my mother sent and took out the pieces. I wasn't handy in the least, but I thought I owned a screwdriver. After rummaging through my junk drawer, I found a small yellow one. I got to work on the wardrobe.

With my new dog sleeping and the rush from the first few days of my new life now quiet, I finally had a chance to reflect on the transformation that had happened in only a few days. This little fluffy creature had unconditional love to give. Having her meant I had a pass to a whole new world of activities with people just like me, and I'd already met several eligible bachelors, even if they would never be eligible for me.

In this experience, I felt God's love profoundly mirrored in that of my new pet. I was no longer *lonely*.

"Dear Jesus,
Thank You for bringing unexpected love into my life.
I didn't recognize it at first, but she certainly fills the void in my heart.
You are good, all the time.
In your name,
Amen"

After an hour of assembling the solid wardrobe, I realized I needed to make space somewhere for it to go, or it would just be sitting in my living room forever.

Opening the hallway closet, on one side was my stackable washer and dryer. The other side had shelving and places to hang coats, with a mid-level shelf that was perfect for it. I just needed to clear everything out. I carried out the pieces one by one. A shoebox full of DVDs, a small bin of souvenirs from the few trips I'd taken to the coast, and a sewing machine. I'd forgotten about the machine, but there was a time when I would sew my own blouses and scarves. A blazer here and there. Once, I made a lined tweed jacket, but I'd messed up on the sleeve and my right arm needed to lose a few inches before I could wear it. So, I took my seam ripper and tore out the inside stitches, enabling my arm to fit, but the entire sleeve tore open when I lifted my arm to adjust my glasses at the Monday morning meeting an hour later. I wasn't sure anyone noticed. Though if they heard the '*RIIIPPP*' noise, they didn't acknowledge it. I couldn't lift my arm and lived with it glued to my side the rest of the day.

The problem with that was, there was an appropriate amount of movement you should expect from your arms when you walked. Too much movement, and you risked looking like an ape— but too little, and you look like that one kid we all knew in middle school that grew up to be a billionaire. This kind of walking was often paired with rolling the ball of your foot like you're stepping on your tiptoes with each slide.

I think I'd rather have that gait than the one I was born with, however. Being pigeon-toed wasn't very glamorous when they forced you into giant brown leg braces as a child. Though I believed we peaked as a society in the 1990's, it wasn't exactly the pinnacle of healthcare. Anything that could be fixed now with a shot and a special sock, like my feet, back then needed experimental surgeries, heavy duty hardware and years of childhood torment. The only thing worse than this was my parents' generation where the treatment for anything from a headache to a bad mood wasn't heroin like you'd think— no, it wasn't cocaine either. *It was an enema.*

Underneath the sewing machine was a small box of fabrics, nothing larger than a foot in length— there in case I ever had a project that required such a small piece. My mother came to mind yet again, her voice telling me to hang onto the scraps when she taught me how to sew all those years ago. "You never know when you might need a piece that size, Katie." She scolded me as I had a 1x2 inch piece of fabric left over from a lap quilt, and I was dangling it above a trash can.

Looking at my sewing machine, I suddenly felt a pang of inspiration. My apartment was torn apart now, with piles of stuff from my newly emptied closet, the mysterious leftover parts from Dolly's new dog wardrobe, and all the hangers waiting for her clothes, which were also laid out.

My apartment looked like a bomb had gone off in a beauty pageant supply store for elves. Everywhere you looked was some miniature bedazzled accessory or outfit. But I set up my machine on my kitchen table anyway, pushing my puzzle pieces out of the way– another hobby I hadn't had much attention for this week. I pulled my few supplies out of the tray beneath my machine and took some measurements. I cut and cut until the scissors hurt my hands, making some sort of patchwork material since I didn't have enough yardage to just use one color. I lined it up the best I could in places where it mattered, and I used some fasteners. Velcro would've been better, but I used what I had.

It was now ten o'clock and, in my hands, I held a dog dress that looked like a quilt. It had simple construction and crude details, but I excitedly put it on Dolly– after waking her up to do so. It was a little too tight in places, but the thrill of accomplishment and a new hobby pulsed through my veins.

Something in the back of my mind was awakened after a very long hibernation. Creativity flowed through me for the first time in years. In my work, creativity wasn't at the top of the list for researching, and I forgot just how intoxicating it felt to craft something beautiful with my own hands.

I took the dress off Dolly and hung it up on a hanger, placing the wardrobe in my closet. I will leave the sewing machine out for now. Just looking at it sparked my mind, and I spent the rest of the night cleaning up my apartment, while working out the details on how I could've made the dress better.

By the time I went to bed it was past midnight, and I couldn't remember the last time I'd stayed up so late. I carried Dolly into her bed to our room, turning out the lights, and fell asleep nearly instantly when my head hit the pillow.

The next morning, we both slept in and decided it was much too dreary for the Art Walk. Since we've been *go go go*, I decided today would be a lazy day. Tomorrow was our pet owner's class, so I planned that we'd make a day of it and do fun things beforehand.

After drinking a half cup of coffee, I decided to try a few more rounds on my sewing machine. I was rummaging back through my fabric scraps when I found a larger remnant that could be a layered bandana, so I tried my hand at sewing that. What seemed like a simple project took over an hour as I first needed to iron the fabric, then starch, then I ironed it wrong and started over. Now I was out of starch, and I didn't properly latch the leg of the ironing board, and it crashed down, knocking over my cup of coffee into my lap.

Thankfully, Dolly was across the room, but she was upset at the sound nonetheless, and I had coffee-soaked undergarments, nearly burning a hole in my carpet.

Sewing the bandana for Dolly was easy and it turned out cuter than I imagined. I had an old headband with a cheesy bow on it that I took apart and fastened the bow to her bandana. It was darling. Did it look *homemade?* Yes, it did. But these weren't the jeans I was wearing on my first day of high school. It didn't matter if Dolly wore something homemade because I was the only one seeing her today. I shuddered at the memory of the outfits I felt so proud of that I wanted to debut them to a school of two thousand unruly kids who'd steal your lunch and give you a swirly for wearing last year's mall trends. Thankfully I didn't get the latter treatment for my horrible clothes, but it was only because the lunch lady happened to be in the bathroom at that very moment.

She was a large, mysterious woman with a lethal combination of strength and a vague air which led me to believe in military influence. What she lacked in the mustache-plucking ability, she overpowered in fear tactics and true grit. Rumor had it she was a bodybuilder in her time off. Others said she was working on an invention of a plastic glove that was not only food safe but also contained hidden brass knuckles inside.

I still send her a Christmas card every year. Once, she sent one back. A picture of her wedding anniversary announcement, taken somewhere tropical. Her husband was about half her size in height *and* width. Judging by the look on his face, he looked very happy. But the death grip of her arm around him told me this could also very well be *a cry for help.*

I started to brainstorm all the items I could make Dolly, and I decided a trip to the fabric store was in order. But there was no fabric store like the one at *home.* My mind went to my mother again. This weekend we will visit. I would go to the fabric store while there. I vaguely remembered the last time I went, which must have been five years ago. There was a woman with three chihuahuas in her cart.

The memory stuck to me because I found it so unusual that in her cart– that she was using giant bolts of fabric to contain, was full of fluffy chihuahuas. She told everyone she passed that they were famous and had just been cast in a movie.

My mother took a picture of them, but I never found out what movie it was until later in the day when I heard an advertisement on the television while I was helping my mother wash dishes. They really were famous chihuahuas! Maybe Dolly would be famous someday, and I'd be buying bolts of fabric with her face on them.

That was a few days before I moved out here. It had been a big day of errands. I got a new car battery, tire check, and oil change. I had to pack a few more items and get some moving materials. But the biggest chore– and scare for my mother– was that I was simultaneously changing banks in the process of moving. My old bank was just a small branch, and where I was moving, didn't have that chain. So, that morning, our first errand was to close my bank account.

I asked my mother three times if she wanted to go inside with me, but she said she was tired. Tired or not, she was having feelings of disbelief that her offspring was fleeing the coop— no matter how old I was, and the fact that I hadn't lived at home in years. I turned off the engine and absently took the keys in the bank with me.

I was at the teller's window, asking for my account to be closed and cashed out while they worked on a few pieces of paperwork for me to sign. We heard a car alarm in the distance, but no one looked up as it is not unusual for this neighborhood. The windows were all double or triple-paned glass, whatever is normal for a bank, but the wall facing the parking lot was completely glass and the door included.

We all heard a bang. The teller braced herself for whatever was *attempting* to come through the door. *Was it a robbery? Were we about to meet a gunman?* I turned, wincing, but I saw it was just my mother, who'd pulled on the door when she should've *pushed,* and now she had banged her forehead as she doubled over, holding it.

"Oh my." I saw that my headlights were flashing as she came inside, disoriented.

"Katie, your car keys, PLEASE!"

As she held the door open, the noise was ringing in the bank while people in the cubicles thought it was the security alarm. Most of them had hit their security buttons and crawled under their desks.

"At least you were closing your account, not opening one." She brightly told me on the drive home.

CHAPTER 14
BONE APPETIT

My phone buzzed, bringing me out of memory lane. *It was Eli.*

Hi Katie. Carter and I are going to the Bark Park today if you ladies want to join? (dog emoji) (twins emoji)

I looked over at Dolly who was *snug as a bug* in her bed. It was pouring outside, and I was still exhausted from staying up so late. Plus, the whole Carolyn thing lingered. I appreciated that he wanted to maintain a friendship 'for the dogs,' but I didn't know if I was capable of such a thing without my feelings getting in the way. Besides, if Mr. Right fell from the sky, I wouldn't want to be distracted by Mr. Not Right Now, although I very much wished Eli was the one.

Thank you for the invite. We were up late and just having a lazy day. (nap emoji)

My phone buzzed again.

Okay. Rest up. No emoji?

I started to overthink it and realized he probably thought I'd been *out late* with Taylor. Which was fine, although I'm a good, proper woman and wouldn't want to stay out late with a man like him, it didn't matter because Eli wasn't single.

My phone rang. It was Judy.

"Good morning sunshine!" Her voice on the other end brought warmth into my heart.

"Hi Judy!"

"I thought I'd see how you girls are making out this week. Lots of adjustments I'm sure for both of you."

"Yes— and you're not going to believe the week I've had. Dolly and I were out late last night playing Bingo for charity at a dog diner!"

"What in the world is a dog diner?" Judy's voice went serious.

"It's a diner where you can bring your dog. They have a little menu for them and everything."

Judy laughed. "Wow— my mind went in another direction— and I thought I'd heard it all! That's great, sweetheart. And your date?"

It seemed like an eternity since then. "It was very short-lived. He was infatuated with the waitress."

"Oh no! Tell me— hold on, let me get in my comfy chair for this. Oh, dang it! I've left my grapes in the dining room. Just a second, sweetie. I'm listening. I just want to hear it all and I have a feeling I'm going to be sitting for quite some time."

I laughed and tore into the story and included every little detail big or small, remembering what they all wore, and what I wore—fashion was very important to her. Then I told her about Eli and Carolyn being engaged *again,* seeing her at the pet store, and so on.

"That brings us up to speed." I'd been going on for a long time because my phone was hot against my face. "What do you think of it all?"

"I think that there is more to Eli than we think."

"Yes, I agree with that. But he's engaged!"

Judy was quiet for a minute, then spoke.

"But is he?"

"She's wearing a *ring.* "

We both sighed. Judy interjected first. "Maybe she's engaged to someone else."

But if she was, why would she be spending time with Eli?

Judy and I went back and forth for a few more minutes. "He's just not the one, Judy. Trust me. I wish he were single. I'd probably ask him out myself!"

We laughed, knowing good and well that would never happen. But a girl could dream.

"Should we get together soon?" My voice squeaked, showing my fatigue from the week.

"Yes, dear, I'd like that. But I'm afraid I'm booked up again tonight. Pastor Bill and Julie were wondering if I could bring my ambrosia salad to the church tonight. Remember that couple, Reece and Tracy? They are getting married today— just the two of them. But tonight, there's going to be a potluck at the church hall, and, well, there's only one ambrosia that's up for the job. Of course, it's my recipe. Suzie Lambert uses that artificial sweetener in hers. I can't take all the credit, because if it wasn't for Betty Crocker, I'd still be putting hot dogs in gelatin like we did in the 70's."

"Ooh, how appetizing." I gagged at the imagery.

"Just be glad you weren't alive in that decade, my dear. Strange things were eaten— even stranger things were done. I do miss the fashion however."

"Don't you own a pair of go-go boots, still?"

"Not since your mother borrowed them." Judy chuckled.

"Speaking of… I am visiting my mother this weekend, so I won't be at church on Sunday. I'll try and stream the sermon from her house, though. And I'll miss seeing you!"

Judy was elated to hear I was visiting my mother. "That's wonderful news. Go, enjoy time with her and we can catch up when you get back."

"I'm expecting to come home Monday, as I have to return to work Tuesday."

Who knew, maybe I'd just extend my vacation time and stay an extra day. I hadn't taken any time off in the years I'd worked there.

"That's great. Let me know when you get home. Well, I better let you go sweetheart. I don't have the ingredients for my salad, and you know I like to beat the crowds at the supermarket."

The second we ended our call, my phone buzzed. It was Samantha.

"Hi, Samantha!" I eagerly answered. I could hear heavy breathing and multiple dogs in the background.

"Katie," *Bark! Bark! Bark!* "Can you hear me?"

"Yes, are you okay?"

"Yep- I'm fine. Just completely swamped down here. Our shelter has just received a big shipment of t-r-e-a-t-s, and it seems the dogs already know what it is. I'm afraid they are going to overthrow their leadership and take this place over if they don't get one soon!"

Bark! Bark! Bark!

The visual was hilarious but I held back my laughter.

"But that's not why I'm calling. There's been an influx of adopters— like I told you before. Anyway, we've had to split our pet owner class into two nights. I've been calling to reschedule some. Are you available tonight instead? I'm sorry it's the last minute. And I'm still available for dinner before, of course."

"Yes, that works for me fine. Our new carrier hasn't arrived yet, but I'll return the one I borrowed the moment it does."

"Wonderful. Shall we meet at the *Barker & Walk Cafe* at around five? It's off Springhill Drive. The class tonight will start at six. That should give us enough time, don't you think?"

"That sounds fun. What kind of dog do you have?"

Samantha laughed. "I have several dogs. Six, to be exact."

Six dogs! Wow, I was stunned.

"How do you handle that?" I asked, laughing.

"I don't, but thankfully, they are all little dogs. Tonight, I'll be taking my dog, Stevie. You'll love him, he's very shy and sweet. And he's met Dolly, they get along just fine."

"Perfect. You better get those doggy's some treats!"

"Yes, I need to. I have to escape for a bit today because our washing machine needs to be repaired, but we desperately need to wash some of these blankets. So, Tommy will take over the t-r-e-a-t giving, and I'll go get to spend a relaxing afternoon at the laundromat!"

"Well, enjoy some time to yourself. I'll see you tonight!"

"See you then, Katie!"

The laundromat was a weird place in my book. Essential to society, absolutely. But it was classed in a small group of places where you actively work to not make eye contact with the other patrons as there's a good chance, they are there laundering items from a crime scene. Even if they are just there to wash the ketchup out of an entire outfit, no one is there to chat.

The last time I'd gone to one was back in my quilting days. I'd just finished a huge king-size spread for a Christmas gift when it needed its final wash before being finished. I was elated to find I was the only one there. *Whew. That was close. I nearly had to coexist with society.* After the wash cycle, I put it in the dryer for a long air dry and it had a timer on the machine saying I had over thirty minutes remaining.

The laundry mat was in a strip mall, and I was right next to a juice store. After watching car after car pull up and leave with delicious-looking concoctions, I took a calculated risk of my sopping wet quilt being stolen and ran for a fruity drink.

I came back seven minutes later. *Seven.* Before that moment, I had no idea what could transpire in such a short time frame.

Hesitating before I opened the door, as I wondered if my Booyah Juice was spiked— yes, maybe I had *just* been chloroformed and wasn't seeing what I *thought* I saw. I returned to an entire Christmas party assembled, complete with tables covered in cookie trays, slow cookers, *music,* and a large group of people.

Another person who came in with a towering basket of *questionably stained* clothes locked eyes with me. I wouldn't normally engage with someone holding clothes with claw marks, but in this extreme situation, the lines were blurred. I put my hands up slightly, in the universal 'I don't know' gesture, and he whispered over to me. "A Christmas party? *In a laundromat?*"

That was the last quilt I made. I had forgotten why up until now.

Dolly and I spent the rest of the morning lazing about. I made a few tweaks to my plans and decided we would leave tomorrow morning for our road trip to visit my mother. I thought I'd call her now and share the good news.

"Katie?!" Every time she answered the phone, she would call

out my name and I wasn't sure if it was in disbelief that I was calling her, or that she assumed someone else was using my phone while I was hog-tied and hanging upside down from a ceiling.

"Guess what?" I felt a surge of excitement rush through my veins. And my coffee just kicked in.

"What?" She didn't like surprises, and that was quite possibly the only thing we had in common.

"We are coming to visit you *tomorrow.*"

"What! Oh, my word. My house is a mess and I've turned your room into my closet. Where will you sleep? Don't worry about that. I'll make room for you and Dolly. Dolly! I'll have to put Edward away, but oh, I'm so excited!"

"Okay, good. What does that mean for Edward? He won't be stuffed into some old broom closet, right? Wait. My old room is your closet? I thought it was going to be an office."

"Well, the office didn't work, and the gym equipment wouldn't fit through the door, so that's now in my living room— not that I've used it, but it makes great for hanging my laundry when it's raining outside. And don't worry about Edward. I'll just keep him with your dad in the bedroom. *We won't even know they are here.*"

"Um, okay? So where is your office now?"

"Well, the desk is in the living room too, but my television is sitting on it. I was going to move it and get one of those fancy televisions that mount on the wall, but the McCleary murder trial was on that week, and I couldn't miss it. I'm still not satisfied with that outcome. I just *know* there was a dirty cop in there somewhere."

"I have no idea what you're talking about, but, alright. Maybe I can help you get situated while I'm home. And I would like to see dad if he's able to come out of the room. Dolly likes other dogs, I don't think– "

"No, I don't trust Edward around Dolly." She cut me off. "He was playing nice with the neighbor's dog last summer and it got to the point I *nearly* let them play off leash, but the moment I turned around he tried to lift his leg on her."

"He wanted to… Pee? *On* another *dog?*"

"Yes, but I'm not surprised. Thankfully Susan was able to pick up Little Susan in time. It really could have fractured the relationship I have with the Susans. But you can't blame Edward, *he's traumatized.*"

I wasn't sure where to begin with that one. My mother would spend the rest of her days justifying Edwards' quirks because of his 'childhood trauma,' but no one could really confirm what that trauma was. I think he was just an oddball. Mostly harmless, unless he saw a pair of shins that offended him. But something still *had* to be addressed with this entire situation. "She named her dog… After herself?"

"Yes, but don't worry about it. We will catch up on the neighbors and their dogs when you get here, and it will all make sense. They just look so much alike, you see. Little Susan even has the same high step as her mother. Oh, I better get going or you won't have a place to sleep!"

"Okay. We will see you tomorrow."

For once, my mother didn't remind me she would be tracking my location or needing me to check-in every three hours with a video call. She was just *happy.*

"I can't wait to see you."

We ended our call, and I made a list in my head of everything I'd need to do before we left.

Laundry. Pack enough underwear that I could change 3x daily and still have enough.

Wash my hair to save time tomorrow.

Eat anything in the fridge that might go bad in the next four days.

No, scratch that. Already my pants feel tight from all this dining out.

~~*Eat anything in the fridge that might go bad in the next four days.*~~

…

It would be wasteful not to eat the food before it perishes. Has your mother taught you anything?

Eat anything in the fridge that might go bad in the next four days.

…

Restock treats from doggy bakery, and something for Edward.

Double-check all driving routes for road closures and suspicious detours that lead into the backcountry.

Create a shopping list for anything I need to buy from the fabric store.

Check tire pressure on the car.

Get a burner phone with an out-of-state number and call Eli as many times as it takes for him to pick up and ask him if he's engaged whilst doing my best British accent.

… Make that Australian. I've watched one too many episodes of Crocodile Dundee and feel I could pull that off more realistically.

… Seek psychiatric care.

With my day being almost entirely booked before our evening with Samantha and our class, I got the wind under my sails to get moving.

While my hair was up in a towel and my bathrobe on tight, I started multi-tasking around the house, giving my frizzy hair time to dry out before I blow-dried it. Opening the fridge, I found a half-eaten container of vanilla yogurt and some eggs. The latter wouldn't spoil, so I took the yogurt and cut up the borderline bananas that were browning away on my counter and mixed them in, adding in a few pieces of shaved chocolate. The fridge was already emptier. It sure felt good to accomplish something for the day.

I opened my laptop while I munched on the snack that wasn't nearly as tasteful as I thought it would be, and I checked my driving route. It had been some time since I'd made the journey, and it appeared a new freeway had been constructed since the last time, cutting our driving time down by an hour but also introducing unfamiliar territory in its place.

"What do you think, Dolly? Should we take the shortcut tomorrow?"

She tilted her head at my question. I closed the laptop and felt a mental breakdown coming on. The events of the week were fun but also very tiring. I didn't realize until now just how much I needed a trip home to recharge and regroup. I choked back tears, remembering breakdowns were things we needed to schedule in advance.

"Virtual assistant: Schedule my complete mental breakdown sans head-shaving for let's say… next Tuesday at 5:30. That will give me time to change my clothes after work."

(No response)

"Virtual assistant?"

I looked over at my little machine and saw the light wasn't illuminated. How strange. I followed the cord to the wall and found it unplugged, remembering I had to plug in my iron instead. I used to talk to this thing several times a day as if it was my friend, and now it had gone *unplugged* for an entire twenty-four hours? I found that amazing. Maybe I was getting normalized into society.

But probably not.

After doing my hair and minimal makeup routine, I decided to jazz it up a bit considering I was going out tonight, thinking about meeting Samantha at the restaurant. I reached for the black matte shadow. Oops, too much. As I buffed it out, it got taller and darker, blending its way into my eyebrows which, let's face it— darker brows don't look good on anyone. As I tried to buff things out, I pictured Samantha and I meeting a couple of single guys who were out with their little dogs, after they sent over a couple of Pina Paw-Ladas to our table. We would wave back, and my eyes would be extra sparkly since I was now wearing dark green glitter on my lids, as I really needed the contrast to break up the two black eyes it looked like I had now.

Glitter eyeshadow had come a long way since the 90's. But in place of the 'cake and flake' that we'd all come to rely on in the days of iconic pop stars influencing us to wear butterfly clips, three belts worn simultaneously, and a popped collar, the glitter went on smoothly now. The catch? Once applied, *it never truly came off again.*

Sure, you thought that powerful waterproof eye makeup remover would do the trick? *Fat chance.* The glitter might be gone from your eyelids, but like a skin rash, it only resurfaces on another part of the body.

I always forget this fact when applying the magical sparkle makeup. Once it was on, I wondered why it was not a regular part of my face routine. It brightened my complete appearance. The sterile lighting of my bathroom gave it an extra kick. It brought out my inner celebrity, and I was accepting my imaginary Oscar when I remembered why I didn't do it more often. By then, it was too late. I could be sitting in a pew the next morning, praying my fellowship would be forgiving to the blinding shards stuck in my pores. They had no idea I was up late choreographing a new dance for a twenty-year-old song and not out standing on a street corner, *or worse,* in a line longer than I could comfortably walk at my age about to see a pop singer so young, I could've given birth to.

It wasn't until after I applied *too much* dark green glitter to my black *smokey* eyelids that I remembered immediately following the dinner I'd be sitting in a plastic folding chair under the glow of the bright, sterile lighting at the animal shelter. My pink silky top with sequin bangles would give the wrong impression for that setting. I started to panic as I smudged the eyeshadow, needing to take some of it back, but it didn't want to budge except to slide downward. *The migration had already begun into my pores.*

Time for eye makeup remover– except after rifling through my drawers for nearly five minutes, I remembered I was out of it, and on the occasion when I had used the remainder, I was in too large of a hurry to add it to my virtual assistant's list.

CHAPTER 15
A TALE OF TWO KITTIES

I dug through my purse and found my sunglasses. Rarely did I need to utilize them with our rate of rain, but I was thankful to have them as a trip to the drug store was urgently needed.

I momentarily considered wearing a ski mask I'd bought at an off-season sale a few years back. It had only gotten cold enough to wear it a few times since then, but I always experienced strange things when wearing it. Once, I went to the Beany Genie for a coffee, and a small family screamed and ran out when I entered. The man at the cash register dropped his pen that he was using to incorrectly spell names on cups and put his hands in the air. Since no one was ahead of me in line now, I went ahead and ordered my large decaf espresso, no foam, extra whip, three pumps of vanilla, and two pumps of that sugar-free, banana milk latte.

They made it at record speed, all the workers assisting and saying things like "yes ma'am, just one second ma'am."

When I put the ten-dollar bill on the counter, they all looked at each other suspiciously while the cashier slowly took the bill and counted out the change. He gave it to me with a trembling hand and I nodded, while another barista came over and personally delivered my drink. I took a sip and started to leave when I turned around and hollered out, "Wait!"

Two out of the three baristas fell to the floor for some reason and the cashier had his arms back in the air.

"You gave me an extra dollar back."

He wouldn't put his arms back down, so I just laid it on the counter and left.

Add this experience to another time I wore the mask. Someone at the discount store nearly shot me in the rear with a blow dart, only to miss and take out a giant inflatable pool toy display. I remembered telling my mother what had happened, and surprisingly she didn't bat an eye despite near *violence* occurring.

"What caliber blow dart was it?" Was her only question.

"Uh... How in the world would I know!? They blew it out of a straw-like contraption. I saw it on the ground afterward."

Didn't she care that it nearly took out my *backside?*

She didn't miss a beat. "How fast did the inflatable go down? Slow and steady or did it nearly burst?"

"I don't know. It fizzled, I guess."

"My guess, it was a .40c but without seeing the wreckage of the inflatable whale, I can't say for certain. But don't worry. Though this is a more common occurrence than you'd expect, I don't think it has anything to do with society's disdain for your butt. I told you to throw those *boho* pants out. They make you look like you're wearing a diaper."

Now as I considered the ski mask again, I was starting to think it was bad luck. Realizing it would still show my eyes anyway, I decided to leave it at home.

"Dolly, I'll be right back."

She looked up at me from her cozy bed and broke into a wide yawn.

I grabbed my pink raincoat, threw it over my black jeans, and slipped on the muck boots that were still by my door. I was wearing a white t-shirt with the word "YES" written on it from one of those inspirational seminars that Judy found in our area last year that promised you would leave with a new extroverted attitude towards life. Much to Judy's dismay, the lessons didn't stick, but I did find a renewed strength in my desire to never go to a seminar again— or be anywhere that group chanting might occur. Now, the free promotional shirt made a great buffer for protecting my skin from the fallout of hair coloring, toilet scrubbing and loose glitter applications, as most of those chores had splash back. The sooner you learned that the better off you'd be.

It was now a tactical mission to the drugstore. I would be in and out, I assured myself as I stomped down the stairs and sprinted for my car, noticing that the sky was too dark for the sunglasses I wore. No one would see me. "Everyone's at work," I whispered as I started my car and backed out of my spot.

A man walked in the distance had Eli's build. I drove hastily away. "That was a close one." I wouldn't want him to see me wearing night makeup when I told him we weren't leaving the house today.

I pulled up to the drugstore and sighed with relief when only one other vehicle was in the parking lot, and it wasn't anyone I recognized— but then again, it probably was. I ran in, hesitantly lifting my sunglasses onto the top of my head. Briskly moving around, I found the eye makeup remover and cotton pads, and threw them into a basket and went to the cash register. But halfway there, I walked past the pet department and a little sparkle leash caught my eye, leading me into a small collection of organic treats made in Iceland, and winter pet clothes on clearance. Minutes later I'd filled my basket with marked-down goods, and I was intensely staring at the instructions for a set of doggy ice skates when someone tapped on my shoulder.

Wincing, I peeked over my shoulder, but it was Pastor Bill and his wife Julie. I was so excited to see them I temporarily forgot about my appearance.

"Well, hello, Katie!" Pastor Bill exclaimed while Julie hugged me. "And what are you up to today?" He looked at my outfit in wonder. Julie, always kind, didn't miss a beat. "Oh, I like what you've done with your eyes today." I felt my face redden immediately.

"I'm here buying eye makeup remover! Things got out of hand this morning when I tried to put just a little on." I gave a flat smile, showing my embarrassment.

"I know how it goes. We have teenagers!" Pastor Bill nodded

and crossed his arms, pointing at my basket. "Are you stocking up for the next ice age?"

My basket was filled with dog coats, hats and even a little scarf. "Yes, I suppose I am! It's just all on clearance. Some of it may not get much use," I said as I held up the pair of dog coveralls, not even realizing I was still holding the ice skates, "but better to have…" They both laughed.

"We heard all about your new addition from Samantha and Judy. I'm so happy that you ladies found each other! We hope to meet her soon. Maybe at next week's church picnic? If the weather holds. Lord willing, it rarely does."

"That would be amazing. I would love to bring her!"

"Perfect." Julie lifted her sleeve to reveal a few scratch marks. "Our little additions are proving to be quite feisty."

My eyes grew big as I examined the scratches.

"But they are at the vet right now getting claw covers so they won't do any more damage to my arms."

"Or the couch!" Pastor Bill exclaimed.

"I saw at the pet store they have big scratching posts. Would they enjoy that?"

"We are heading there next after we pick up the antiseptic for Julie's wounds." Bill cringed referring to the scratches.

"Let's just say, they *know* we are going to keep them forever." Julie rolled her eyes and smiled. "We love them, though. At the end of the night, after they are done flying through the air and digging their claws into me and the couches, they become the sweetest, cuddliest creatures on earth. We must get past the lashing out. The vet says they are decompressing after a very long stay at the animal shelter."

"Oh, that makes sense. How long were they there?"

"Eleven months!"

I gasped at the thought.

"Poor babies!" They nodded, agreeing that it was very sad.

"We just gotta give them time and space. And in the meantime, the claw covers are going to help immensely!"

The overwhelming urge for picture-sharing came over me. "Here, let me show you Dolly." I fumbled through my phone to pull up the photo. They both shrieked in joy.

"She's so cute, Katie! I would've swooped her up too."

Pastor Bill had a soft spot for animals, I could tell.

"Bill, do we have any photos of the kitties? I thought we took one for your sister."

Pastor Bill patted down his pockets, looking for his phone. "Yes, that's right. I have it here somewhere." He finally found his phone and pulled it out of his shirt pocket. He looked at the screen and they both laughed.

"When Bill wasn't looking, I made the picture his screen saver!" Julie handed me his phone so I could get a closer look.

"WOW THEY'RE HUGE!" I didn't mean to react so loudly, but it was a very unexpected sight.

From the pages of Katie's Dictionary:

obese

ō-bēs′

adjective - Extremely fat. *synonym:* fat.

When describing something unusually large, meaning it was not *designed* to be anywhere near that size, sometimes the phrase *obese* is tossed around. Though it is a technical term, people found it offensive. And what little I had learned about the pet world, including my multi-day ownership of my own animal, once you adopt a pet, you take *credit* for its abilities and dashing looks. This also translates into taking the blame for its misgivings. While I do not advise objective comments of animals, aka '*furbabies,*' my foot was already in my mouth. Thankfully, I knew these people *well enough* to ask the real questions, but I sensed I had tread into unknown waters.

"They are huge..." I gaped at them wide-eyed, hoping that didn't come off as disrespectful, but then again, these cats were *adopted* and not raised by them.

"Huge *love muffins.*" The words came out singsong as my eyes couldn't look away from the two massive calico cats covering the screen. They were so big in this photo of them lounging on a couch, I couldn't see their entire bodies. Like the Lord, there was no beginning and no end to the shapes of their bodies.

"I know! Aren't they adorable?" Julie gushed. They looked like a wheelbarrow was required to transport them around.

"Oh, I mean, yes, they are just so… They're BIG cats!"

Pastor Bill laughed. "Yeah, the vet thinks something might be wrong with their thyroid. We will get that test done."

"When you said they were flying through the air, I didn't expect– ", I paused, realizing I might be crossing the point of no return, "– so you're telling me, they are quite sporty despite being such big kitties, huh?" My analytical mind just couldn't imagine it.

"They are so playful. Speaking of which," Julie saw something out of the corner of her eye. "Are those cat toys, Bill?" She pointed to the aisle behind me.

"Yes, they have dog *and* cat toys on sale!" I ran over to the cat section, where all the toys were catnip-infused and had long dangles of ribbon trim, bells, and feathers.

Julie picked out a set that looked like sushi, complete in a small tray. Each toy had little sparkling faces on it. "How adorable is this?" She showed Bill and he smiled in approval.

"Okay, we better get going, but now we need this too." She hugged me once more and Pastor Bill waved.

"See you Sunday?" Julie asked as they walked away.

I'd almost forgotten. "I'm afraid not. We are visiting my mother this weekend. But I'll tune in online, so I don't miss anything!"

"Oh, I'm so glad to hear that. Have a fun and safe trip. We will see you soon!"

They left the aisle and headed for the checkout. I took one last stroll through and made my way up to the front.

The cashier gave me a side eye as she rang up the eye makeup remover, nodding in approval. "That'll be $58.16. Cash or card?"

I held up my card.

"Insert the card into the chip reader. Would you like a receipt?"

"No, thank you." I noticed in my peripheral that the front doors were whizzing open and closed. Suddenly a lot of people were arriving, and I wanted to flee. I slid my sunglasses over my eyes in preparation for walking out any second.

"Sorry for the delay. My chip reader is very, very slow today. The stormy weather is interfering with our satellite connection."

As slow as the chip reader was, the cashier spoke at even more of a glacial pace. "Oh my. I forgot to scan your rewards card. May I have it?" Someone came through the front doors and paused briefly, looking in my direction. I turned the other way to see if anyone was standing near me in line, but it was just me.

Jesus, I know you only give me what I can handle. But please don't let that be Eli.

"That's okay, I'll skip the rewards this time." My heart rate was increasing.

"But you don't get the sale price if I don't scan it. Here, I'm canceling this transaction. Let's start over."

The person kept walking in my direction. I heard the front cooler open, and the clink of a drink being dispersed— then a crinkle of someone grabbing a bag of tortilla chips. The squeak of a small dog toy. The footsteps slowly walked toward me as I still waited for the chip reader, dressed in my bright pink coat with sunglasses on.

"I'll pay double the price if you get me out of here as soon as possible." I whispered in desperation to the cashier, but she just shook her head and laughed. She thought I was joking. "I'm as serious as the plague. Please help me get out of here!"

"Alright. Here, let me scan these again." *Beep. Beep. Beep.* Not only was she moving slowly, but she wanted to look at each item to analyze what I was buying before she scanned it for the second time. *It was the perfect storm.*

"Good choice on this. My little Leroy has it in blue." She held up the pink dog beret.

I let out a whimper as I considered walking out without my items. Did I have *anything* at home that could remove this makeup? Could I use canola oil? Toilet bowl cleaner? *A trip to the emergency room?*

"Hmm. Something's still not working on my end. Try pulling out your card and reinserting."

I followed the cashiers' instructions.

"Okay, I think it'll work this time. Let's just wait a minute."

The presence behind me in line was so familiar I could feel it, but I didn't look over.

"Hi." A quiet voice whispered behind me.

"Hello, sir." The cashier answered and I smiled.

"Hi, Katie."

Now I'd been called out and it would be crazy not to turn around.

I turned my head, looking at Eli's face, but didn't make eye contact, still wearing the sunglasses. "Hey."

"What's going on, are you alright?" He sounded genuinely concerned.

"Yep, just making a quick errand."

"Same." He gave the small bone-shaped toy a squeak and it echoed through the store. All of us, including the cashier, let out a laugh.

"Do you want to go to the park later?"

The register opened and my receipt printed.

"Have a nice day, *ma'am.*"

Ma'am. A word that only brought the thought of cow udders, bonnets, and *girdles* to mind. A word so unflattering that it should be removed from the English language.

"Thank you," I nodded to the cashier. "I can't today. I bet Carolyn would."

I wasn't prepared to make such a snotty comment, and truthfully, I felt terrible the moment it came out of my mouth. But if I wanted to find a husband, I couldn't be idling with unavailable, dead-end situations.

Eli gave a flat-lined look and nodded, *agreeing with me.* There you go, I told myself. It's an open-and-shut case, as my mother would say. I hoofed out to the car, the raindrops hitting my head like coins on the way out.

My words stung as I drove home quickly, knowing Eli would be right behind me any second. Hopefully, he paid with a card as well so I could buy myself a few minutes considering I hit every red light on the way back. I pulled into my parking spot, grabbed my bags, and ran the short distance to my stairs.

Dolly was at her water bowl when I stormed through the door, shaking off my wet raincoat outside before hanging it on the rack over the tile floor. "It's raining cats and dogs!" I hollered over to her. "Time to go potty?"

Her grass pad was getting more and more convenient as the weather raged on. Thankfully there was a small covering to our balcony, so she didn't need to get drenched.

I sat her by the door to see if she needed to go and she quickly ran out, did her thing, and ran back in.

"Good girl," I robotically spoke to her, but I felt a heaviness. I felt overwhelmed. I wanted to apologize for my rude comment to Eli, but I also didn't want to get in any deeper than I already was. It was quite a conundrum.

Once Dolly was inside, I let her see her new outfits.

"For next winter!"

She sniffed each thing, before finding the little toy I hadn't realized I'd put in the basket. The same toy Eli bought Carter, except pink. Dolly picked up the pink squeaky bone and started chewing on it immediately.

"Do you like that?" The squeaks were loud and funny, a deeper noise than I'd heard from other toys. This one was like a low squeal from a disgruntled pig. I gave her a quick pat on the head before I headed to my vanity to fix the mess on my eyes.

The cotton pads came up black and sparkly. I looked much

younger suddenly, having removed the excess color from my appearance. I let my skin dry and then applied a little eye cream and some pale shadow that just enhanced my eyes instead of adding depth and drama— two things no one needed to see on a school night at the animal shelter.

I felt much better once changing out of the errands outfit and into a casual, but fitting, pair of light wash jeans and a black long-sleeved sweater. I finished my look with a few accessories— a black headband, my pink stud earrings, and my rose gold watch. Casual with a touch of 'I haven't given up *yet.*' Exactly what I was going for.

I ate a light lunch of salad to use up my lettuce, and topped it with some lunch meat, a few crushed up tortilla chips and an avocado that had been sitting on my counter so long it was almost to the point of growing legs of its own and leaving. A large drizzle of ranch dressing and voila— a salad fit for the garbage disposal. It was better than the yogurt concoction, but still wasn't very high on the list.

As I ate, I absently went through the box of fabric scraps once more, thinking of ideas of what I wanted to buy. Dolly was still squeaking her toy, looking up at me every few minutes as if to say thank you.

After lunch, I got out my duffel bag and travel kits, but immediately decided I didn't have the energy to pack today and would do it first thing in the morning, which meant tomorrow would be hectic and rushed, and the rest of the to-do list except for *Wash my hair,* would also be put off.

We had just enough time to watch a made-for-television movie before leaving to meet Samantha. It was about a vacation rental owner who unknowingly had a realtor stay a weekend at the house who ended up showing it to a family and then sold it to them. The plot, as always, was just the background noise for our short nap.

When I opened my eyes, the vacation rental owner had just discovered the new owners of his home were his long-lost relatives who'd been in witness protection for the last decade after watching a dinosaur costume company get robbed by a gang of bandits who were disgruntled from being fired from their theme park jobs. The realtor was arrested for forging documents, but the family was allowed to stay in harmony and the homeowner married one of them.

"They are really running out of ideas, Dolly."

I clicked off the television, checking the time. We slept longer than I'd realized and now had to get going in about fifteen minutes. The rain had slowed. I dressed Dolly in a sportswear ensemble with her harness. A knock at the door startled me and Dolly looked up, wide-eyed with her tail straight in the air. She barked out a small, meager noise that wouldn't do much for intimidation, but it was the cutest attempt. I looked out the peephole and saw it was the front office.

"Hi, Rachel!" I swung open the door, holding Dolly.

"Hello, Katie. You got this box in the mail. Sorry I'm just bringing it to you. The road only just opened."

It was Dolly's new carrier. "That's fine and this is perfect timing! Thank you."

"I heard about your sweetie, here. We were expecting you to stop by anytime now, but it's fine that you haven't. How about you come by next week and sign our pet forms? We are just catching up with all our paperwork."

"Oh, sorry I haven't come by yet! Things have been a little hectic this week." Lame excuse as I'd just awoken from a nap, but alright. "I'll be there– probably Tuesday, as we are traveling this weekend. Does that work for you guys?"

"That works for me. Have a good day!"

I shut the door and tore open the box, pulling out the shiny new carrier that had special clip-in technology for car seats and converted it into a stroller. "How fun is this?" I snapped together the pieces to make the stroller and used one of Dolly's blankets as a pad for the bottom. Perfect to take to the dog diner.

I carried Dolly inside her carrier down the stairs, then pushed it as a stroller to my car to test it out. It was surprisingly smooth, and I was very pleased. Once in the car, I used the other attachment that was under my arm to install it in the back seat, effortlessly unhooking her from the stroller and into that.

We left our complex and headed to meet Samantha at Barker & Walk. When we arrived, it was off-street parking, and we had to cross a busy road. I was thankful for the stroller conversion but felt self-conscious pushing it through a crosswalk, lest someone think I had a secret child. But when we got to the restaurant, I was elated to see many of the dog owners had their dogs in similar carriers and strollers.

Samantha was already inside when I slid the stroller in the door first, the hostess running to hold it open for me.

"Thank you," I said to the smiling blonde woman. "I'm meeting Samantha." I pointed to her as she waved back at me, excitedly.

"Have a wonderful meal." The hostess had a permanent joyful expression, and it was contagious. This felt like a happy place the second I walked up.

CHAPTER 16
YAPPY HOUR

"Well look at you!" Samantha stood, looking me up and down as I wheeled our stroller over to her, and presumably, Stevie, who was a white fluffy dog that had the same essence as the hostess—smiling ear to ear.

"Dog motherhood looks really good on you, Katie." Samantha smiled sincerely, then giggled as she touched everything that she was enjoying; she gave the stroller an exam, tugged the collar of my pink raincoat and greeted Dolly, who was adorably dressed in a colorful tracksuit.

"Well, thank you! If I had known it would be this fun, I would've accidentally adopted a pet years ago."

Samantha was too busy looking at Dolly's set up to hear what I said.

"I mean it. You look different, in a good way." She picked up her dog who was wiggly with excitement as she let him sniff Dolly. "This is Stevie. He's a little ham."

"He's so cute! What is he?"

"He's a Pomeranian and was the runt of the litter. He came into Newtown after the breeder couldn't get him enough nourishment from his mom. I had to bottle feed him."

The visual was about as cute as I could imagine.

"That is so sweet! What are your other dogs?" We both slid into our chairs, Stevie on Samantha's lap as if there was no other option for him to sit. Dolly was content in her stroller as far as I could tell.

"Believe it or not, I have three more Pomeranians and yes, it's about as yappy as you'd think. Then I have 2 Chihuahua mixes. It's a lot of potty trips outside. I've considered just setting up a tent in the backyard since I'm out there so much."

"There's a guy at the pet superstore with four Pomeranians!"

"Really? Is he my future husband?" Samantha and I both laughed. "No really, is he cute? He sounds like *the one*, that's for sure."

"He was very charming in his own way, I suppose. Boyishly cute, but don't take my advice. I can't pick them. I'm currently crushing on someone that's engaged." I rolled my eyes at the thought. It sounded even worse coming out of my mouth. But then I felt shameful at the revelation. It took me saying it out loud to realize what I had been doing. *Coveting someone else's partner was a sin.* I had to let it go immediately and ask the Lord for forgiveness.

"Well as it turns out, I need to make a trip there to set my monthly bulk grooming appointment." She winked at me, breaking me out of my heavy thoughts.

"So, you're single then?" She didn't have a ring on her finger, but I was surprised considering her co-worker was extremely handsome.

"Yep, with no prospects in sight, unfortunately. Except for the mystery pet store man! Can you imagine if we got married? TEN dogs under one roof?"

"I can't!" I laughed. "What about Tommy? I mean, he's cute, right?" A blind person would have known he was a perfect ten, there was no reason to dance around that one.

"Yeah, he sure is alright. Just zero chemistry. He's more introverted and I know I need an extrovert." She shrugged. "I'm at the painful part of my life where I must choose as much with my brain as I do my heart. I'm not worried, though. I very much want to get married one day, but if I don't, God just has other plans for my life and that's okay, too."

"Amen to that. I'm in the same boat." Our waiter came over and announced himself.

"Good evening Pawrents and pups, my name is Jeffrey and I'll be fetching all of your treats tonight." Stevie's ears perked at the word. "Oops, sorry, that's a hot word around here. Since it's *Yappy Hour,* may I offer your pups a complimentary biscuit?"

Samantha and I both offered a resounding *yes.* He turned and picked up a long silver tray of individual dog treats, each sitting inside a paper cupcake liner.

He leaned in so we could each select one. "Now, then. What may I get you ladies to drink?"

"Strawberry lemonade for me, please." Samantha ordered right away, and he turned to me. "Oh, that sounds good. I'll do the same."

"Two Barkberry lemonades coming right up."

We giggled as he walked away. "How can he say that with a straight face?" Samantha whispered to me.

"I have no idea. But I love it!"

These dog restaurants were my new favorite place, and I was thankful to come out here tonight with a friend.

"So, tell me about the engaged one."

"Well, it's kind of a funny story that I met him. He has a dog that's *identical* to Dolly. Same age, everything. We think it must've been a litter mate."

Her jaw dropped. "What are the chances of that?"

"I know, it was awfully strange. And I find him, Eli, very attractive."

"The dog or the dad?" Samantha chuckled.

"The dad! His name is Eli."

"Oh yes, the man who called! I almost forgot; it's been such a wild week. I love that name, Eli. Very masculine."

I agreed with her.

"So, he asked us for a playdate, and I was thrilled. It went so well, and it seemed like we connected effortlessly on a deeper level, you know what I mean? It wasn't this shallow connection that guys just pretend is there these days. It felt real."

"Okay, so what happened?" Her brow furrowed.

"Well, then, at the end of the playdate, at this point it had been going on for HOURS, he told me his ex-fiancé had just gotten back in touch. And he seemed happy about it."

"Oof, they have history. How do you compete with that?"

"Exactly. Well, guess what? I ran into them at the Bark Park later and not only is she gorgeous, but she's wearing a big sparkly diamond ring."

"NOO!" Samantha's animated howl made heads turn. The waiter dropped off our drinks. "Shall I give you ladies a few more minutes to look over the menu?"

"Yes, please." Samantha said, barely turning to the waiter as she was so engrossed in my story.

"Very well then." Jeffrey walked off.

"So, what was it all for, then? Was it *really* just about the dogs? I mean, I doubt that..."

"Yeah, I'm afraid it was just about them. But it's okay. He's still texting me, and I ran into him this morning. I froze him out badly, and I feel bad about my snarky comment. I just don't want to be wasting time with a man who's *unavailable* and miss meeting Mr. Right, you know what I mean?"

Samantha nodded dramatically, taking a long sip of her drink. "Yes, girl. Amen to that."

Clinking our glasses together, we both picked up our menu as Jeffrey returned.

The rest of our dinner was smooth, and disappointingly, no men sent over drinks or other contact information. We split the tab, and each left a tip. Jeffrey was a great server.

"Okay, well, I'll see you in a few minutes at Newtown! You know… Tommy will be there." She winked at me. I hadn't given Tommy much thought past the adoption moment since I assumed they were together. But now, the prospect seemed exciting.

"Oh, will he now?" I laughed back, both of us knowing full well he would have to make the first move for anything to come out of that.

"Shall I let him know you are single?"

I cringed at her words, but I had consumed so much sugary lemonade during the last hour. I felt a sense of hope. "Sure, why not?" We both laughed as the anxiety trickled into the back of my mind.

After we let the dogs roam the grass patch near our cars, we loaded them up and I waved to her saying she would follow me out.

We arrived at Newtown within seconds of each other and all the lights were illuminated, casting a warm glow on the sunset shadows around the building. Sitting momentarily in the car, I saw Tommy inside, unfolding the chairs. He lifted a stack of chairs and then dispersed them individually. For a moment, he appeared to be very strong, but then I remembered the chairs only weighed a pound or so. Still, you couldn't deny him in the looks category. But what was he like?

Samantha waved me out of my car, pulling an imaginary rope after I got Dolly's carrier out and walked towards her. "Come on, he won't bite!"

"Shhh! Don't let him hear you!" My cheeks were reddening as he looked out the window and extended a smile when he saw us. Then he was smiling at me. Maybe there was something here after all?

"Hi, Tommy. You remember Katie, don't you?" Samantha held the door open while I walked in, giving my entrance announcement.

"Hey, Katie! And Dolly! How's it going with you ladies?" He had kind eyes. He was the easy kind of attractive– the type of guy that would have his shirtless picture on a shopping bag if he were more muscular. He wasn't lanky, though, just an average build, but a beautiful face– the type of face that was so unusually striking. He had light brown hair and eyes that matched an olive complexion. There was a slight freckling over his nose and bright white teeth with a gap between his front two. He was taller than me but didn't tower over me. He seemed athletic in a hiking sort of way.

I must've been lost in his looks because Samantha nudged me with her elbow. "Katie," she whispered.

"It's– it's been great! Yeah, we are doing just great. Really great week so far."

"That's... Great." He winked and went back to his chairs.

Samantha raised her eyebrows at me, mouthing *really?*

I shrugged, knowing that was so completely lame, but she expected too much of me if she thought I could open up to him that quickly.

Samantha glanced at her watch. "Class starts in a few minutes!"

"Are we all set up? Do you need anything from me?" Samantha asked Tommy.

"I'm all set, thank you."

"And remember I have to set up tomorrow, and lead the class, so I better pay attention tonight so that I learn what NOT to do!" She teased, but I didn't know what Samantha was talking about. It seemed like they had wonderful chemistry.

People started filling in and Tommy had a look of mild panic on his face.

"Is he okay?" I whispered to Samantha.

"Yes, he's just having stage fright. He will get over it... I hope." She gave me a flat look, suddenly worrying this was a bad idea. Tommy started running his fingers through his hair and his breathing quickened.

"Is he having a panic attack?" I asked Samantha.

She stood up and went over to him, and they talked for a few minutes while people sat down. Then, Tommy came and sat beside me, and Samantha took the thick pen from the dry erase board and wrote out her name.

"So, you're off the hook then?" I peeked over at the gorgeous guy sitting next to me. He nodded rapidly. "Yes. What a relief! She's a good friend." He smiled but didn't look in my direction.

I wanted to make conversation but had nothing clever to say except, "She's pretty great!" He nodded and turned to look in my direction as people were sitting down all around us. "So, tell me about you, Katie." He reached over and gave Dolly a pat on her forehead as her carrier sat in my lap.

"Oh, well, where do I begin? I've recently become a dog-mom." I smiled, hoping he would find it charming and not creepy as we were sitting very closely together.

"Yes, I do recall that. When I saw you last Sunday, I immediately thought of Dolly."

"And why is that?" I was curious how these dog-matches worked.

"Because you are both very cute." He gave a sheepish grin and his cheeks turned pink, pale in comparison to the raging red mine were turning.

"Oh, is that so." I laughed and felt at a loss for words.

"Good evening, group. Welcome back to Newtown! Thank you for joining us for this class. I promise to keep it short and sweet, just like your new animal companions!"

A small clap took over the crowd and Tommy, still half turned in my direction, moved his arm so it was bent on the top of *my* chair. I could feel my heart racing as I sat next to him. Something about his *presence* that made me feel faint.

"Dear Jesus,
Please guide me. I don't know what I'm feeling. Is there something more to this?
In your name,
Amen"

I prayed hard for the next several minutes and completely missed Samantha's first three topics. When I was back and refocused, my feelings were no longer intoxicating in Tommy's favor, and I felt a little more in control of myself. Samantha's scrawl across the board read:

Must Haves: Nutrition, Playtime & Love

Funny, because those are the three things I wanted, too.

She was finishing up a Venn diagram of how the three of them equaled happiness when Tommy whispered to me. "What are you doing after this?"

Yikes, I had no plans, but I'd already done something. Now, to do more? "I don't know yet. No plans." I whispered back, not making eye contact.

"Do you want to come over to my house?" *Red flag.*

"No." I blurted out, at normal, talking volume. Samantha cocked a smile at me before continuing with her class.

"I mean, I just barely met you." *And I wouldn't come to a strange man's house at night anyway.*

He nodded, not deterred in the slightest. "How about dinner?"

"Just ate, I'm afraid." I didn't mean to keep striking out, but I wasn't about to eat twice, plus I was slightly bothered about the first invitation. Was that the kind of girl he thought I was? Or was that the *kind of guy he was?* I didn't know which was worse.

"Well, how about this— tomorrow I will take you out to an

early, proper dinner."

I shook my head, smiling. "Going out of town first thing tomorrow."

He laughed. "Okay, when do you get back? Now I *really* want to take you out!"

"Next week."

I didn't want to get too specific because I knew if he wanted to go out, he would make it happen. But also, since I prayed about it, I didn't feel peace. The only person I found myself focusing on now was Eli.

Dolly stood in her carrier, and I whispered I was going to take her outside for a moment and excused myself. It was the perfect moment to get some air and analyze my thoughts without his pressure.

To my surprise, he stood up as if he was going to accompany me. From the POV of my mother, this was good to fend off potential nappers and killers that could be hiding outside behind a parked car or defunct dumpster, but if he was the killer of the story, it was his perfect chance.

"That's okay, I'll be right back." I put my hand up, showing I did not need or *want* him to accompany me. He paused, then sat back down. *Whew.*

I stepped outside, picking up Dolly from her carrier and taking her leash, and we walked around for a while. She hadn't had much exercise today and she didn't need to go to the bathroom. I think she needed the air as much as I did.

"Thank you, Dolly, for getting me out of there." I pulled out my cell phone as we walked around the large yard next to Newtown.

"Hi," I said to my mother as she answered on the first ring.

"I'm almost ready for you to visit!" She hollered, huffing, and puffing. "I've just torn the linen closet apart, and the couch is now a bed!"

"You didn't have to do that but thank you." My voice was low as I wasn't sure if it carried inside.

Her voice turned low in response. "What's wrong?"

"I don't know. I'm here at the pet owners' class, sitting next to a gorgeous guy who's very interested, but it's just… Not the one."

"That's okay, Katie! Just because he's gorgeous doesn't mean anything. Looks fade, but personality is forever."

"Yes, but his personality is nice too."

"So, what's wrong, then?"

"He invited me to his house after the class."

"Um, absolutely not! Did you tell him you're not like that? What is he thinking? Is *he* like that?"

"That's what I was thinking. Okay, I better get back in there, I just needed to bounce that off someone. Thank you, I'll text you when I get home."

"Okay. Don't go over there. I know you wouldn't. Right? Tell me you *wouldn't.* For so many reasons!"

Talking to my mother was my daily reminder that she apparently knew absolutely nothing about me.

"Trust me, I wouldn't. I gotta go. Talk soon." I hung up, took a deep breath, and prayed.

"Dear Jesus,
I praise you for this week. What lessons You've taught me
about life. I will continue to be patient for the right one.
In your name,
Amen"

I waited around another minute, Dolly standing and staring off in the distance.

"Are you ready to finish this up?" I whispered to her and looked inside Newtown. No heads had turned in my direction and people were raising their hands as Samantha called on them. I picked Dolly up and put her back in her carrier and we walked inside, but instead of sitting next to Tommy, I took the first seat open on the aisle by the door. Tommy, stiffened as he heard my steps and peered over his shoulder to look back at me, smiling slightly.

"That's all for tonight, and I thank you from the bottom of my heart for adopting from Newtown. It means the world to me to be able to send our animals off to wonderful homes like yours." Samantha started clapping for everyone in the audience, and Tommy stood, echoing her clap.

People began to stand and mingle as they made their way to the door. It was now or never, so I slipped out quietly and took the opportunity, feeling the sting of Tommy's eyes on my back.

As I clicked Dolly's carrier into the car seat, I wondered if I would ever meet a man with the same values. *That wasn't already engaged.*

While I was willing to give a non-Christian man a chance to learn about the Lord, I wasn't willing to compromise my desires to stay pure until marriage. Purity, to me, meant a few different things: pure in mind, heart, and body. It was the pinnacle of my moral foundation since I was born again.

I got into the driver's seat and pulled out of the lot. Purity in mind, to me, meant acknowledging I was a sinner, and I needed Christ's salvation. In my heart, I had the desire to do His will. And I wanted to save my body for marriage. That didn't mean I had never been tempted. It's very hard in societal standards to be this way, and I never would have thought I would wait this long.

But no matter what, His will took precedence in my life, and if I was meant to marry Eli— I mean, marry in general, then I would, and the waiting would all have been worth it. Alternatively, if the Lord had different plans for my life, I would accept that too. Because His plan was perfect.

I pulled into our complex and navigated the road in the dark. Part of me hoped to see Eli outside, and the other part reminded me of my plan to stay focused on finding someone available.

As I got out of the car and retrieved Dolly's carrier, I walked slowly, but I didn't see him. My feet dithered, wondering if maybe he would come out at any moment. I saw my neighbors sitting out on their porches and they waved.

"Hello," I called out, louder than normal.

But he wasn't here, and I went up my apartment steps, opening the door and locking it behind me.

My phone buzzed. It was Jenna asking me about the dress code at Three Maples. My heart sank that I'd forgotten to tell her I wouldn't make the Sunday service after all.

Come as you are. I usually wear something like I would to work, because my closet is just full of frumpy clothes. (laughing emoji) People wear jeans and shirts, or some dress up. Whatever you are comfortable in is fine.

I hit send, immediately starting my next text.

I'm so sorry but I won't be there this Sunday after all. I'm going to visit my parents, but I will be there next Sunday.

She replied quickly.

That's great about the dress code. And don't worry, I'm going to be fine. My husband agreed to go with me, and the kids will attend as well. Have a safe trip!

My heart warmed learning that she was taking her whole family to church.

I had set my alarm as I would for a workday so that we could hit the road before nine. I analyzed the route. It was about a six or seven-hour drive if you counted traffic, but there were some beautiful picnic areas along the way that I mapped out where we could stop for Dolly's potty breaks and to stretch our legs. Each place was popular and out in the wide open, complete with playgrounds for children and families. Never would I be alone in an area off the interstate— that I agreed on with my mother wholeheartedly.

When I moved out this way, I was alone. The drive wasn't unbearable, but without a companion, I decided to break it up into two days, so I never had to continue driving while feeling exhausted. But I made the mistake of drinking too much water and had to take a few emergency bathroom breaks. I found most rest stops were manned by a staff; a man and a woman had a table set up serving coffee and cookies. Truckers, families, and police would be in and out daily and relied on the support. But for a young woman traveling by herself, I was relieved that I wasn't the only one there.

Except for the one stop where there was no staff.

There were no cars. No trucks. I just knew there was a killer inside waiting for me. But nature called. I drove around the lot that backed up into the woods. Of all the places to hide out waiting for a potential victim, a rest stop has got to be the worst place. Imagine all the good places being taken. Do serial killers draw straws to decide who gets the public restrooms?

Opening my kitchen drawer, I found a small can of pepper

spray I'd been meaning to put into my car console and added it to my luggage.

All I had left to do was figure out some food options for the drive. I opened my fridge to see what makings I had to scrape together a meager lunch for myself. In all this week, I hadn't found much time for grocery shopping. *Next week I must return to meal prepping.* After all, it's only been six years since I bought all the containers for it. But yes, *next week I will change everything about myself to instill that new habit.*

Wrapping up my lunch in beeswax paper, I filled my thermos with hot coffee, put fresh water in my large jug, and packed a few snack bags of crackers and grapes in my lunch bag.

Moving on to my closet, I packed a large duffel bag with clothes for the weekend, plus a few supplies for Dolly. I rationed out small baggies of her treats, a large Ziploc of her food, and packed plastic bowls to bring along for the ride. Tossing in the little dog dress I sewed last night, at least my mother would get a laugh from it. The bag was full. We had more than enough in case of emergency, flat tire, or somehow taking a wrong turn and getting lost in a desert that didn't exist in a 1000-mile radius for a period of 37 days. My mother would be pleased.

Thinking of her, I knew my mother would want to see the outfits she bought Dolly, so I took the little hangers out of her miniature wardrobe and folded the micro clothes into our bag; removing a sweater of my own to make room. The last outfit, a little snowsuit, was so tiny and cute it brought tears to my eyes.

"Dolly, are you just my little sweetie, or what?" I asked her, as she patiently watched in silence.

God sent me this selfless, loving little furry creature to comfort me. I was no longer lonely. I was no longer feeling insecure. She reminded me of God's unfailing, unconditional love and His never-ending blessings for my life. Dolly being the biggest of late.

And it was then that I realized the Lord did send me love right when I needed it. Just not in the way I thought it would be.

CHAPTER 17
TAKE A PAWS

I grabbed the bags to make the first trip to the car, when I heard a knock on the door. "That must be our mail." I announced to Dolly, racing to the front door.

It was Rachel from the front office.

"Good morning!" I greeted her with enthusiasm, I didn't realize I was capable of this early.

"Why, hi there, Katie!" She craned her head to look behind me. "Oh, there she is. Hi sweetie!" She gave a little baby wave to Dolly.

"How are you, Rachel?"

"I'm doing great, thanks for asking! I won't keep you. I know you are leaving town. I just wanted to hand deliver this note that was left for you anonymously under the lobby door. I can't even tell you who left it, because the concrete guys accidentally hit our power box at the office, and we've been scrambling ever since to get back online."

"Oh, how weird." I was analyzing the envelope like a fine diamond.

"I thought so. I mean how does a truck back up that far on a sidewalk? The good news is they are going to jackhammer out all the concrete that they mistakenly poured *inside* the building."

The envelope just said *Katie in #818*, which thanks to Rachel's fine detective work, was my apartment number. I started opening the envelope while Rachel stood there. She seemed just as curious as I did.

Then I considered the note might contain something embarrassing, like photo blackmail of me wearing a bucket hat and braces in the fourth grade. Or someone had a telescope lens and captured an image of me in my apartment wearing bathrobe belt braids.

"Thanks, Rachel. I'll come see you next week, I promise."

She seemed disappointed but nodded and left. "See you then, Katie! Drive safe."

I closed the door and slid to the floor, ravishing the envelope open. Inside was a small invitation card with calligraphy writing.

Your presence is requested tonight, April 25th, in the year of our Lord 2023, at 5:30 pm at the finest Bark Park.
We do hope to see you there, Ms. Katie and Dolly.

No return address, no hint of who sent it, and the worst part… now I was *curious*.

I felt horrible that I wouldn't be there tonight, but I was hitting the road, and they didn't leave any contact information. Also, I was not about to walk into a den of murderers. So, while I find this sort of charming as I'm easily impressed (though treacherously jaded), I didn't do the whole *anonymous* thing.

My bags were still sitting at the door. This note made me feel like I was being watched. I grabbed my keys, the bags, and told Dolly I'd be right back.

"If I'm not back in five minutes, Dolly, make sure they use the right picture for my Dateline special."

I stepped out my door and spun around, locking it behind me. Looking both ways was moot, considering to the left was a concrete wall. I still gave it a solid once-over and ran to my car with the finesse usually only seen in a three-legged jaguar.

Using my key fob to unlock the car, I hit the button twice and then struggled to open the back door. I was in the middle of sliding my luggage all onto one arm, sufficiently cutting off all circulation, when someone said my name right behind me. I let out a shrill scream for the ages. No one was touching me, and I wasn't being attacked, but I blamed the cryptic note and years of my mother telling me to be afraid, be very *afraid.* If the police weren't on their way after that call of the wild, I'd be horrified. It was all I could do to not wet my pants. *At least I have 37 pairs packed.*

"I'm so sorry to scare you, Katie."

It was none other than Eli.

As I turned to face him, he was holding a bouquet of beautiful blooms in varying shades. There were so many flowers; in fact, a bee landed on one. My neighbors hustled outside, one of them still in her bathrobe, rubbing her eyes. I must've awakened her, but instead of asking for help, she fumbled to get into her chair to watch.

There wasn't too far to go from screaming like a banshee when the only threat at this moment was a bee sting.

"Hi, Katie. I hope you are alright."

I looked at the flowers, imagining Carolyn lighting up when he handed them over. "I'm alright, thanks."

"Are you going somewhere?"

Never let people know when you're leaving town, a top rule from my upbringing which was also hilarious because we never, ever, *ever,* went anywhere. Mainly because my parents were homebodies to the point where I'd consider them shut ins. Not only did they travel in a five-mile radius and only because there's a good thrift store that benefits animal rescue at the edge of this radius, but also, they lived with all their windows covered with curtains for the last eighteen years.

"Ye-no, not really, I mean– "

Ugh, do I lie and commit sin, or do I announce to my entire complex I will be going out of town if anyone wants to stop by and loot?

"I'm going to see my mom, but I'll be back soon."

There you go, vague, direct, not misleading but also aloof. I could use a little more mystery anyway. *Thou shall not lie.*

"That sounds fun. You'll have to ask her if she's following the Crane trial."

"She sure is. It's all she could talk about last week."

"I'm about to see my mom, too. It's her birthday."

I felt relief wash over me when I realized the flowers were not for Carolyn.

"She will love the flowers. Lilies are my favorite."

"These are so strongly scented. I hope she doesn't find them overpowering." He motioned to the bouquet, and I couldn't help myself. I leaned in to smell them, but the longer I breathed in the intoxicating scent, the closer I found myself getting, and I'd forgotten I was holding up the hatchback of my SUV. When my hand wasn't pressing on it anymore, it swung open hard and fast, nearly knocking me out in the process. I fell sideways, the duffel back padding my fall.

"Oh, my word, here, let me help you up."

My arm was so tangled in the bags I'd been holding I couldn't seem to get off the ground.

He held out both hands to me, the flowers still in one. I reached up but grabbed the bouquet instead.

"Sure, I guess you can have those if you want. Did you hit your head?" He hovered over me and started holding up fingers and asking me to count. "When is your birthday? Do you know what day it is?"

"The door got me a little bit, but not too bad. I'll be okay—December 14th. And I can't see your hands over this bouquet. I'm sorry, here, give these to your mom."

I handed him the flowers back and successfully broke free of the luggage straps. I grabbed a bag on each side of me so I wouldn't pull a shoulder out when I got up– or, at least, that was my logic.

He must have seen how poorly my mind was at problem-solving, so he set the flowers down in the back of my SUV and hoisted me up under my arms like you would a baby. For once, I hadn't been stressed about the state of my armpits when now I had two handsome hands in them. Suffice it to say, things were not going as planned today.

He pulled me up, and suddenly, we were *almost* in a hug. Had my arms not been wrapped around myself like I was wearing an invisible straight jacket, we could have embraced. And I might have done that as a platonic way of saying thanks, but my lower back was a little sore, and I wasn't sure how far I could lean over.

There was electricity between us that I hoped he felt, too. I looked up at him, and I noticed he was sweating slightly. It could be that the sun was finally emerging, or maybe I was just much heavier than I appeared. Probably the latter, considering I was holding all the bags.

"You got a little something on your nose." His words were smooth, and I could almost feel a cool wave from his minty breath.

I found myself basking in the romanticized near-embrace of him holding me up by the armpits. What a terrible time to remember just how ticklish I was.

Imagine the horror of finding out the hard way that your ticklish reflex was to kick your leg. I will never be welcomed back into that salon for a pedicure ever again, and Eli will not be impressed with getting kicked in the shins. It was, however, a surefire way to end contact, promising I could forever hide from my shame for being so rude at the drugstore, so again, I was toying with the idea.

Here I went again. My mind always loved taking me on these detours while someone tried their hardest to tell me something. He started making those facial gestures, like when you're plucking your chin hairs or applying mascara to discreetly let someone know something *was wrong* with their face– *my* face.

"What is that?"
"It's the pollen from the lilies."
I didn't dare step away or try and crank my neck to see my reflection in the car window. No, I took the approach where instead of acknowledging there was gum in my hair, or I'd just sat on a melted candy bar on a bench outside Mervyn's while wearing white jeans, *I would just ignore it until it went away*–the boldest approach for those without bravery. People would think you did it intentionally or you truly *didn't give a rip.* And while it would haunt you every time you tried to fall asleep for the rest of your life, eventually, they would stop laughing in a few years. *I called that a win.*

But sometimes longer. Much, much longer, in fact. Once, I saw a man wearing a full cowboy outfit get out of a vehicle and step onto a sheet of solid ice at a movie theater. Cowboy boots and ice are like oil and water, with the same effect. Though the movie I saw that day had long been forgotten, I still remembered the horrific fall eighteen years later. I could still hear his rear slamming down on that ice patch.

Well, it wasn't horrific, because his ego was the only thing injured. Again, this was an assumption because the crowd that gathered around him had been laughing too hard to see if he even cared. Sure, he may have just pretended, *"I meant to do that"*, but when he bottomed out on that ice and slid all the way to the box office window, the little spurs on his boots making sparks, *it was impressive he didn't need an ambulance.*

But the ego is the most fragile part of the human body. He may have been so internally wounded, so scarred. Regardless, he got up, sat through a three-hour matinee of Titanic, and ate handfuls of popcorn a 48-ounce soda, and finished it off with a box of some rock-hard gummy candy, only to leave the movies and drove himself to the emergency room.

"It's all over your nose and cheeks. It's— everywhere." Eli let out a short laugh after he couldn't take it anymore and stepped back from me.

I started to fall backward out of fright once I realized he wasn't holding me up anymore, and quickly, he caught me by the armpits and pulled me up to his level.

Motioning to my bags, he had to break the silence. "Man, what did you pack in there? Rocks?"

I shrugged. "My dad has a new rock tumbler I want to test out."

"Oh, okay. Well, I hope you have a good time."

He was still just an inch away from me, like at any minute we were going to dance. I could practically see those baby hairs that lived between eyebrows, only to be seen in direct sunlight— like the ghost of a unibrow. I felt all sorts of things and needed immediate willpower to walk away from the forbidden fruit.

"Dear Jesus,

I do not know what on earth is happening here, but please give me the strength to keep this... Proper.

In your name,

Amen"

More than anything, I wanted Eli to throw caution to the wind and whisper something romantic in my ear.

"I think you look good with bright orange pollen all over your face. If it weren't for my allergies, I'd rub noses with you so we could match."

He finally broke away from our stance, and I found myself letting out a sigh of relief. I didn't remember ever feeling so *attracted* to someone before Eli. But since he was in a relationship— *engaged,* after all— I needed to remember that this was a dangerous line to walk, one that would always lead to sin.

Katies Biblical Application

"You shall not covet your neighbor's house. You shall not covet your neighbor's wife, or his male or female servant, his ox or donkey, or anything that belongs to your neighbor." Exodus 20:17

Picking up his flowers, Eli nodded at me over his shoulder and walked to his car, parked a few spots away from mine. I dropped the duffle bags into the back of my SUV as the door was still open.

"Eli," I hollered over, my voice cracking like a preteen boy going through puberty.

He turned around, his eyebrows raised quizzically. "Yeah?"

"I'm sorry for being rude the other day. At the drugstore. That wasn't cool. I'd been having a little eye makeup emergency before going out and— well, that's a poor excuse."

He nodded and didn't say anything for a moment, causing me to hold my breath and wait.

"Okay."

"Can we still be friends?"

I wasn't sure that part was a good idea since I felt strong feelings toward him, and he was taken, but I wanted to know he didn't hate me at least. It didn't mean I had to see him, but if I casually ran into him and Carolyn, at least we wouldn't have this elephant between us.

"I don't know."

My heart stopped. Was he really *that* mad about one-off comment, even after I apologized?

"Oh, okay then. Well, take care." I closed the back of my SUV as I waited for my inflamed shoulders to settle before grabbing the heavy hatchback.

Eli was still standing there, facing in my direction but not quite looking my way. His eyes were up, as if he were gazing at a cloud formation, trying to decide if it was a cat riding a unicorn or just your typical stratocumulus formation. With him not leaving, I felt like I should loiter too, so I reached down to tie my shoe, but that was not something I could do without announcing.

"Better tie my laces. Wouldn't want them to come undone on my big drive." I mumbled loud enough that the neighborhood ladies surely heard, as one commented, *"Make sure they are tight."*

Eli glanced at me as I was tying them. He must have expected my eyes to be on my shoes, but in fact, I could multi-task— such as cracking an egg while brushing my hair. The fact that I dropped twice as many eggs as I consumed really had nothing to do with the fact that I *could.*

I waited for Eli to say something, but after making eye contact, he turned and walked away. Running my fingers along the side of my head under my hair, I could feel a large bump forming. *How embarrassing,* I thought. At least it didn't pop up while he was still standing here. Yes, better for all injuries to reveal themselves after the handsome man had left.

I hit the lock on my key fob and marched back to my apartment to get Dolly. The sun coming out felt like a great blessing for my day of driving as I was concerned we'd hit rainstorms.

After washing the last of the pollen off my face, and the bit that spread to my hair and teeth— I was finally ready to depart. I fetched Dolly, who was wagging her tail as we got her harness on so we wouldn't have to fumble with it on the road. She seemed very excited, and her joy was contagious.

Once back outside, I triple-checked my door was locked and felt assured I'd unplugged everything inside and had my living room light set to a timer. The neighbor ladies waved me off.

Dolly quickly got into her car seat, and I felt emotion coming over me. There was only one thing left to do. I put my head down in my hands and prayed out to God.

"Dear Jesus,
I don't know how I royally messed things up beyond repair with Eli. I'm so sorry for being rude to him. I just want Eli to be happy… even if it's with someone else."

It was such a relief to feel the words of my prayer come out. Just then, Dolly let out a little yawn, and I smiled.

"And Jesus, thank you for this little creature. You really did send me love when I asked for it, just in another form that I wasn't expecting. She has brought me so many interesting things in just a few days. I can't wait to see what else You have in store for us."

Yes, I still had a deep desire for a husband, which was a different kind of love, but there was no mistaking that God had answered my prayers.

"You have shown me nothing but love in my life. Bringing Dolly to me has shown your love even more. I have complete trust in You for my future and will not worry about anything, as you've commanded us not to, but instead will cast that all upon You, oh Lord!"

I wiped the tears from the corners of my eyes as I felt overwhelmed with God's love and the presence of the Holy Spirit. I lifted my face and was ready for the journey, looking out my rearview mirror to see it was clear. Turning on my car, I backed out of the parking spot and drove off into the day.

By the time I'd reached the first stop sign in my apartment complex, my phone buzzed. It was probably my mother, stating that she saw I was finally on the move and to be careful at the next four-way stop, but since my car wasn't in motion and no one was behind me waiting, I peeked at the phone in my purse. *It was Eli.*

I'm sorry Katie. I don't want to be friends.

My heart stopped again. Why did he feel the need to tell me *again?*

He was typing, surely to tell me why and how come and

because of this and that. I knew the day I first saw Carolyn I wasn't anywhere *near* his type physically. No need to rub it in.

I replied.

Okay, I understand.

And truthfully, it was fine. I thought back to when I first prayed about finding a husband. I had asked God if something was right "open all the doors, and if it's not- close them shut forever." This was the latter, unfortunately, but I'd accept it because God had something even greater out there for me. My mind whispered back, 'but who is going to be more perfect than Eli?'

I shuddered at the thought.

My car was now in park, as the typing bubble continued. I was a glutton for punishment, so I waited to read why I wasn't his ideal woman.

Because I want to be more than friends. I thought you would have received the invitation I sent by now, and you would know that.

A car pulled up behind me. No one was at the other stop sign, so it would be fine for them to go around me. They didn't, but I was consumed with reading that text over and over.

Wait, what? My brain felt like it was swimming upstream through a landslide. It still hadn't hit me what he meant, and now the car door behind me was opening.

Just then, my mother decided to video call. I answered, talking fast as I needed to hurry up and drive away. "Hi! I'm just hitting the road. But you won't believe who just texted me to say they want to be *more than friends.*"

"OH MY!! Does this mean I have not one but TWO grand dogs now!?"

"I don't want to get ahead of myself— but probably— maybe. Let me call you back in just a second. Someone stopped behind me, and they just opened their door."

"WHAT? I'm not going anywhere. Keep me on the phone!"

"Okay. Just hold on a minute." I set the phone in the holder attached to my dash as I'd need it for my GPS anyway. I flipped the rearview mirror back to downcast headlights and put my car in drive, only to jump out of my skin in a blood-curdling scream when someone knocked on my driver's side window.

"What is it, Katie! Who is it? Is it Ted from your work? Or your mailman, Ron! I knew it. It's Ron, isn't it?"

"How do you know who my mailman is…? Wait, never mind, I don't want to know. And it's Eli, who has now been watching me and probably thinks I'm talking to myself. Just be quiet in the background, okay?"

"I'm as quiet as a church mouse. You know me, Silent Suzie is what they refer to me as."

"Maybe *on opposite day...* And that's not even your name? Okay, just *shhh.*"

"And let him think that you are talking to yourself. It makes you more unpredictable; it's like I always say, 'a little crazy keeps the killers away.'" My mother winks and gives a dramatic thumbs up, pretending to zip her mouth shut.

The embarrassment was still fresh, and I knew my face was swollen, red, and blotchy, but I peeked out the window and saw Eli sheepishly grinning at me. I just stared blankly until he motioned to roll down my window, using the old-fashioned gesture of cranking it down. I reached for the crank when I remembered my car had automatic windows.

"Will you give me a chance to explain? I'd like to tell you about Carolyn first."

What about her? "Okay."

Since he was towering over me, I needed to get out of my car door and stand for this. I was getting a sore muscle from cocking my head in this position for so long. Carefully putting my car back in park and then shutting off the engine, I cautiously opened my car door, clipping Eli in the process.

"Ouch, sorry about that." I motioned towards the door.

"Looks like we may need to call your SUV in for assault," he softly said as he lifted my hair to see the swelling. The slightest touch of his hand on my face sent shockwaves down my body and caused my skin to blush shyly.

"So, Carolyn..." he began. "We started talking again, and yes, I invited her to the Bark Park, but that was before I met you. It was the first time I'd seen her in YEARS. After I met you, I kept the date with her because I wanted to tell her it was too late *in person.* I wanted to give her that. Imagine my surprise when she showed up wearing the engagement ring I gave her all those years ago."

Yes, now that he said it, it *was weird.*

He waited for me to say something. Anything. But I still looked like a surprised beluga whale, half agape and afraid to move because I couldn't remember if I was wearing my TMJ headgear as I needed to do while driving because I always clenched my jaw on long trips. My hand crept to my chin, and I felt relief wash over me realizing I hadn't put it on yet.

He frowned, watching my fingers frantically wander over my face as if I'd forgotten to wax my mustache, but he continued. "But whatever was between us back then is gone now. The person I was when I fell in love with her all those years ago is gone. She has changed with time, matured, and we are complete strangers aside from the brief history we had when we weren't even adults yet."

He went on, giving his shoulders some slack. "We want completely different things, her and I. Church is very important to me, whereas she worships the gym. I want to see the world— she wants to explore Ikea. She wants twelve children, and I can't see myself having a family with her at all. Believe me when I say Carolyn and I were a good part of each other's lives, but only in the past..."

"It's none of my business, Eli." I swatted away all my stoic feelings momentarily and tried just to listen. Technically, it wasn't my business, but I wanted to hear it anyway. I hoped he would continue.

"But I want it to be your business, Katie."

My cheeks reddened. Is that so?

"It was too late for Carolyn because I want to be with you. I knew it from the moment we met, just those few days ago. I know it sounds crazy, but my soul recognized yours. I've been praying about it and… from the moment I saw you, Katie, I knew you were going to be special to me. I just surprised myself at how fast it happened. You are all I can think about."

I didn't know how to respond. Inside, my heart was doing a victory lap. I needed to sit down before my legs went weak under me.

"I'm about to go visit my mom."

"So– if I'm not overstepping here– " Eli tried to change the subject back, or at least I think he did because I interjected.

"Yes, I'll go out with you!" I still hadn't let go of my car door.

He laughed wholeheartedly. "How about I properly take you out when you return?"

"I'd like that a lot." I felt overwhelming joy.

"Hi, Eli?" We both looked at each other in fear. He didn't know where the voice was coming from, and me, because I did.

"This is Katie's mom! I am listening to your arraignment, I mean– disclosure, gah, I'm sorry, proclamation– " a part of me died inside as she spoke, "– and know that I couldn't be more thrilled about this whole thing, but could you be a dear and just quickly give me your social security number and mother's maiden name, and I'll be out of your way."

Eli's eyes went to the inside of my car where the voice was

coming from and saw my mother on the video call. Or at least saw the center of her glasses as the phone was much, much too close to her face to make out even a sliver of her appearance.

"Of course, I totally get it. How about I text it to Katie, and she can forward you that info?" He laughed, flashing his perfect smile, and I melted into him for a hug.

The second of silence turned out to be too much for my mother. "Just to be safe, why don't you send me Carter's, too?"

Dolly let out a small bark at the sound of Carter's name.

"MOM!" I called back, giggling in embarrassment.

We all laughed, and I again felt the peace of the Holy Spirit wash over me.

EPILOGUE
FROM WAGS TO WEDDING BELLS

After a wonderful season of dating, all my previous romantic failures became clear to me. Eli and I were meant for each other and blended into each other's lives nearly effortlessly. We quickly fell into a great routine. On Friday nights, we would go to dinner and a movie, while on Saturdays, we would take the dogs on long walks and to the park. It was interesting to see that anything from sitting next to him in silence at the movie theater or eating a plate of messy spaghetti to walking uphill while trying not to sound like I needed an oxygen tank— everything with Eli was exciting. And the best part was that he felt the same way about me.

As a couple, we decided as a couple that he would start attending my church on Sunday mornings, and he'd continue being a youth leader during the week at his church. And immediately, he wanted to get involved at mine, and so after the first service, he talked to Pastor Bill and Julie about a new idea for a fellowship program that he wanted to hold weekly at the Bark Park. They loved the idea, and every Tuesday night after that, a group of members would head to sit on the Pawrents park benches, where we would share laughs and wisdom, such as my advice to always wear muck boots to the dog park.

On a crisp Sunday morning, Eli and I walked up the steps at church where we were greeted by Pastor Bill and Julie at the door. Pastor Bill chatted up with Eli momentarily, asking him about the game yesterday. Julie said a few people were inside waiting for me in the pew.

As I peeked in the doors, Judy was standing where we normally sat, motioning me over. She saw Eli and hugged him. Jenna and her family were filling half the pew, as well as Samantha and Mitchell from the pet store.

"I took your advice and went to the pet store you recommended. I may have found just what I was looking for." She blushed and Mitchell laughed.

Then, to my disbelief, I scanned the pews behind us and found Micah sitting with Carolyn. Eli and I looked at each other in wonder, both mouths agape. Thankfully they took the cue and answered the unspoken question. Micah had been attending since the week we met, but the coupling was very surprising yet made total sense.

"We met at the gym last week." Carolyn shrugged, grinning ear to ear. "I told him I was looking for a new church since moving back, and he said he heard great things about this one."

"I'm happy for you both and hope you get as much out of the services here as I do," I replied with pure-of-heart intentions. It felt so good to be free from the weight of sin.

Pastor Bill and Julie walked down the aisle, Julie holding her phone up to me. "Katie, your mom just video called. Say hello to her."

"What? Okay, uh, hi mom!"

"Hi, Katie."

"What's up?" I started to whisper, feeling a little unsure, but everyone around wore the same smiles. A tap on my shoulder had me spin around to Eli, who was down on one knee, holding a squeaky toy that looked like a diamond ring.

"Katie Fitzgerald," my jaw dropped, and I felt tears well up. "After praying for my future wife for years, I knew you were the one the moment I laid eyes on you. These last few weeks have been the best days of my life since finding you. And I don't need any more time to know that I want you to be my Paw-rtner for life."

Everyone let out a giggle at that.

"Will you marry me?" He looked at me with his perfect green eyes.

"Yes, I will!"

Clapping and cheering took over. He handed me the squeaky toy, and I laughed again, a few happy tears escaping.

Everyone settled down but I felt like there was more to come.

"Give the toy a squeak, Katie." Eli was smiling as wide as I'd ever seen. I gave it the biggest squeak I could, and suddenly, running down the aisle was Carter!

"He's got something for you." Eli cheered on Carter to make sure he made it all the way over to us and did not get lost in the sea of people.

Carter made it to us and immediately pawed for Eli, wanting to be picked up. Eli obliged but held him out towards me. He was wearing a tiny little blue backpack.

"Go ahead, Katie."

I reached inside the backpack and pulled out a delicate ring box. Eli waved Julie over, and then my mom was there, too. Inside was a beautiful honey-colored gemstone with two accent diamonds on the sides. It was beyond anything I'd ever seen before, and I loved it. The tears took over again once he slid it on my finger, and it was a perfect fit.

As I looked upon my loved ones around me, I praised the Lord for all that had transpired.

ABOUT THE AUTHOR

Cassandra discovered her passion for writing at the age of seven when she purchased a diary at the Scholastic Book Fair. What began with journal entries about her school and home life later evolved into a collection of poems, short stories, and novels.

Her hobbies include skiing, traveling around the Rocky Mountains, and reading. Much of her writing inspiration stems from her love of dogs, her Onondaga heritage, and her Christian faith.

Cassandra's favorite genres of books are Christian fiction novels, Thrillers, and anything British.

She is a full-time writer and resides in the mountains of Wyoming with her husband, Chad.

OTHER BOOKS

Fetching Love- Book #2 in the 'Dog-Mom Rom-Com' series!

Three couples, three journeys, and one hilarious adventure on the unpredictable path to love.

Katie and Eli are ready to say "I do," but the days leading up to the wedding are full of surprises— especially when Katie's mom's true crime sleuthing lands her in a pickle.

Samantha and Mitchell seem perfect together, but hidden struggles test their relationship. Can they find common ground, or will their opposing desires pull them apart?

Carolyn and Micah have found faith and each other, but their surprise romance leads to a sudden, life-altering decision.

As these couples follow the Lord, they find joy and laughter along the way.

Genre: Christian Romantic Comedy

Stay tuned for the next installment of this series!

The Après-Ski Proposal: A Romcom About Love Off-Piste

She came for a fresh start… Not a fake boyfriend. When Claire Riley gets dumped on the eve of her 30th birthday, she's blindsided. A spur-of-the-moment ski trip seems like the perfect escape, until she runs into her ex... With his new girlfriend. Shocked and desperate for a lifeline, Claire accepts a proposal from a charming stranger to pose as her fake-boyfriend. What begins as a simple act of saving face turns into a journey that reveals a fresh start in life and love— the kind that only God could have planned.

Genre: Christian Romantic Comedy

The Curse of Josephine Bagley

Over the course of a century, three individuals are woven together by a decades-old curse:

William, after surviving an Indian raid on his orphanage due to his facial disfigurement, goes on to live among the tribe. But when misfortune befalls them, he is quickly traded away and faced with a pivotal choice that changes his life forever.

Josephine has faced immense loss. Despite her granddaughter's efforts to help her find solace in faith, she finds she can't let go of the past and falls further into her belief that she's eternally bound to darkness.

Saraphina, a fledgling antiques dealer, gets the surprise of her life when a courier delivers notice that she's the last surviving relative of the Bagley Estate. What seemed like a windfall that could help her career now causes her to question her own reality.

In this tale of intertwining mystery, loss, and faith, these souls navigate through nefarious trials to find the gift of grace and forgiveness that extends to us all.

Genre: Christian Gothic

www.ingramcontent.com/pod-product-compliance
Lightning Source LLC
Chambersburg PA
CBHW020339010826
48970CB00012B/1573